SPACE Viking's THRONE

John F. Carr
& Mike Robertson

Pequod Press

SPACE VIKING'S THRONE
A Pequod Press Adventure Novel

Printed in the United States of America

First Printing, 2012
V 10 9 8 7 6 5 4 3 2 1

ISBN: 978-0-937912-19-5

Cover art by Alan Gutierrez

Pequod Press
P.O. Box 80
Boalsburg, PA 16827
www.Hostigos.com

DEDICATION

To Dwight Decker: We started corresponding about H. Beam Piper in the late Seventies and are still going at it. Dwight was also one of the first readers of the original "Last Space Viking" manuscript. He had this to say: "By the way, other than the use of the contemporary term 'man-up,' I could have sworn reading this that it's an unknown MS found in the bottom of Beam's trunk…"

And to Steven Carr: who, on more than one occasion, has said that *The Last Space Viking* is his favorite of all my novels.

Space Viking Era
CHRONOLOGY

The Atomic Era is reckoned as beginning on the 2nd December 1942, Christian era, with the first self-sustaining nuclear reactor, put into operation by Enrico Fermi at the University of Chicago. Unlike earlier dating-systems, it begins with a Year Zero, 12/2/'42 to 12/1/'43 CE. With allowances for December overlaps, 1943 CE is thus equal to Year Zero AE, and 1944 CE to 1 AE, and each century accordingly begins with the "double-zero" year, and ends with the ninety-nine year—H. Beam Piper.

(All dates in the Space Viking Era Chronology are based on Atomic Era dating. jfc)

782   Foxx Travis born.

839   System States Alliance secedes from the Terran Federation.

842 - 854 System States War.

855   Ten thousand refugees from Abigor flee the Terran Federation for unknown worlds. They end up in a star cluster, they call the Helm, several thousand light-years from the Federation and settle an earth-like world, Excalibur.

895   Sword-Worlds Joyeuse, Durendal and Flamberge colonized from Excalibur.

915   Sword-World Haulteclere colonized from Joyeuse.

935   Sword-World Gram colonized from Haulteclere.

950   Aditya abandoned by the Federation, as it pulls back from the frontiers.

1000   The Interstellar Wars begin, a series of wars and uprisings which lead to the break-up of the Terran Federation.

1100	The final dissolution of the Terran Federation as war breaks out on Terra and the Sol System. The colony worlds turn on the mother world.
1200	The Interstellar Wars come to an end, more through exhaustion than desire. Only a dozen or so worlds still have the capability for interstellar flight.
1242	A fleet from Osiris attacks Poictesme and is repulsed after heavy damage, including the nuclear bombardment of the capital, Storisende.
1268	First Gilgameshers arrive on Vishnu.
1450	First Sword-World ship returns from the Old Federation. Aditya occupied by Morglay.
1533	Wulf Hellmut raids Baldur and a dozen planets in the *World Smasher* and brings home over a billion and a half stellars of plunder back to the Sword-Worlds.
1572	Captain Erlic Sanchez, the Planet-Buster's, raid on Isis is one of the richest Space Viking raids ever made in the Old Federation.
1595	After an unsuccessful raid on Aton by six ships from Haulteclere, Space Vikings no longer raid 'civilized' worlds in the Old Federation.
1602	Aditya is abandoned during a dynastic war on Morglay.
1615	Skathi, a Space Viking base world, is abandoned.
1650	Marduk-Odin "fake war." Both navies make a lot of fireworks, then each side goes home and claims victory.
1665	Planetary Nationalist Party takes control of Aton during the crisis after the war with Baldur.
1716	Lucas Trask, seeking revenge for the death of his new wife, leaves Gram aboard the *Nemesis* for Tanith in the Old Federation.

1718   The Battle of Beowulf.

1723   The Battle of Adhumla between Trask's allies and Andray Dunnan's Space Vikings.

1723   Dagon, a Space Viking base world, is raided by Otto Harkaman for attacking Ganpat, a Tanith trade world.

1725   Battle of Marduk between alliance of Lucas Trask's allies and loyalist Mardukan forces against Andray Dunnan's Space Vikings and Zaspar Makann's Mardukan rebels.

1730   King Lucas of Tanith and Prince Simon of Marduk establish the League of Civilized Worlds.

1734   Arthur Trask is born.

CIVILIZATION LEVELS

Civilization Levels (usually referred to as Civ-Levels) were invented by Otto Harkaman because he thought the former Federation Civilization Index, which only went to 5, was not descriptive enough for those worlds who had survived the fall of the Federation and the Interstellar Wars which had followed.

Civ-Levels are used throughout the Sword Worlds and Old Federation to rank worlds and their stage of civilization, or decivilization, however that might be. Space Vikings use Civ-Levels to rank Old Federation worlds in terms of fighting capability and potential loot. These are a holdover from the Federation Civilization Rankings that were included in the *Astrogator's Guide to the Worlds of the Federation*. Space Vikings find the ratings very useful as a shorthand when discussing past raids, future targets and dream scores.

They are usually expressed in writing as Civ-Level 1, Civ-Level 2, etc.

Civilization Levels (Civ-Levels)

Level One—Blasted back to the Stone Age.

Level Two—A pre-mechanical world at a Dark Ages equivalent. Fighters use swords, bows and arrows and bone and leather for armor.

Level Three—Medieval equivalent. Pre-mechanical world, but with steel plate armor and castles for defense.

Level Four—Late Medieval. Some hydraulic powered machines, gunpowder, and the printing press.

Level Five—Early steam technology, paddle wheelers, rifles and dynamite.

Level Six—Steam age with locomotives, heavy machinery, ocean liners and telegraph communications.

Level Seven—Gasoline engines, early autos, first airplanes, telephones, moving pictures and radio.

Level Eight—Jet planes, solid-fuel rockets, computers, chemical-explosives and television.

Level Nine—Semi-Civilized World, atomic power, the atom bomb, television, super computers, interstellar travel.

Level Ten—A civilized world, with nuclear power, collapsed matter, hyperspace technology, with their own space ships for trading and protection.

PART ONE

H⊕TH

I

Commodore David Morland found himself nervously looking out the viewscreen at the gas-giant Loki, which was striped in white and orange like an oversized children's ball. Loki was a massive gas-giant, almost large enough to be a star. According to his well-preserved copy of *The Astrogator's Guide to the Worlds of the Federation*, Loki was only a few Jupiter masses from deuterium fission. Had it been large enough to ignite and go brown-dwarf, it would have become a binary star and there would have been no life on the planet Hoth.

What was bothering Morland wasn't the huge orb, but the lack of any Hoth naval vessels patrolling the solar system. On their last visit, almost four years ago, the *Skull Splitter* had been met by Hoth naval ships once after their last micro-jump and another time just outside the orbit of Loki. He'd have felt better if he'd brought along a real flotilla instead of just the *Pay Dirt*, since he didn't know what he was getting himself into. However, the other ships were needed to guard Poictesme, their base world of sorts.

The original plan, after their latest series of successful raids, had been for DeBorder to return to Tanith, to reimburse King Rodrick for ship repairs to the *Pay Dirt*, then travel to Joyeuse by himself for trade and to pay off their investors. At the last minute, Morland had changed his mind and the mission. Ever since the attack by the Mardukan ship, *Challenger*, he'd been worried about Captain Vandarvant and where and when he might return to hunt the *Skull Splitter* down.

Morland needed to learn more about his adversary and he'd quickly come to the conclusion that he wasn't going to get that information by laying low on Poictesme. So he'd left the *Faerie Queene* back at the Gartner Tri-System and made way, with DeBorder, to Hoth to sell and trade some of their goods, before traveling to Tanith.

This left the expedition more exposed than he liked. If they ran into a Mardukan squadron in this sector, it would be all over despite their precautions of changing the *Skull Splitter's* name back to the *Nebula* and claiming to be merchants from Poictesme. One on-board visit by a Mardukan ship's officer would blow that sham to Nifflheim and back since the ship was too well-armed to be a freighter.

Morland was beginning to wonder if their stop at Hoth wasn't a big mistake. On their previous visit, there'd been several ships coming and leaving the system. So far, signals-and-detection hadn't picked up a whisper from another living thing.

One of the Communication officers said, "Sir, an incoming message from Captain DeBorder."

"Patch him through."

"David, what in Great Satan is going on?" DeBorder asked.

"I don't know, Javen, but I mean to find out."

"What do you think happened?" he asked, his forehead furrowed.

"Something bad. Maybe a raid by other Space Vikings wanting to take over the Everrards' operation? Or a native uprising or revolt. It could be any of a dozen things."

"Yup. And none of them good for us."

Morland found himself nodding his head. "True, but it's important to get to the bottom of it. We need more intelligence about what's going on in Old Federation and this looks like a good place to start."

"Yeah, if there's anyone left alive to question," he answered.

While using their Abbot lift-and-drive to reach Hoth orbit, Morland used the telescopic screen to study the surface. They were out of phase with the Hoth day/night cycle and the spaceport city of Khmun was blanketed in darkness. The only thing that registered with the naked eye were glowing patches—from radiation. Things did not look good. The infra-red scanner showed lots of ruins and radioactive hot spots.

There was no localized space debris, so it looked as if Hoth had been hit and hit hard. The question Morland was interested in: Who'd attacked it and when? If it was just another internecine Space Viking war, then it held no real interest for him; however, if it was a Mardukan attack then it was important that he pinned down all the details he could uncover. Hoth was two thousand hours from Joyeuse and two thousand, seven hundred and fifty hours from Marduk, clearly outside the five-hundred light-year radius of space claimed by the Mardukan Empire. If the Imperial forces were attacking major Space Viking base worlds this far from Marduk, clearly no planet in the Old Federation was safe.

Morland briefly considered sending a pinnace out to gather more intelligence, but rejected the idea since they'd be too dependent upon filtered and enhanced lighting. He wanted a clear view of the damaged capital and spaceport and any dangers they might present.

He talked with Commander Ladbrok, a short man with a powerful build who carried an air of command. Lord Ladbrok was the last of the Gentleman Adventurers from Joyeuse and was now Ground Force Commander of the expedition. When asked how many fighters to take on their reconnaissance mission, he replied, "I wouldn't go down without at least a company, Commodore."

Morland nodded. "It's far too radioactive inside Khmun City to land. Signals-and-detection says the spaceport is red hot. We may have to settle for secondhand information from some of the survivors outside the capital."

Dawn arrived an hour later and Morland took one of the *Skull Splitter's* pinnaces down to Hoth's surface. The sun was rising from the east, bathing the ruined city in a red wash. As they drew closer, Morland could see that the Khmun Spaceport had taken major damage. The spaceport was laid out in the standard octagonal layout with docks for eight ships, but two docks were complete rubble, probably from missiles with atomic warheads, since a thermonuclear would have taken out the entire port. Inside the spaceport remained the hulks of five spaceships, three two-thousand footers and two fifteen-hundred footers. The globular ships were in various stages of demolition: One had been sectioned, as if someone had cut it with a blade halfway down to the ground, showing the interior decks and bulkheads. Another had been breached, but was tilted to one side. A third ship had collapsed into itself from multiple missile strikes and one of the fifteen hundred-footers was completely gutted.

The Royal Tower had twisted and fallen halfway, about a thousand feet down its shaft. Most of the Tower's interior furnishing and support beams had rained down upon the Hoth Mercantile Building, leaving it battered and crushed. Unless Prince Nikky Everrards and his brothers had been out of the Tower, they would have to be counted among the casualties of this horrific attack. The city itself was in even worse shape, as most of the contragravity towers were broken or had fallen down upon the inhabitants.

Using the telescopic screen, he searched the city and found no movement or evidence of life—not even a mongrel dog slinking around. "What do you think, Rovard?"

"The radiation detection sensors show high readings throughout the city, sir," reported Rovard Harvan, verifying his earlier reading. "They're highest around the spaceport."

"Is it safe to land?"

"Yes, but only if we wear radhaz suits, sir. But I doubt we'll find any real answers here."

Morland nodded.

"David, I think our best bet would be to visit one of the local towns and talk with some of the locals," Lord Ladbrok offered.

"I agree. Rovard, where's the nearest decent-sized town?"

Before Rovard could reply, there was a burst of static out of the squawk-box on the control board. "Standard Sword-World impulse-code. Interrogative: What ship are you? Informative: provide screen combination. Request: Please communicate."

Morland nodded. "I don't see any problem from the ground. What's their screen-combination?"

"It's the *Grim Reaper's* code, sir."

Morland remembered meeting the *Reaper's* captain, Anse Shawley the last time he was on Tanith. Shawley was a big man with the strong aura of command, almost the archetypical Space Viking. "Give them our code."

The communication screen flicked, then lit up. There was a ghost-effect around the edges of the screen.

"What's that?" he asked.

"Radiation interference, sir," Rovard answered. The screen went gray, then the colors popped again with only the outside edges showing the ghost-effect.

The gray-haired man peering into the screen was seated in a wooden chair in what appeared to be the basement of an old house. "Raff Dondaldson reporting, sir. Is this Captain Morland of the *Skull Splitter*?"

"Yes, although it's Commodore Morland now. And who am I speaking with?"

"Sorry, Commodore. Sir. I'm the Signals-and-Detection Officer, *Grim Reaper*, sir."

"What the hell happened here?" he asked.

"A stealth attack by the Empire," he replied. "The bastards came in using Sword-World codes as Space Vikings. Once they took out Everrards' outriders, the Mardukans hit Hoth with everything they had."

"How's Prince Nikky?"

"Missing and presumed dead. He was residing in the Royal Tower when the backstabbers hit it with a missile barrage."

"Did any of the Everrards survive?"

"None that were on planet. The youngest, Stefan Everrards, was off-world, but we haven't seen hide nor tail of him. In fact, we thought maybe you were Duke Stefan returning from his trade-and-raid run."

"How did you escape?"

"The Captain took us out of Khmun for some R&R. He thinks the crew gets better service away from the sharpers and high-priced merchants at the capital. We left a skeleton crew aboard the *Grim Reaper* and the rest of us were at Darrak Town, some two hundred miles southwest of Khmun."

Rovard reported, "Found it on the map, sir."

"I'd like to meet with Captain Shawley in person," Morland said to Dondaldson.

"I'll send him a message you're coming, sir."

"Anything we can do for you and your crew?"

"No, sir. This is my post until we find a way off this hellhole."

II

Darrak Town was the usual Neobarb settlement, mostly three and four story wooden buildings at the center of town, with some larger houses at the northern edge. Darrak was located at the confluence of two major rivers and there were a number of boats at the docks, but little water traffic. Morland suspected that the bombing of Khmun had had a bad effect on business. There was no wall or fort, but he reasoned that would change now that the Everrards were out of the protection racket.

He doubted that Duke Stefan could hold Hoth together with just one ship and that once it recovered, if ever, Hoth would become just another chicken-stealing world for out-of-luck Space Vikings to raid. It had a mild climate, but it was a dry world. Its only oceans were at the poles. The countryside below the pinnace was desolate, mostly desert and hard-scrabble land with only a few Terran-introduced trees.

The local plants were mostly shrubs and long vines with yellow-green leaves the size of hands. According to the *Bestiary*, there were no native edible plants or wild life. The local animals were low on the evolutionary scale, mostly cold-blooded life forms that looked like early amphibians. Settlers had introduced jackrabbits and sheep, but nothing much larger flourished in the wild, due to the scattered and limited vegetation. All the local cattle and horses were imported, including the Gram bisonoids, and had to be kept on large ranches that grew their own feed.

They set the pinnace down on a small airport just out of town. The dirt field and its hangers were home to half a dozen propeller driven planes, two old battered aircars and three ships' pinnaces that looked as if they'd seen better times. Morland left with Lord Ladbrok, First Historian Ulrik Selner and a maniple of five ground fighters in a combat car driven by his trusted aide, Sergeant Xavier Burris.

Burris landed the combat car in the town diamond, a remnant from when the locals traveled by horse and buggy and used the open space to turnaround. From what he'd read in the *Bestiary*, Hoth was poor in fossil fuels. They'd be back to horse-drawn carts and buggies in another generation, if not sooner, he mused.

Their combat car drew a lot of local attention, everyone came out of the local shops eager for news. Morland suspected that habit would die as soon as the first off-world raiding party arrived. He disembarked with Lord Ladbrok, Ulrik Selner and a squad of fighters.

One of the better-dressed locals, who introduced himself as Mayor Argant, asked them to retire to the local tavern. Drinks on the house. The Mayor was surprisingly young and didn't wear a beard, unlike most of the locals.

After introductions and when they were seated, the Mayor asked, "Has anything changed at the capital?"

Morland shook his head. "I doubt there's a living being in all of Khmun. Somebody hit it fast and hard with several atom bombs."

The Mayor shook his head. "We heard the bombing from here, it sounded like distant thunder…we knew it was bad. I had one of our marshals do a flyover and he said the city was a goner. That was a couple of Galactic Standard months ago."

Morland nodded. "The attackers weren't satisfied with blowing Khmun Spaceport to kingdom come and back, but dropped several atomic bombs on the city itself. I'm surprised they didn't bomb every major city on the planet."

The Mayor paled. "Khmun *was* the only large city on the planet. All the other towns and villages are scattered all over the upper latitudes. If you hadn't noticed, Hoth isn't the most welcoming world to life—too much damn desert, and very little water."

"It doesn't seem that bad here in Darrak Town," Lord Ladbrok said.

The Mayor laughed. "That's 'cause we're at the equator. It gets dry as Hell's lava in the summer."

Morland noticed, when he brought another round, that the bar was tended by a human bartender, not a robotender. Without some outside help, Hoth would drop down to a Civ-Level of 3 or 2 within a generation.

"How long before we can do some salvage work in Khmun City?" the Mayor asked.

From the look of desperation on his face, Morland knew this was a question of some import. "It all depends upon the radionuclides. Most have brief half-lives, but some last for years, even decades. From what I saw, most of the blasts were groundside and that means more long lasting radionuclides. The spaceport took a lot of hits. The worst of it should be over in another five hundred hours. I wouldn't send anyone in without a hazrad suit any sooner than that."

The Mayor shrugged. "Who has one of those? Any that were on this planet were in Khmun City."

"I've got two or three I could sell you, but it would have to be for fresh meat."

The Mayor smiled. "We've got lots of meat since the attack. We were a major transit point to Khmun for all the ranches within a thousand miles. Now that the city's gone we're running out of feed for all the cattle we've got on hand. And our refrigeration units are stacked to overflowing"

They shook on the deal and Morland sent Burris back to the ship with a load of fresh meat and a message for the Second.

"I have another little problem that maybe you can help me with," the Mayor said tentatively. "I've got a number of former space visitors who can't go home."

Morland kept the smile that threatened to break to himself. *I don't doubt that: What with most of Shawley's crew stuck here and who knows how many other present and former Space Vikings are in town.*

"I might be able to help you out there. First, I'm looking for a Captain

Shawley—"

"Oh, Shawley!" interrupted the Mayor. "Former Captain of the *Grim Reaper*. I know him well. I'm sure he'd love to meet with you. An old friend, maybe?"

"Not quite, but we've met. On Tanith."

The Mayor nodded. "Let me send for him." He spoke to one of his hangers-on and directed him to bring Shawley to the tavern.

Morland listened while the Mayor gave him the chamber of commerce spiel on Darrak Town. He thought it was strange how people stuck to their "normal ways" even during the most extraordinary of times. *Must be some survival mechanism bred in the bones of the Terro-Human species,* he decided. *He doubted the next ship to land would find anything close to 'normal' when they arrived at Darrak Town.*

He saw Shawley come in through the tavern door and waved him over. Shawley, who looked exactly the same as he had in the Riff-Raff Tavern in Rivington, walked over to join their table.

Morland stood up and they both knocked fists. He turned to the Mayor, "Mayor, I would consider it a favor if you would leave and allow me and my old friend to catch up on our affairs."

The Mayor, who looked as if he was planted for the duration, nodded begrudgingly and got up and left.

Shawley took his vacated seat at the table. "Look at you, Morland, a Commodore now. And here I am shiftless and ship-less. Last time I was on Tanith, all I heard was talk about your successful raids and shiploads of loot." He paused to rub his glove-sized hands over his eyelids. "I should have joined up with you on Tanith…."

"I wish you'd joined up with us, Captain Shawl—"

"Call me Shaw."

"Okay, Shaw. We've been working a sector of the Old Federation that's seems almost untouched since the Interstellar Wars. More than enough booty for a dozen ships."

Shawley let out a sigh that ended with a groan. "We didn't do so well with our four-ship squadron, or Black Band as we called it. Our first raid at

Liothe went pretty well, although the world was more advanced than we'd expected. With four ships, their ground defenses folded pretty quickly and we left with a reasonable haul."

Morland nodded. "Captain DeBorder hit Liothe alone in the *Pay Dirt* and got mauled. He ended up on Tanith with a damaged ship he couldn't afford to repair and refit. He ended up going into hock to King Rodrik and joined up with us out of sheer desperation." He paused to grin. "DeBorder's done pretty well ever since. At least, I don't hear any complaints."

"I wish I'd been half as smart. Anyway, there are too many armaments on Liothe for just a single ship and the Liothians as fighters are as rough as cobs. Our next raid was even worse. We hit Tetragramaton and found a squadron of Imperial ships waiting for us—"

"Was it an intelligence slip-up or were the Mardukans just lucky?" Morland asked.

"Nah, we didn't even pick it as a target until after we left Liothe. It was one of a dozen possible worlds we'd planned to hit. Not even the Imperials have enough ships to cover every world. Still, Tetragramaton is over six hundred light-years from Marduk, so we thought we were well outside of their so-called Imperial control zone…."

"Ha!" Morland chortled. "I'm beginning to think the Mardukans don't see any boundaries at all. They want to rule the entire Terro-Human universe."

"That makes sense," Shawley said, nodding in agreement. "Why else would they have attacked Hoth unless it's an undeclared war against Space Vikings."

"None that I can think of, Shaw," he replied. "How did you escape them?"

"We tried to fight, but were outnumbered six ships to four, and one of ours was a fifteen hundred footer. When two of our ships went to em-cee-squared, we ran for it and jumped into hyperspace as soon as we dared. Unfortunately, we took a shipload of damage and had to limp into Hoth for repairs."

"Did you take out any of the Imperials?"

"Yeah, just one. I saw it blow when the *Victor's Wreath* rammed it."

Morland signaled the bartender for another round of Durendal draft, the favorite beer of Space Vikings everywhere. While they were waiting, he said, "Let me introduce you to my officers. Captain Shawley, this is Historian Ulrik Selner and Commander Ladbrok."

They bumped fists.

Then Shawley said, "Former captain might be my current title. My ship the *Grim Reaper*, may she rest in peace, was in the docks when those Mardukan bastards blindsided us."

Ladbrok nodded. "We saw. I thought Hoth was safely outside their five hundred light-year boundary."

"So did a lot of others until last year. It's not 'official,' but that boundary's been extended by another five hundred light-years. Or at least the Mardukan Navy is acting as if it has been—especially when it comes to Space Vikings."

"I know," Morland answered. "We had our own run-in with the Mardukan Navy off Rhiannon."

"Rhiannon? Never heard of it."

Morland knew that Shawley, like most Space Viking captains, kept a mental library of every world listed in the *Bestiary* as well as any planet they'd ever heard mentioned by another captain. "Rhiannon's a Civ-Level 1 or 2 world that we first learned existed in the Vishnu Civic Library."

Shawley's face broke out in a cat-who-ate-the-canary smile. "Those Old Federation libraries can be worth their weight in gold."

Morland nodded. "We'd uncovered an old uranium mining complex on Rhiannon and we were busy stripping it when a Mardukan ship, the *MINS Challenger*, arrived. We gave it a good drubbing and might have destroyed their ship if we hadn't been low on defensive missiles."

Shawley nodded. "I know how it is. A good Viking captain's gotta know when to quit, as well as when to press hard. But, by damn, I sure picked the wrong base world for repairs."

"Don't beat yourself up, Shaw. The way the Imperials are gunning for us, I don't think there's a safe port outside of Tanith in the Old Federation.

And who knows how long Tanith will continue to be an independent."

"This reminds me of the British expansion back on Terra during the settlement of the Americas," Ulrik Selner said. "They were always testing the boundaries of the Spanish Empire with their privateers and buccaneers. If you look at the Sword-Worlds as Spain, the Mardukans as the British, you have a pretty fair analogue as to the present situation."

Morland shook his head. "Up to a point, but where your model breaks down is that none of the Sword-Worlds will spend a sol or send a single warship to help the Space Viking base worlds, not even when it's one of their own bases."

"Too much fighting amongst themselves," Lord Ladbrok offered. "Plus, it's a one-way street. The Sword-Worlders want all the gold and goods to come to them, not the other way around."

"If the Sword-Worlds don't change their policy, they'll find there isn't any place left to raid or trade in the Old Federation since the Mardukans will have cobbled up all the Old Federation worlds into their empire," Shawley observed. "By nature, I'm a lone wolf, but even I can see the handwriting on the bulkhead."

"I'm glad to hear that," Morland offered. "How would you like to join up with us?"

"I'd love to, Commodore. Just one problem, I don't have a ship."

"You have a crew, don't you?"

"Sure, and a damn fine one, at that. Although, they're starting to go to seed in this backwater burg."

Morland smiled widely. "Well, we've got our own shipyard on Poictesme. There are a couple of half-built ships still in their cradles. It might take a while, but they should be able to knock out another ship in a few thousand hours or so after we return."

"You mean it?" Shawley's eyes were as wide as a little boys on his first birthday.

"You have my word on it, Shaw. Of course, it'll be standard Sword-World shares for you and the crew. As owner, I'll take ten percent off the top, as captain your share will be five percent, two percent for the five chief officers, one percent for regular officers with the rest to be shared out equally among the crew and ground fighters."

"What about the cost of the ship?" Shawley asked. "We're flat broke and don't have more than five thousand Tanith stellars among the lot of us."

"The standard buyback rate is fifteen percent off all plunder, plus the owner's cut; that's what we're paying the New Base Venture, Ltd. on Joyeuse. The cost of a two-thousand foot ship in the Sword-Worlds is roughly six to eight hundred million Sword-World Stellars. Ships are more expensive on Excalibur because there's more demand at her dockyards and they're better built, or so they claim. Our cost at the Koshchei shipyards is about half of that, say four hundred and fifty million stellars since most of our equipment came with the planet."

Shawley nodded, "That's more than fair, Commodore. You've got yourself another captain and his crew."

"Good," Morland said with a smile. I'd also like you to pick out the best crewmen from the other stranded Space Vikings."

"Done, Commodore," Shawled said. "I know them well, since we're been sharing mess and drink."

They bumped fists and exchanged sworn oaths. Then he told the waiter to bring them a bottle of Baldur honey-rum to commemorate the deal.

III

They had to send down more pinnaces to pick up not only Shawley's crew, but another hundred and seventy hand-picked Space Viking recruits, most of who didn't want to be stranded on Hoth. The *Pay Dirt* took another three hundred. If they'd had room aboard the *Skull Splitter*, they could have taken three times that number.

Morland called a meeting in the great room so he could introduce Captain Shawley and his officers to his own crew, First Officer Laz Rivera, Second Gytha Valkanhayn, Third Reese Duggan, Fourth Reginald Mathes and Fifth Rovard Harvan. The new recruits were awed by the stories about their raids on Nissaba, Mara, Lyonnesse and Tashmetum. He also filled them in on their base at Poictesme and their shipyard on the dead world of Koshchei.

"It looks like you have yourself the makings for a great base world," Shawley offered.

"Not yet," Morland said. "Poictesme took a lot of damage after the breakup of the Old Federation and the Interstellar Wars. It was the base of the Third Federation Force Group. I doubt there are twenty million inhabitants on the entire planet; a far cry from what we need for a good working base world."

Shawley nodded. "Bigger does seem better these days. Look at Hoth. They had five ships, but only three were in fighting condition when the Mardukans attacked. Plus, their security was almost non-existent. Enough to keep their Space Viking visitors and merchant ships in line, but clearly lacking when major trouble arrived."

"Exactly," Morland replied. "I want a world with a large enough population and industrial base that we can counter any of the civilized worlds of the Old Federation."

"That's going to take a while," Laz Rivera said. "But, I must admit, we've made a good start."

"Since the holds are filled, where to next?" Shawley asked.

"Tanith," Morland replied. "We can sell most of our swag there. I was hoping to sell some on Hoth and at the other Space Viking base worlds but, after what happened to Hoth, we don't even know if they're still in business."

"Why not go back to the Sword-Worlds? You'd get good prices for most of this cargo."

"The political situation in the Helm is in shambles," Morland said, "when we left Joyeuse, rebels were still shelling Longinus City. Plus, I don't trust King Alwyn. He's one of our Base Venture investors and I think he'd like nothing more than to have us return to Joyeuse so he can commandeer the *Skull Splitter* and add her to his navy. If he's still in charge, that is."

"Excalibur is still stable," Shawley pointed out.

Rivera shook his head. "True, but everyone else knows that, especially the merchants and trading houses, so it's hard to get a good price."

"I agree," Morland said. "Plus, I want to talk with King Rodrik and find out what he's heard about Mardukan expansion beyond their so-called 'borders.' Also, Tanith's got some ship fabricating machines that I'd like to get my hands on for our shipyards on Koshchei. Rodrik knows more about the Space Vikings in the Old Federation than anyone else in the Old Federation."

DeBorder spoke up, "Besides, it'll give me a chance to pay-off my repair bills for the *Pay Dirt*. All thanks to the Commodore and his nose for plunder. Hot damn, will that be a relief!"

TANITH

I

With so many Space Viking recruits from Hoth, the *Skull Splitter* was as tightly crowded as a Gilgamesh freighter on the way home. They'd put together some temporary bunks in one of the empty cargo compartments, but until then it had been hard on the crew. It didn't make things any easier that the hyperspace journey to Tanith was slightly over a thousand hours.

There had been some trouble between the newcomers and Morland's crew as they sorted out the new pecking order. The fights stopped when he threatened to drop the guilty parties off at the closest Neobarbarian world. Shawley's crewmen were well behaved; it was the independent Space Vikings who were the biggest problem. He'd already interviewed them during the hyperspace voyage and drafted all the willing hands that'd been officers or had special skills. The rest were passengers and would disembark on Tanith.

And good luck to them, he decided. *If things are as tough on Tanith as I suspect, they'll be marooned there for a long time.*

Morland believed the era of independent Space Viking raiders going wherever they wanted and doing as they pleased was almost over. Hoth was good proof. The only Space Vikings who'd survive these times were those who banded together, or had major support from one of the Sword-Worlds. At one time—maybe a hundred years ago during the time of Otto Harkaman and Lucas Trask—the independent Space Vikings, with support from the Sword-Worlds, could have put a fleet together that would have brought an end to Marduk's dream of empire.

Not today, though.

He would have preferred to return to Poictesme, dropping most of the recruits off there, but he hated backtracking and, more than anything else, he needed good intelligence about what the Mardukans were up to. He doubted that the Hoth attack was a unique event. If the Imperials were targeting Space Viking base worlds, he wouldn't be surprised if planetary security on Tanith was a lot tighter now than it was during the *Skull Splitter's* last visit.

With all these questions and full cargo holds, Morland heaved a sigh of relief when they reached the Ertado System. As he peered through the outside viewscreen, he watched as the gray of hyperspace turned into a tumbling chromatic dispersion as the hyperspace field collapsed. No two eyes saw it the same, but most appreciated its ephemeral beauty. Ever since its initial discovery, in the Third Century, Atomic Era back on Terra, artists had attempted to recreate its beauty, but most had failed.

Suddenly the viewscreen displayed a black field dusted with sparkling stars in all their majesty. Morland slowly exhaled, releasing the breath he'd been holding in his lungs. Like the evening sunrise on Joyeuse, this was a sight he could watch over and over with awe and wonder. For the first time in a long time, he wondered what was happening back on his homeworld: Was King Alwyn's head still on his shoulders? Were the revolts still wracking Joyeuse? Would the war continue for generations, like on Durendal, with seesawing political factions?

At the center of the star field, he saw the golden coin of Ertado's Star, the G3V-class sun of Tanith. Right after they came out of hyperspace, they were met at five light-minutes in-system by two Tanith interplanetary warships and boarded. They were boarded again before they reached Tanith orbit, the second time just outside Shiloh, Tanith's moon. The Tanith officers were polite but uninformative. He wondered what kind of reception an unknown vessel might receive.

From their intelligence files, Morland knew that the League of Civilized Worlds' Navy had maintained twenty-two capital ships. Since the League had been an association of worlds, not a federation, the League's Navy had disbanded upon its dissolution. Now that most of its member worlds were part of the new Empire, he wondered how many warships King Rodrik had at his disposal. No more than eight or nine, at best—certainly, not enough to ward off an Imperial attack. *King Rodrik*, he thought, *is probably wondering when his neck is going to be the next one on the chopping block....*

It took almost twelve hours to reach Tanith, and then they had to wait several hours more to get proper permission to land both the *Skull Splitter* and *Pay Dirt* at the Rivington Spaceport. Morland didn't want to waste time using the pinnaces to haul the ship's cargo to the surface. He wasn't sure what was happening on Tanith, but he doubted that they'd want to stay for too long.

Tanith Spaceport was designed like an eighteen-pointed star and was one of the largest ports in this sector of the Old Federation. As they descended, the first thing he noticed was that there were only five ships at the spaceport and even fewer at the shipyard. He had observed three times that number on their previous visit. Nor were there as many aircars and flitters above the city as there were the last time he was in Rivington.

As they drew closer, Morland saw that there weren't any Gilgamesher ships at the docks which was most unusual. Gilgamesh ships were noticeable as they were shaped like onions, for religious reasons he assumed, rather than globes like almost every other spaceship. He would have to look into their disappearance since the Trasks were the only Space Vikings on friendly terms with Gilgamesh. Most Space Vikings viewed the Gilgameshers as interlopers, at best; or religious maniacs who should be exterminated, at worst. They were, however, the most successful traders in the Old Federation and Gilgamesh itself was the Holy Grail of Space Viking planetary targets.

II

As soon as the *Skull Splitter* landed, even before the flight crew could disembark, the head of King Rodrik's Houseguard approached the gangway, asking to speak to "Captain Morland." He was brought aboard and taken to the bridge.

"Captain...I mean Commodore," the Houseguard said, after seeing Morland's insignia. "I have been ordered by the King to take you directly to His Majesty's private Presence Chamber."

"May I bring my sergeant-major and fellow captains?"

"I'm sorry, sir. For security reasons, the King asked to speak to you alone."

His Executive Officer, Laz Rivera, looked worried. "I'm not sure that's a good idea—"

"It's fine," Morland said. "I'll go alone." *If things have gotten to the point where I have to worry about being assassinated by King Rodrik, then there's not a safe harbor for any of us inside the Old Federation's borders.*

The captain escorted him to a fancy combat car with the Trask blazonry—a skull impaled on an upright sword—on the door panels. As they traveled up over Rivington City, Morland looked over at the Gilgamesh Quarter where the Gilgameshers' compound was located. The surrounding walls and buildings were intact, but there was no sign of life inside. It appeared as if the Gilgameshers had decamped en mass.

Morland pointed to the compound. "What happened?" he asked.

The guardsman shrugged. "The gilgies all left about six S.G. months ago. Never said a word to anyone, they just up and left, taking their goods and ships with them. Haven't seen a single one since. Good riddance, I say."

Morland kept his own thoughts to himself. Trade with Gilgameshers had been one of the cornerstones of Tanith's prosperity. Whatever had caused them to leave Tanith, must have been something major. The question was: Did they leave on their own, or were they sent away by Rodrik? He knew that whatever the answer was it would have repercussions beyond his visit.

The captain landed on one of the private landing pads at the Trask Tower, the tallest building in Rivington. The royal palace occupied all the floors from four hundred to six hundred. The guardsman ushered him inside the tower anteroom where the Chancellor was awaiting him. Morland realized that his star had risen on Tanith; on his last visit he'd been ushered to see the king by a mere attendant.

The Chancellor looked put out by this duty, but kept his thoughts to himself. They went up a contragravity lift to a portal from where he was quickly taken into the king's presence chamber.

King Rodrik was seated in a comfortable chair; he motioned with one hand for Morland to take a seat and, with the other, to have the room cleared. Rodrik looked as if he'd aged a decade in the five years since their last visit. He still had the same regal hawk-nose, but his hair was all gray and the edges of his brown beard were edged in white, as if by hoarfrost. There were lines etched into his face that Morland didn't remember seeing before.

Rodrik was still sharp, noticing his new rank first of all. "I see you've been promoted."

He nodded. "We've had some successes, Your Highness."

"So I heard from Captain DeBorder during his last visit. He seems quite taken with you."

Morland smiled. "As he would be with anyone who helped make him rich, sire."

"Rich enough to pay off his debts?" Rodrik asked, raising his eyebrows.

"Yes, he has the hundred and fifty million Sword-World stellars necessary to pay off the final installment of what he owes you for the *Pay Dirt's* ship repairs. I had him set aside a quarter of the *Pay Dirt's* share of our takings to buy back the ship. "

"Excellent. That's the first good news we've had in some time. It's a damn good thing I'm king; if this were a parliamentary planet, I'd be thrown out of office."

"Things are that bad?"

"Worse," Trask replied.

"What happened, Your Highness?"

"The Empire happened. After they killed off the League of Civilized Worlds, they started going after the independent Space Vikings with a vengeance. It's not enough that the Viking ships stay out of their self-proclaimed Imperial territory, they've been hunting them in packs far outside their so-called boundaries. As you can see from our near empty spaceport, there are damn few Space Vikings left in this sector."

"Then the destruction of Hoth begins to make sense."

"What—Hoth? What are you talking about?"

"We stopped off at Hoth first to sell some of our cargo. The Everarrds have always been good customers."

Rodrik winced. "Their Mercantile Center—has hurt us more than once. So what did you find there?"

"Khmun City and the spaceport, all destroyed. The Royal Tower in ruins. A-bombed. Not a living thing left in the city. According to the locals, the Mardukans used Sword-World codes to identify themselves, then turned on the Everrards and destroyed the capital. They left the hinterlands alone but, in a couple of generations, Hoth will have fallen back to complete barbarism—Civ-Level 2 maybe...."

"Well, Hoth was never a paradise at its best."

"Now, it's an abattoir."

King Rodrik shook his head in dismay. "I'd heard about the attack on Jagannath. The Grathams fought back and were able to turn the Mardukans away, but they lost half their ships. Now, Hoth and the Everrards.... All of them?"

"Nikky's youngest brother was off-planet when the Imperials attacked so he may have escaped."

"This is bad for all of us."

Morland nodded. "I know. We've had our own problems with Marduk.

We were in the middle of loading radioactives on Rhiannon when the *Skull Splitter* was attacked by the Mardukan Imperial Navy ship *Challenger*. Rhiannon is a Civ-Level 1 world with some still functioning automated breeder reactors we were able to repair and get running. It's hundreds of light-years outside the Imperial boundaries so we were totally unprepared for their attack. Before we returned to Rhiannon to pick up the plutonium and radioactive isotopes, we'd taken a beating on a raid on Mara which used up most of our defensive missiles. We were at a disadvantage when the *Challenger* arrived, but managed to outfight their ship. Now I'm worried that they'll be back for another round. This time with an entire squadron or fleet."

"Did you kill their ship?" Rodrik asked with apparent concern.

"No, but I think we'd have been better off if we had. Their captain, last name Vandarvant, promised us dire consequences upon his return. I believe he meant it."

"*Vandarvant*. I've heard that name before. Conrad Vandarvant is one of Emperor Lucas's intimates, a duke if I recall correctly. He's part of the militant expansionist wing of the Mardukan aristocracy. A real imperialist. This Captain Vandarvant may be a son or nephew. I'll have my secret service check our files."

"Thank you, Your Highness."

Rodrik smoothed his hand over his forehead back through his thick hair. "It's best that you didn't destroy the *Challenger*, David. If you had, they'd have sent half the Imperial Navy to hunt you down. The Mardukans are making examples out of anyone with the audacity to fight back. God help anyone who actually destroyed one of their ships! Now that you're on the Empire's radar, your best bet might be to return to the Sword-Worlds."

"Not now. Not when I'm so close to establishing my base. I've already got a major shipyard at my disposal—"

"What did you do, conquer Isis or Aton? Those facilities don't grow on trees."

"Better than that, Your Highness. We discovered a former Federation shipyard on an airless planet in the Gartner Tri-System. It's a remnant of the Third Federation Force ship facilities from the System States War. Apparently, it was abandoned after the System States surrendered and the locals, who've reverted to almost total barbarism, had no use for it, or any way to get to the shipyard. It's been abandoned for almost a millennium. I've got some of my best men rehabbing it.

"I know it's hard to believe, but some of the ships were almost finished and were just abandoned there on Koshchei. It's like they were frozen in time. Most of the fabrication places and factories had automated cleaners and robotic repair units and are in surprisingly good shape. We're going to need some new milling machines and other machinery, but—"

"If you're really going to dismiss my advice and try to make a go of this base world of yours, I have a lot of silent factories and idle machinery right now. As I'm sure you noticed coming in, our repair docks are almost empty and most of our shipwrights are out of business. We've called a halt to all new ship construction. We've got a lot of great machinery that we can sell at a good discount."

Morland rubbed his hands. "Excellent. And we've got lots of power cartridges to sell or trade, as well as uranium, luxury goods and the usual Space Viking cargo."

"I'll take it in trade, but I think you're making a mistake trying to set up your own base world with the entire Old Federation in a state of flux."

"I appreciate your advice, but this is something I need to do. The Sword-Worlds are finished; even before the Empire, they were in a state of decline. It's like that famous quote of Otto Harkaman's: 'Civilizations die from suicide, not by murder.' What's happening on the Sword-Worlds today is a slow case of self-extermination. All the men with any gumption or ambition have fled to the Space Viking base worlds, or are off aviking. Other than Excalibur, they're all in a state of decline. There's no future for us there."

"Sometimes, I just wish"—the King splayed his hands out— "I could do what you're doing and start anew myself. Of course, it's impossible; too many responsibilities and the family to take care of. I'll just have to find some way to muddle through our current problems until Tanith gets back on its feet."

Morland couldn't think of anything to say that might be encouraging. Things in this sector were going to Nifflheim in a handbasket and it didn't look like they were going to get any better for Tanith, or the independent Space Vikings.

"If you'd like," Rodrik continued, "you might consider hiring some of our shipwrights and shipbuilders. Many of them are already on our benefit rolls; I'm sure they'd rather be working."

"Are you sure?" he asked. "If things turnaround, you might find them hard to replace."

The King made a funny little laugh. "I don't think there's much chance of that unless someone puts Marduk out of empire-building business. And I don't see that happening anytime soon." The King shrugged. "Maybe if they encroached far enough into the Confederacy's territory...?"

Personally, Morland agreed. He didn't see much chance of Marduk running afoul of the Odin Confederacy; at least, not yet. A century ago, Odin herself had been expanding, but that had been brought to a halt by a coalition of Space Vikings. The Confederacy was still too big and strong to roll over for the Mardukan Empire—for now.

Nor did he think there was much chance of Tanith's economy turning around any time soon. Tanith was in the early stages of a depression from which it might never recover. Certainly, it was clear that the Space Vikings, Tanith's major business clients, were being run out of the Old Federation and there was nobody who was going to take their place. As far as trading, even their biggest trading partner, the Gilgameshers, had left Tanith high and dry.

"I don't mean to pry, Your Highness," Morland stated. "But, as we were flying over Rivington, I couldn't help but notice that the Gilgamesh Quarter appeared deserted. Where did they go?"

Rodrik shook his head in mystification. "They all bugged out. Most of the Gilgameshers are standoffish, but I've made friends with a few of them over the years. Some I even grew up with. My father encouraged them to attend the University of Tanith, but only a few went. Most of them returned to Gilgamesh for their higher education; I guess, for fear of religious contamination. Some of the locals are pagans and there's a small Church of God community. However, most of us are just hardheaded pragmatists, like most Sword-Worlders."

Morland nodded, as that certainly described himself.

"One of my friends, Mordecai Veltrin, told me that back on Gilgamesh the Elders had received word from their Avatar Merlin to leave Tanith. He didn't know why, just that they were to leave."

"Merlin!" Morland sputtered. "I've heard that name back on Poictesme. I thought it was the name of one of their military leaders or presidents. I wonder what role it plays in their religion."

Rodrik shrugged. "I'm almost embarrassed to admit how little I know about Gilgamesh religious practices or their beliefs."

"The Gilgameshers have always struck me as a pragmatic people, except for their religion."

"But that doesn't explain why the Gilgameshers have stopped trading with Tanith," Morland said.

"He wouldn't answer that question," Rodrik said, clearly perplexed. "He just does what he's told. I've talked with several space traders and merchants since they left. They claim the Gilgameshers have become sparse throughout this sector."

Morland chewed over that for a bit while Rodrik took out his pipe and began to load it with Haulteclere tobacco. For some reason it was almost orange in color, but pipe smokers swore it was the best leaf anywhere.

"Do you think they left their colony on Tanith because the League of Civilized Worlds has disbanded?" he asked.

After he finished lighting his pipe, Rodrik said, "That's something I never really thought about. Gilgamesh is over fifteen hundred light-years from Tanith so I've never seen them as a military threat. As far as I know, the Gilgameshers have established colonies on only those worlds that are considered civilized, the most prominent being Odin. I've never heard of them attacking anyone or colonizing any Neobarbarian planets in the Old Federation."

"No, they keep to themselves, all right," Morland said. "And their merchant ships are heavily armed, almost in the same class as your typical Space Viking ship. No sane Space Viking views them as easy pickings. Yet, they're always around during political upheavals and planetary uprisings. I also find it interesting that they completely eschew trading with the Sword-Worlds."

"That's easy to understand, it's because they wouldn't be welcome," Rodrik said firmly. "You and I both know there's a *lot* of anti-Gilgamesh prejudice in the Sword-Worlds. Isolated and thousands of light-years from their homeworld, the Gilgameshers would have to be crazy to try to trade with the Sword-Worlds. The League of Civilized Worlds was responsible for increasing interstellar trade along the edge of the Old Federation, by policing those worlds and providing protection from outside interference, mostly Space Viking raids. I've always believed that was why the Gilgameshers helped grandfather back when the League was in its infancy. We've always promoted a good-neighbor policy and good trading relations. The Gilgameshers have always been merchants—first and last."

"Or so they've appeared," Morland offered.

"Maybe you're letting your prejudices show, David, " Rodrik countered. "Sword-Worlders are brought up to disbelieve in any religion. They love to scorn the Gilgameshers because of their funny appearance and strange ways."

Morland, who thought of himself as far more enlightened than most of his Sword-World kin, tried not to take umbrage at the King's conclusion. "You may be right. I've never gone out of my way to befriend a Gilgamesher. Although, I've always thought that I might, if given the opportunity. But they have as great a distaste for Space Vikings, as we do for them. I suspect they hung around Tanith because your grandfather gave the Gilgameshers special privileges in exchange for their help, which from what I've read in Otto Harkaman's history—*The Trials and Tribulations of Gentleman Privateer*—were mostly in the area of intelligence."

"I wouldn't have admitted this before the League broke up and they left, but there's some truth to your words. All arriving Gilgamesher traders

have always shared *sensitive* data with Tanith's Off-World Intelligence."
Rodrik's face paled. "I didn't realize how much safer that made me feel
until they all left. I wish I knew what they were up to. Do you have any
ideas, David?"

"I can't think of anything. For some reason, they're pretty scarce
around Poictesme and I'm beginning to wonder why."

"What I want to know is this," Rodrik said. "What's in it for them?
Gilgamesh is one of the wealthiest and most civilized worlds in the former
Federation. So why were so many of them in this sector? Just what is it that
makes this part of the Old Federation so important?"

"Those are good questions. For the last hundred years, it was probably
the League of Civilized Worlds. Maybe the Gilgameshers wanted to
keep an eye on the League in case it expanded into their sector of the
Old Federation. Now that the League has disbanded that threat is gone.
Or possibly their Avatar has some religious reason, something we don't
know or can't even imagine. Religious pronouncements often mean little
to outsiders.

"But, there's one thing I do know, when I get back to Poictesme I'm
going to get to the bottom of the Merlin rumors. There's always been
something odd, or off, about the Lord High Mayor of Litchfield. I've never
looked into it because I had other more important things to worry about.
Now, I'm going to do some serious digging."

"Good. And, David, let me know if you learn anything."

Morland smiled. "You can count on it. Likewise, let me know if you
learn anything more about my Mardukan nemesis, Captain Vandarvant."

"We still do some trading with Marduk; I'll have our people keep
their eyes and ears open."

III

The *Skull Splitter* spent almost a Galactic Standard (G.S.) month on Tanith, unloading cargo and loading machinery. Morland spent much of that time in the Riff-Raff Tavern, sifting the gossip and rumors he heard for kernels of truth. He sold about half their cargo on Tanith; the rest he had transferred to the *Pay Dirt's* cargo holds for transshipment to the Sword-Worlds. With the cargo holds of the *Skull Splitter* emptied, there was plenty of room left for most of the Space Vikings they'd picked up on Hoth as well as several hundred shipwrights, machinists, machine operators and other skilled spaceship workers who wanted to emigrate from Tanith to Poictesme.

Morland knew he was transferring some of the best brains and talent Tanith had to offer and he valued them more than all the gold and goods that he'd transferred to the *Pay Dirt*. The best part was that these new citizens were just as happy to leave, and be able to continue to do their work on Poictesme, as he was to get them. It wasn't as if King Rodrik didn't know what he was losing, but the Tanith shipyards were now operating with a skeleton staff and things on Tanith would probably get worse before they got better—if they ever did.

As a matter of course, King Alwyn would never have allowed such a transfer of talent off Joyeuse; he would have kept the skilled workers there and out of work rather than let someone else benefit from their skills. This was what made King Rodrik an excellent ruler and good example for Morland to follow. However, the expansion of Mardukan power, at Tanith's and the other Sword-World base worlds' expense, presented Morland not only with opportunities, but grave problems.

He'd already had one run-in with the Mardukan Imperial Navy and that presaged future contacts that might not always end in his favor. This meant he needed to accelerate his search for a better base world and start preparing for future hostilities. Rodrik had strongly suggested that he retire to the Sword-Worlds and take over one of the lesser worlds. "If you landed your three ships on Gram, you could probably take and hold the entire planet," he'd said. "I'd bet my last stellar that the people there would welcome you with outstretched hands and open hearts, especially if they thought you could bring an end to the wars of succession. Then maybe we'd see the beginning of a Sword-World renaissance."

Morland had rejected that idea for the same reasons he'd left the Sword-Worlds in the first place. The Sword-Worlders were too set in their ways and mostly looked to past glories, not future ones. He wanted a world that was a clean slate so he could create something new and better than anything the Sword-Worlds had to offer.

But first, Morland had to return to Poictesme and find out all he could about Merlin and have his scouts keep their eyes open for Gilgameshers. If they were spies, he couldn't begin to imagine their motives, but whatever they were—if they favored the new Mardukan Empire—they were counter to his best interests.

There was a lot of gossip at the Riff-Raff about Space Vikings staying away from the territory included in Marduk's new Empire. There was also some bluster that a few ships were still raiding in Imperial territory, but Morland didn't buy half of it. Most of that talk was under the table since there were plenty of independent traders who'd happily sell that information to Marduk for a centistellar. In general, the Mardukan claims had put a damper on Space Viking raids.

He was mulling this over when Captain DeBorder arrived at the Riff-Raff Tavern where he sat with the Ship's Historian and Commander Yorick Ladbrok. He was using this opportunity to talk and share information with the different Space Vikings and off-world merchants. The few who were still on Tanith were worried about their futures and several of the Space Vikings were talking about returning to the Sword-Worlds for good. He'd told them of his own successes and welcomed them to take their chances in this new quadrant of the Old Federation. Two of them were interested and he provided them with Poictesme's coordinates.

"Hi, David," DeBorder said, as he took a seat at the table. Then he turned to the robot-tender and ordered a glass of Excalibur red whiskey.

Morland nodded in return.

"Would you like a glass of whiskey? My treat."

"No," Morland said, pointing to his half-empty glass. "I'm drinking Poictesme melon-brandy."

DeBorder looked around. "So are half the customers in this place. What did you do, sell them a few barrels."

"I gave them a small cask as a sample. Then sold them a dozen barrels. Before we leave, they'll want to buy whatever we have left."

"Don't sell it all or you'll have a mutiny on your hands," DeBorder joked.

Morland took it as a sign of just how contented his crew was that DeBorder could joke about the worst disaster a ship could encounter; after all, they'd made enough stellars on the last few raids that even the cabin boys could retire.

"Is Poictesme where you're headed after we finish up here?" DeBorder asked.

Morland nodded. "I've got a ship full of engineers and shipwrights. Plus, I want to get to the bottom of this Merlin business that King Rodrik brought up."

"I don't blame you," DeBorder replied, "The last thing we need are any homegrown Gilgameshers. There's always been something *off* about that Lord Mayor. Nothing I could put my finger on, but something a bit askew...."

"I've felt it too," Ladbrok said, "and I don't like mysteries."

"Yorick, you did the initial contact with the Poictesmians," Morland said. "Did anything strike you as odd or unusual?"

"Yes, that whole business with the Lord High Mayor Fitch, on my first visit to Litchfield. It was very stilted with a creepy sort of audience.... I didn't like the Mayor then, and I don't like him now. Fitch acted as if his welcoming us was doing us some huge favor, when in truth we were bringing the fruits of civilization to a broken-down world, one that had fallen into near barbarism and remained there for centuries."

DeBorder rubbed his gray beard. "I don't know. I think that a fairly typical reaction from a planetary ruler, or whatever this Fitch is. These local potentates always want you to think they've got something in reserves, when in actuality they're living on the thin edge of disaster."

"You may be right," Morland said. "I'm still going to look into it when we get back. What I really want to know is: Why did the Gilgameshers leave Tanith in such a hurry?"

DeBorder looked around at the half-empty tavern. "Stab me, but I'd leave this place, too. In another ten thousand hours it'll be as dead as Melkarth. This planet has no really valuable mineral resources, like plutonium or gadolinium. Nor anything else of value to trade. They've made their living off us Space Vikings, buying our goods and reselling them at a good profit. Repairing and fixing our ships. What else does Tanith have to offer?"

Morland had to agree that DeBorder had made a good point. Tanith wasn't even centrally located; its importance had been magnified by the League of Civilized Worlds. Now that the League was disbanded it was just another Neobarb world living on its past.

"You're probably right," Morland said, shaking his head. "Still, it just doesn't feel right that the Gilgameshers would leave their colony so quickly…."

The Ship's Historian spoke up. "I think it's possible you're making too much out of isolated events. Let's look at the historical picture: From what all the surviving evidence shows, Gilgamesh was a relatively unimportant world during the time of the Federation. They are rarely noted in the histories and there's no mention of them being interstellar traders, either. However, they were staunch supporters of the Federation during the System States War. Yet, after the Big War, we don't find any mention of Gilgamesh. The first information we have on their god Yah the Almighty doesn't appear until almost a century after the Federation's fall."

"Now, the fall of the Federation is a controversial subject, Ulrik,"

Morland argued. "Almost every historical school has its own interpretation of how and when the Federation ended."

"I know, Commodore. That whole period is an enigma historically as most of the Terran Federation's records were lost when Terra was destroyed, while others disappeared during the collapse that followed. The Gilgamesher traders are very canny and tight to the vest. They never reveal any information about their homeworld. There's very little known about them before the System States War. However, they were hit hard a number of times during the dark night of the Interstellar Wars. After the economic collapse that occurred Federation-wide after the fall, my guess is that there was some kind of religious mania or revival on Gilgamesh. It's not uncommon for people during times of decivilization and decline to look inward for salvation and answers.

"Their new religion gave them a focus, and I'm sure that their early contacts with other worlds quickly taught them caution. Which in turn reinforced their religious beliefs, leaving them more secretive and withdrawn, as outsiders derided them or took advantage of them during their first forays into the former Federation. Now, they've become so wealthy and insular that this pattern has become ingrained."

"Look, I don't blame them for their paranoia," Ladbrok offered. "Space Vikings have been drooling over the possibility of sacking Gilgamesh since the days of Wulf Hellmut."

"Agreed," Selner said, "still their reticence and secrecy goes beyond any other civilization I've run across in my studies. I believe they make a deliberate effort to keep their homeworld hidden through deliberate obfuscation."

"As if they have a secret that they want to keep from the rest of humanity," Morland suggested.

"Exactly. It's almost impossible to break their covenant of secrecy."

"Well, they may have made a mistake by abandoning Tanith," he said, "because to me it looks as if they only used the Trasks for gathering intelligence. My question is: Are they going to start working for Mardukans, which would mean they're using the new Empire, too? We'll have to keep our eyes and ears open. I don't know what the Gilgameshers are up to nor the whys and wherefores, but I'd like to get to the bottom of it."

The Historian's face flushed. "There might be a whole new field opening up of Gilgamesh studies. If I were the first one to crack their shell of secrecy and write a treatise...."

DeBorder was the first to speak. "This is not just some dry scholarly mystery, Selner. Cracking the Gilgamesh secrets, may give us the leeway we need to survive the Mardukan threat."

"Yes," Morland said. "If we're going to survive and flourish we need any and every advantage we can find. Javen, I know your first stop at the Helm is going to be Excalibur. I'd appreciate it if you'd have your ship's historian check out the libraries there and what data you can find on the first Space Viking contacts with the Gilgameshers. Maybe there's something buried there."

"Sure, David. I'll put him to work and try to recruit two or three more ship historians, now that I've seen how important historical knowledge has been for our previous raids."

"Good, and while you're there, see what you can learn about the Mardukans. I'd also be interested in what Excalibur's position is regarding the new Empire."

"Okay, David. My ship will be lifting-off this evening."

"I hate to see you go."

"Me, too. We've had an unbelievably successful series of raids. Now that Rodrik is paid off, I feel as if a huge weight has been lifted off my shoulders."

"Yes, congratulations are in order."

"Well, if they are David, it's thanks to you."

"I couldn't have done it without your help, Javen."

"Thanks, but to be honest, I did my share of foot-dragging in the beginning. Now, I own my ship and have a top-flight crew, and it's all thanks to you. I won't forget."

Morland tried to keep the pleasure he felt from flooding his face. They were now both very wealthy men, rich enough to buy their own patents of nobility on any Sword-World, including Excalibur, and retire in style. "Be sure and come back, now."

DeBorder laughed. "I'm having too much fun to retire. Besides, I'm a space dog at heart. And there's still a lot of the Old Federation left to see. One day I'd even like to visit Terra."

Morland snorted. "I didn't know you were a sentimentalist, Javen."

"I'm not, just curious."

"I talked to a captain from Hoth, on my first visit to Tanith," Morland said, "who claimed to have landed on the Homeworld. He said it's just like any other Neobarbarian world, except worse. It was bombed back to the Stone Age during the Interstellar Wars and hasn't recovered."

DeBorder shook his head. "Every Space Viking who's made over two raids into the former Federation claims to have visited Terra. And most of them are only kidding themselves. I won't believe a word until I see terra firma with my own two eyes."

P⊕ICTESME

I

Lord-High Mayor Morgan Fitch was seated at his desk, his fingers nervously playing a sonata on the desktop. It had been over ten Galactic Standard years since the last courier ship had visited; today it was arriving at the spaceport right on time. He wished he'd had some way to let them know about the off-worlders before they landed. If there ever had been such devices, they'd been lost or destroyed during the economic and social collapse that had followed the Great Exodus.

The Space Vikings kept a careful eye over their own communications equipment, not that it would have done him any good, since he didn't know how to work it. Their arrival was unprecedented; for the past two centuries very few of their ships had ventured into this sector of the Old Federation, only one of which had landed on Poictesme previously, almost three centuries ago.

The Space Viking's leader, Prince David, was a man of great foresight and ambition and he had created unprecedented changes in Poictesme herself. Prosperity had come to Litchfield and with it many newcomers from the Sword-Worlds and Space Viking base worlds. Their industry and independence was rupturing a social fabric that had continued for centuries without change. Such things were unprecedented on Poictesme since the Time of Troubles and he suspected that the Caretakers would not be happy with the changes that had been wrought in their absence.

Fitch's worry was that somehow the Caretakers would blame him for what had occurred instead of the Oracle for not having predicted this very thing. *Or did it*, he thought, *and they just didn't bother to inform us.* Not unprecedented, since the Caretakers, who cared for the god-machine they called the Oracle, often assumed airs and acted as if they were demi-gods, not mortal men.

No matter how hard the Caretakers strove to kill the age-old rumors of the god-machine Merlin, it still persisted in old Poictesme legends and in song, seemly impossible to stamp out. Fortunately, the newcomers had focused most of their attention on the long abandoned space facilities on Koshchei and had shown little interest in Poictesme herself.

Frankly, Fitch rather admired the Space Vikings' industry and curiosity. *I've lived too many years with true-believers who question nothing and continue to stagnate*, he decided. The Caretakers ship had arrived only hours before and he wondered how they would view all the changes. *Not well, I fear.*

He heard the ringer go off and picked up the phone, another old invention reinstalled by the newcomers. "Yes."

"It's the Scion and his party, Your Worshipful."

"Tell them to come in."

"Yes, Your Worshipful."

The Scion, the young Maxwell, entered with Sylvester Zareff, the Arch-Archivist and interpreter of the Charter. Zareff was a tall man with long limbs like sticks. The Arch-Archivist bowed, saying, "Your Worshipful, I received your message."

"Good. Then you know that the Caretakers have arrived."

"Yes, Your Worshipful. Right on time. I fear they will not be pleased at all with the changes brought about by the infidels."

Fitch nodded. The Charter told them to serve the newcomers, but made no distinctions between who they might be or what they might do. Nor had it provided any provisions in case they might be potential enemies of the Oracle. In the past, such directions had not been necessary; Poictesme had been bypassed by raiding parties due to its obvious poverty. However, that had not dissuaded *this* group of Space Vikings. *Could this be a fundamental error in the Charter?* he asked himself.

Best not go there, he decided. Next he might be questioning the Oracle Itself and that could easily be seen as heresy. It had been a long time, at least two centuries ago since the last Lord-High Mayor had been boiled alive in oil for questioning the Charter. That was one custom Fitch would prefer not to see revived.

"What happens if the Space Vikings return before their ship has left?"

The Arch-Archivist deferred to the Scion, who had the Maxwell traits of height and broad shoulders. The Scion's deep blue eyes peered into his own as if they could see the thoughts behind them. "It must not happen. There must be no link between us and the Resettlement."

"Then they must make their survey quickly. It's been almost eleven Earth Standard months since their departure. Morland or another of his ships could return at any time."

"The Rector is incensed that we have allowed the barbarians' access to Koshchei and the shipyards."

"It wasn't our decision," Fitch replied. "They discovered them on their own. Who expected them to put a permanent settlement here in Litchfield or refurbish the shipyards on Koshchei and use them to build new ships. Not I."

"The Rector has not made a final decision," the Scion said, "but I have recommended destroying the Space Viking settlement, killing all the intruders."

The Lord-High Mayor lowered his head, "As I have argued before, Young Maxwell, killing all the Space Vikings living here would only cause the barbarians to look closer at what we are doing. Prince David is not your typical Space Viking, but a man on a mission—one he may not completely understand. Morland would not forget or dismiss the destruction of his settlement, but would worry it like a wolfhound with a bone. He's a dangerous man and a threat to the Mission."

"I agree," the Arch-Archivist said. "The smart thing to do would be for the Rector and you to leave immediately—doing nothing—before the Space Vikings return."

The Scion looked at him as if he were a bug under a microscope.

"There is much you two do not understand about the Plan. There is no place in it for these barbarians. They must be destroyed."

"You don't understand the danger we face from the Space Vikings," the Lord-High Mayor said. "You have stayed in Oracle House and refused to meet or talk with them."

"I will not debase myself by communicating with such scum," the Scion pronounced, brushing his hands against his robes as if to dislodge something distasteful.

"Then you cannot know them as we do," the Arch-Archivist put it, as his fingers twisted like large worms. "Killing them could endanger the Plan and bring retribution from those who are off-planet."

The Scion shook his head. "You both have been here on Homeworld too long. Your perspectives are distorted.

"Scion, it is you who are wrong in this matter. Tell him this, my advice is that the Rector leaves immediately before the Space Vikings return, meanwhile doing nothing to annoy or bring attention to our Mission."

II

This time there was no advance warning of their arrival. The Rector, a large man with a long black beard flanked by two burly Brothers, pushed his way into the Lord Mayor's office with the Arch-Archivist trailing behind. In the background, he could hear his assistant's cries.

Fitch rose to his feet. "What is the meaning of this breach of hospitality?"

The Rector stared at him icily. "Is it true, as the Scion claims, that you have become a lackey of the Space Vikings?"

"I work with them, as directed by the Plan. They appear to be honorable men and I have treated them likewise."

"What have you told them about the Oracle?" the Rector demanded.

"Nothing. They heard rumors of Merlin and asked the usual questions. They appear to have accepted the rumors as hearsay and legends. I have told them nothing more."

"Have they asked about the Mission?"

Fitch shook his head. He didn't understand why he was in so much trouble. *If the Space Vikings were to be diverted or shunned, why wasn't I told beforehand? Has the Oracle been in error?*

"Well, they are our enemies now," the Rector said. "We shall destroy their henchmen in Litchfield, and then annihilate the shipyards on Koshchei. It should have been done long ago, but we have been lulled into complacency by the lack of visitors here in the past. The Space Vikings will find nothing left upon their return."

"But they'll blame us," the Arch-Archivist wailed.

"The Oracle said there would have to be sacrifices."

The Rector's eyes looked at him coldly as if he were already dead and dissected. Fitch backed up against the wall, his eyes searching for a weapon. The two Caretakers advanced, each one grabbing one of his arms. He tried to kick his feet out at them, but a hard slam to the gut by the Rector left him slumped over in pain, gasping for breath.

"Pull up his sleeve and leave no marks. This must look like a natural death," the Rector said, as he pulled out a hypospray and pressed it against Fitch's bicep.

There was a sudden stabbing pain, then his heart started beating wildly against his rib cage and suddenly everything went red as if his eyes were bleeding out—

III

The first thing Morland heard coming out of hyperspace and into the Gartner Tri-System was the beeping of the communicator. For once, he didn't notice the change from hyperspatial gray to the wondrous star-studded black field. "Who is it?"

The Ship's Fifth, Rovard Harvan, reported on the squawk box, "Standard Sword-World impulse-code. It's an incoming message from Captain Vann Stenger aboard the *Faerie Queene*. He wants to talk with you Commodore."

"Patch him through to the Bridge."

"Aye-aye."

"David?"

"Hi Vann, it's me. What's up?" He knew it wasn't good news, or Vann would have waited until they landed at the Litchfield spaceport. *Let it be anything, by Odin's Spear, other than a Mardukan squadron."*

"There's a Gilgamesh ship at the spaceport. It arrived fifty-four hours ago. Upon entering the system, thirty hours previous to your arrival, we did the usual survey of our out-system satellites. Two of them reported the arrival of a Gilgamesh freighter and we decided to stay hidden behind the moon and monitor their activities."

"Good thinking, Vann."

"We've talked about the Gilgameshers before and I know you don't trust them so I thought I'd see what they were up to. I didn't want to show any evidence of our presence until I had further orders. But I fear I have bad news. We haven't heard from Poictesme headquarters since they landed. All we got was a stealth communication from HQ that the Gilgameshers were demanding entrance. Since then, we haven't heard a word."

"You did well to wait for reinforcements, Vann. There's no way you could have stopped them in time alone. I didn't trust the Gilgameshers before I talked to King Trask; now, I don't trust them at all. I suspect they're providing intelligence for the Mardukan Empire."

Vann Stenger whistled through his teeth. "What are we going do with them, David? They've been down on Poictesme long enough to disrupt our operation and cause us real trouble."

"Agreed. We're either going to have to capture their ship, or destroy it."

Vann whistled sharply. "But how? We can't attack them at Litchfield port, sir. We'd damage our own spaceport and maybe level the town."

"I know. We'll wait until they start to leave. Two ships to one should make quick work of them. No matter what it takes, I don't want them leaving the Gartner Tri-System."

"Understood. What are our tactics?"

"We're both going to go into high-earth orbit over Litchfield. Then I'll take the *Skull Splitter* down to the spaceport and order them to surrender."

Vann Stenger looked grim. "I don't think they'll go for it. I've never heard of a Gilgamesher ship surrendering."

"If they don't, we'll wait until they lift. Once they're into the stratosphere, we'll hit them hard. The *Skull Splitter* will stay just above their ship, while you shadow our movements from above with the *Faerie Queene*. With a little luck we can pull a squeeze play."

"If we can hit them from two flanks, we should be able to kill them quickly."

"We have to. If the Gilgameshers can get by us, and far enough out to make a hyperspatial jump, we're all in trouble."

As soon as they passed through Poictesme's magnetosphere, Morland had signals and detection inform their people on the ground of the upcoming attack. Almost instantaneously, missiles shot out from the Gilgamesher ship which sat in one corner of the spaceport like an armored onion. Weapons fired counter-missiles and none of the Gilgamesher's missiles made it through the stratosphere before exploding.

Rovard Harvan reported, "Sir, missile fire directed at the Litchfield Airlines Building and several other places in town."

Morland let off a string of curses. The Airlines Building was their headquarters. Suddenly the entire building blew up. He was happy to see no mushroom cloud.

The onion ship began to rise up from the spaceport, firing at select targets within Litchfield. The *Skull Splitter* fired several of its own missiles to keep them occupied when suddenly the Gilgamesh ship veered off to the southwest at full atmospheric speed.

The *Skull Splitter* dropped down to chase them, firing missiles. Only one missile made it through their counter-fire, shaking the enemy ship but otherwise leaving it unharmed. Morland was holding back on his arsenal of fissionable missiles in order not to create any more collateral damage than absolutely necessary. It was surprising, now that it was under attack, how much he thought of Poictesme as theirs.

The normal-space astrogator said, "It looks like they're headed for the Golfe Du Lion. Do they think they can hide in the Sea of Lion?"

No experienced captain would fight an undersea battle, when all they had to do was leave a ship posted above the Gilgamesher's hiding spot and wait them out. It might take ten thousand hours or more, but sooner or later, they'd have to surface for fresh food. Carniculture worked fine as long as it was provided essential nutrients every eight to ten thousand hours.

Of course, they could stay under indefinitely if they started adding the local fish into the vats to replace missing vitamins and trace minerals. Still, he couldn't imagine them holing up undersea for any length of time.

It appeared the Gilgameshers were headed for deep water as they left the Golfe Du Lion and moved into one of the deeper underwater rift canyons.

"Where are they going?" someone asked, voicing a question running through everyone's mind.

Suddenly there was a massive explosion and a burst of light from under the sea. Moments later the sea below broiled as a huge spout of water shot up into the sky.

"Great Satan!" someone else cried out.

"They blew up their own ship, sir," Rovard Harvan reported.

"Send out a tsunami warning to all seaports and islands within a three thousand mile radius."

"Yes, sir," Harvan replied.

"There won't be any answers coming from that quarter," Lord Ladbrok observed.

"No, there won't," Morland agreed. "We need to get back to Litchfield Spaceport and have a talk with the Mayor."

IV

Morland, escorted by his top officers, headed to the Lord Mayor's headquarters. No one was surprised when they reached the Mayor's office to find him and the Arch-Archivist both dead. They had a medico check them over.

"All medical signs point to a heart attack, sir."

Morland shook his head. "What are the odds of two men in the same office having lethal heart attacks at the same time?"

Ladbrok replied, "Slim to none. They were murdered to keep them from telling us anything."

Everyone knew that under a veridicator the truth would always come out. There was only one way to beat one—and that was to die. In this case, Morland doubted that the two men on the floor before him had any choice in the matter.

"Look at their upper arms," the medico said. "If you look closely, you can see slight abrasions. Once I have them back on the ship, I'm sure I can find the point of entry for whatever killed them."

"Do that," Morland said flatly. "However, I don't believe we'll find the culpable parties on Poictesme. I think they're on the Gilgamesh ship that just blew itself up."

"What does it mean, sir?" First Officer Laz Rivera asked.

"Only that we were right. There was a secret about Poictesme that's so important to the Gilgameshers it's worth killing and dying for."

"Shall we question any of the others?"

"Sure. But I'm sure the only persons of interest on this planet who knew anything either died in this office or elsewhere. The Gilgameshers were here long enough to wrap up any loose ends. And we know they're good at their jobs because up until now no one has suspected them of anything more serious than wearing funny clothes and worshipping Yah the Almighty."

"Any thoughts, Ulrik?"

The Ship's Historian stayed quiet for a few moments, then shook his head. "I'm as perplexed by this as you are, Commodore. Historically, there's never been any evidence that the Gilgameshers are anything other than what they've always appeared to be—successful traders and followers of a small, inbred religious cult. However, their sudden abandonment of the Tanith colony and their possible association with Marduk raises a lot of questions. Questions that may never be answered, if this example proves to be a typical of Gilgamesher response when they are cornered."

"Still," Ladbrok said, "just give me a couple of hours with one hooked up to a veridicator, then we'd learn just what it is they're up to."

"Whatever it is," Ulik said, "they took a one-way road out. I can't understand why, though. The Gilgameshers have always appeared to be observers of the flux and flow of history, not participants."

"Which shows just how little we know," Morland said. He turned to his Weapons Officer, Reginald Mathes, asking, "What do you think about all of this Reg?"

Mathes was the only man in the room who spoke Gilgamesh trade-talk; he knew more about their customs and rites than everyone in the room combined. He spent a few seconds filling his pipe and then lighting it. "It's the strangest damn thing I've ever seen, sir. Gilgameshers live by the Word of Yah, and he doesn't permit suicide. Suicide is a cardinal sin and just about the worst thing one of them can do according to their scriptures and everything I know about them. Whatever secret that ship held, it must have been lethal as all hell for them to face eternal damnation."

Morland ground his teeth in frustration. "I know, none of this makes any sense, but they did kill themselves and destroy their ship. That's an observable fact. Either that ship wasn't a Gilgamesh ship, or there's a secret so important that its crew would face damnation to keep it from us. I just wish I knew what else they might do...."

"Me too," Mathes said. "We're just lucky that ship wasn't here long enough to visit Koshchei and destroy it, too. We've lost some good people and a few buildings here in Litchfield, but what we have there is irreplaceable."

Morland nodded. *Yes, but why?*

K⊕SHCHEI

Giffard Zhorgay, the *Skull Splitter's* Chief Engineer, who was overseeing ship construction on Koshchei was pleased when the *Skull Splitter* returned. He was even happier when he got an eyeful of the construction machinery, skilled technicians and shipwrights that Morland had brought with him from Tanith.

"Now, we can really ramp up ship construction. We've got another interstellar ship ready to be launched within the next hundred hours."

"Good timing, Giffard," Morland said, "since I've brought a captain and crew with me from Hoth. Captain Shawley formerly captain of the *Grim Reaper*, which was destroyed on Hoth by a Mardukan surprise attack. He and his crew survived, but were stranded on Hoth."

"Sir, didn't you meet him on Tanith during our first visit?"

"Yes, and I tried to enlist him in our venture, but he had other obligations. I believe Captain Shawley's going to be a real asset."

"What about Tylor Ragnarsans?" Giffard asked. "Won't he be upset when he learns you're going to give the first ship we've launched to an outsider?"

"He might be, but that's not his decision to make. Tylor doesn't have the necessary experience to captain an interstellar ship. I'll appoint him captain of the first interplanetary warship that comes out of the shipyard. Tylor shows promise, but he needs more seasoning."

The Chief Engineer shrugged, as if to say it wasn't his problem. "How did this Shawley survive the attack on Hoth, if his ship was destroyed?"

"Shawley and his crewmen were away on business when the Mardukans bombed Khmun City to hell and back."

"Ah. I had some friends there…Damn, I'd hate to think what they'd do if they ever found this place," Giffard said worriedly, pointing to the dozens of domed construction facilities that surrounded them.

"Blow them all to em-cee-square."

"Then we've got to keep them away," Giffard replied, looking sick just at the mere thought of such a thing.

Morland nodded. "That's why I'm going to keep two ships in the Gartner Tri-System at all times to keep an eye out for any Gilgameshers or Imperials. I hate to tie down half my Navy just on routine patrol, but we can't afford to leave our assets here unprotected either."

Giffard said, "I was notified about the Gilgamesher ship's arrival. But I thought it was a routine trading stop until they attacked our people in Litchfield. What was that all about?"

Morland shook his head. "I don't know. We may never know… Whatever it was, there's one thing we can be certain of."

"What's that?"

"The Gilgameshers want to keep us in the dark; otherwise, they wouldn't have blown themselves up rather than face capture. Did their ship approach Koshchei?"

"No," Giffard replied. "I didn't even know they were in-system until I got a call from Vann Stenger. They wouldn't have found us unless they were doing a survey of the entire Tri-System."

"Good. Our detection systems are pretty well camouflaged. Still, after they landed it didn't take them long to find out about our presence and react. They put a missile down the stovepipe of our headquarters in Litchfield."

"How many men did we lose, David?"

"Overall, about a hundred of our own men and ten times that number of locals. "

Giffard looked stunned.

"The Gilgameshers bombed most of our supply and residential buildings. Luckily, most of our men were off-planet or scattered around Poictesme doing survey work, or casualties could have been a lot worse. We're trying to keep it quiet. I'm not leaving again until this system is better protected."

"In addition to the almost completed interstellar ship, we've got two interplanetary warships that were nearing completion when the Federation shut down the shipyard," Giffard said. "With additional help, one of them could be rehabbed within a thousand hours, after we finish the interstellar ship. Both of the interplanetary ships could carry a higher payload and more weapons than any vessel that Gilgamesh can send our way. Unless they send a fleet, these ships should be more than able to outmatch anything the Gilgameshers have in their arsenal."

"That's good to know. To be safe we're going to need five or six such ships so that they're spread throughout the Tri-System. The last thing we need is to have enemy warships entering Gartner Tri-System, gathering intelligence on us and then successfully jumping into hyperspace before we can destroy them. We've not only got Captain Vandarvant looking for us now, but the Gilgameshers will be wanting to know what happened to their ship, once it's reported as missing. We probably only have a few thousand hours before they reach the conclusion that it arrived here and never left."

"Well, your timing is close to perfect," Giffard replied. "With all these new hands, we should be able to really ramp up our production. In a couple of Galactic Standard years, we should be strong enough to fight off six or seven warships."

"Excellent!" Morland exclaimed. "The next problem we're going to face is getting enough crewmen to man them."

Giffard looked lost in thought for a moment. "When Vann Stenger was here last, wasn't he trying to turn some of the locals into real spacemen?"

"Yes, but he spaced-out before he really got anything going."

"Maybe we need to create a training program or school?"

"Not a bad idea," Morland said. "Our own space academy, I like it. If we're going to do that we'll also need to ensure the locals loyalty. There's some kind of link between Poictesme and Gilgamesh and, until we find out what it is, we should probably run all our potential candidates through a veridicator before accepting them into the new academy. I'd hate to find out later that we let any Gilgamesher moles on any of our ships."

P⊕ICTESⅢE II

It took almost a G.S. month to find and rehab a suitable replacement for the Airlines Building in Litchfield which had been their headquarters before it was destroyed. It was fortunate that most of the occupants had been in the field running down information on the Gilgamesh ship so the casualty list was just over a hundred men and women—far less than it might have been. The Litchfielders, who had taken the lion's share of their losses, were as angry about the surprise attack as the Space Vikings, putting the blame squarely on the Gilgameshers.

The replacement New Base Venture's headquarters building, the Allied Storage Building, wasn't as large and accommodating as their former one, but, on the other hand, they'd been using less than twenty percent of the available office space in the Airlines Building. The Allied Storage Building was shorter, but much broader and had more docks and storage space. They even found some demolition equipment and robots that could be salvaged and used later for rehabbing some of the older parts of town.

The shipyard had already finished an interstellar ship, which Anse Shawley christened the *Grim Reaper II*, and was starting work on two new two-thousand foot interplanetary ships. For its device, the new ship had a figure in a black-hooded robe holding up a silver sword in each hand with a planet at its feet.

Captain Shawley was already chomping at the bit to go out on a raid-and-trade expedition. "I wanna see what kind of pickings we have in this sector."

Morland wasn't anxious to leave Poictesme until he learned more about what the Gilgameshers had been up to. They were still trying to track down former Litchfield officials and political officer holders who might have answers about Merlin or the Gilgameshers. The results were unsatisfying, to say the least. If anyone knew anything new about Merlin, other than it *might be* the name of the man who'd rescued Poictesme from ruin after the System States War, they weren't talking or they had been eliminated by the Gilgameshers before the *Skull Splitter* had returned.

Finally, in exasperation, Morland called an officers meeting in the new Allied conference room. After the room was thoroughly swept and found to be free of listening devices, the combined officers of the three available ships gathered together and took seats around a large oval table. He'd forbidden robot-tenders so Rovard Harvan volunteered to serve drinks, mostly the local melon-brandy and Nissaba pomegranate wine.

When everyone had a drink in hand and was settled into their chairs, Morland came to his feet and said, "To cut to the chase, we don't know a damn thing more today about why that Gilgamesher ship went haywire than we did the day it happened. There's very little left of their ship; it appears they set off all onboard warheads simultaneously. Frankly, we're lucky that the Gilgameshers eschew hellburners or we'd have had a tsunami that would have scoured the entire coastline of the Lion Sea. As it is, over a hundred fishing vessels were lost as well as eight freighters and several large boats. A dozen coastal towns and villages were heavily damaged with a casualty count in the thousands. But, as I said, it could have been so much worse. For the most part, radiation levels are back to normal except in the vicinity of the Golfe Du Lion. As far as finding out what happened and why, we're still completely in the dark."

"Why don't we run down a Gilgamesh ship and get some answers?" Tylor Ragnarsans asked.

"Because, Gilgamesh ships don't surrender." Morland replied. "We could send a ship to lay in wait for one to arrive on one of their known trading worlds, but I suspect the run-of-the-mill Gilgamesher knows about as much about what happened here as we do. Which means, we'd have to tie-up an entire ship for thousands of hours on a mission that's probably not going to learn anything more than we know right now. I suspect the only place we'll ever get a satisfactory answer is on Gilgamesh itself and that world is the most heavily defended planet in the Old Federation. We'd need a huge armada to even consider tackling Gilgamesh with any hope of success and, at that, we might have to destroy the planet. No, Gentlemen, I fear it's a lost cause, for now."

Almost everyone's head was nodding in agreement.

"As to protecting our assets here on Poictesme, before we leave for our next raid we'll have two heavily armed interplanetary ships on station to protect the system. I suggest we leave another one of our warships on permanent watch inside the Gartner Tri-System. We'll rotate duty and the roster will be drawn up at a later time. For now, we're not going to let anyone who is not a friendly land at Litchfield Spaceport."

"But what about other Space Vikings, Commodore?" Vann Stenger asked.

"They will be allowed to stop, but only if they allow us to board them and determine their prior stops and what they want on Poictesme."

Captain Shawley was shaking his head. "Commodore, that'll never wash. Most independent Viking ships won't allow themselves to be boarded unless they're disarmed and out-gunned."

"Their ship could be a sheep in wolves' clothes for all we know. We Sword-Worlders have bred enough brats throughout the Old Federation that it would be easy for the Mardukans, or even the Gilgameshers, to assemble a crew of counterfeit Space Vikings good enough to fool anyone at first glance."

"I must have left bastards on a dozen planets," Shawley mused.

"Me, too," said several of the other older officers.

Laz Rivera shrugged. "Space Vikings, for the most part, look like everybody else, except for our distinctive clothing. Anyone can impersonate us as a ruse of war. Until now there's never been any reason to do so."

Reginald Mathes interjected, "Commodore, you're on the wrong track. I, for one, don't believe there's much to worry about. I don't see the Gilgamesher's impersonating Space Vikings. First, they'd have to find or steal a ship that doesn't have their distinctive architecture. Then they'd have to shave their beards and wear our clothes; hellfire, there must be a dozen strictures against that in their religious codes and regulations. Besides, Gilgameshers wouldn't know how to act like regular spacers."

Heads nodded in agreement throughout the room.

"I suspect you're right." Morland conceded. "Still, we'll keep a close eye on all merchant ships that enter this system. After all, it's not just Gilgameshers we have to be wary of, it's the Mardukans as well. We can't trust anyone whom we don't know. Unfortunately, Poictesme is too underpopulated to make a good base world, but it will be our temporary base world until we locate a better one."

AGRAᛗᛗA

I

The *Skull Splitter* came out of hyperspace three light-years from Agramma for a site-stopping. Morland liked to have both ships arrive in any new star system together and making a site-stop was the only reliable way for both ships to arrive simultaneously. The astrological problem they faced, when pinpointing a new star system, was that they were basing the star's position on either Otto Harkaman's *The Bestiary of Old Federation Worlds*—which was a hundred years out-of-date, at best—or *the Astrogator's Guide to the Worlds of the Federation*, which was over a thousand years old.

The Astrogator would use his computers and the knowledge of nearby stars to determine the star's current estimated position, then they would estimate a site-stop within a light-year. In this case, Reese Duggan's calculations were two light-years, plus one light-year for observation, off from the star's actual position which was within typical specs. Now that they had a fix on Burlson's Star's position, next time they could jump right to Agramma's solar system.

The *Skull Splitter* arrived first, which gave Historian Walter Ovard a chance to brief them on Agramma. Before they left Poictesme, the assistant historian had spent the last thousand hours poring over documents and old starship logs in the Conn Maxwell Memorial Library in Litchfield.

"From the documents I studied, there was a brisk trade between Agramma and Poictesme in the Tenth and Eleventh Centuries A.E. At first, most of the trade was for fur, amber and precious gems, but as civilization rose on Agramma they discovered deposits of gadolinium—"

"Now that's something we need badly," Morland interrupted. Gadolinium was hard to come by and most of the worlds that had it in any quantity, like Beowulf, were part of somebody's idea of an empire. It was an essential material for the construction of hyperdrive engines and more valuable pound for pound than plutonium. Before they left Poictesme, Giffard Zhorgay had told him in confidence that they needed more gadolinium or they wouldn't be launching anymore interstellar craft.

"Did it give the location of the mines?" he asked.

"Yes," Ovard replied. "However, it's debatable as to whether or not they're still in production."

"If they are, they're probably trading partners with Odin Confederacy or Osiris, which means they may have a naval presence. If not, we have enough gear to cobble together some mining equipment and mine it ourselves. That means that we might be there for a while."

Using an overhead projector, Ovard went on to show them detailed Federation era maps of Agramma, indicating the major cities, seaports and gadolinium mines. Before the briefing was over, the *Grim Reaper II* arrived and Captain Shawley was provided with copies of all the relevant material.

"I like your thoroughness, Commodore," Shawley said over the screen. "How do you want to pick this place apart?"

Morland replied, "I'm going to let the *Grim Reaper II* lead the raids on the major cities. I have no idea what shape they're in since these maps are over eight hundred years old. However, they do provide us with potentially profitable targets. Meanwhile, the *Skull Splitter* will hit the Pennor Mine, right here. Of course, it might have been played out centuries ago, but we won't know until we visit it for ourselves."

Two microjumps later and they were deep into the Burlson System.

"What do you think, Commodore," Mathis the weapons officer asked. The battle-stations board was an arc of red lights for full combat readiness.

Morland studied the yellow orb. From where they were, all he could make out was the single habitable world about the size of a pea. "Signals-and-detection, are you getting any readings?"

"No, sir," Rovard Harvan replied, "there are no detection stations or sensors that we can sense. In fact," he said as he peered into the telescopic screen that showed Agramma at about the size of a pomegranate, "I don't see any evidence of life. Or at least, civilized life—nor any city-light halos anywhere on the dark side that's showing."

Morland pondered what he should do next. They were about 2 Astronomical Units from Agramma and it would take another microjump to put them about a light-second from the planet. If *Skull Splitter* came out of hyperspace any closer to Agramma than a light-second, the collapsing field itself would kick her back out to the heliosphere. The alternative was a couple of hundred hours or more of normal-space travel. He turned to the astrogator, asking, "Can we make it in two microjumps?"

Reese Duggan, said, "Yes, sir, that should do it by my calculations."

Morland nodded. "Jump," he ordered.

Duggan twisted the red handle to the right and pushed it in. The viewscreen swirled with broiling colors. The screen turned a dead gray as the pickups attempted to translate a dimensionless void into something the eye could parse. Suddenly colors kaleidoscoped across the screen again, and now Agramma appeared as a coin-sized blue disc, blotched with brown and gray. The single moon was some eight hundred miles in diameter and eighty thousand miles off-planet.

The next microjump left them a little more than a light-second away from Agramma, and less than thirty thousand miles behind her moon. The last jump was when a ship was most vulnerable, and coming out behind a moon provided some shielding from planetary battle stations. It could be dangerous on a moon with detection systems and missile-launchers; however, that was a moot point here.

Battle stations klaxoned and red lights flashed until signals-and-detection called out, "All clear."

Reginald Mathes, Weapons Officer, was looking at the moon through the telescopic screen. "All clear on this side."

Signals-and-detection agreed.

So did the *Grim Reaper II* which had followed them by about five minutes.

When they came out from around moon, Agramma filled up a third of the screen showing blue oceans, four large continents and two white poles. It was daylight over most of the planet below them and there was still no evidence of civilized life.

A sigh of disappointment that ran through the entire crew.

"It looks dead," Shawley said on screen.

Morland nodded. "Could be. We won't know until we touch down. Let's keep to the original targets and send out all pinnaces."

When Shawley's face winked off, he turned to Walter Ovard, the Assistant Historian. "I want you to go down yourself and give me a report on what passes for civilization."

"We're working in the dark here, sir," Ovard said wincing, as though he took the planet's apparent poverty personally. "It's always a guess."

"I know. We've been lucky so far, more hits than misses. That's why I want you down there on the ground to see if we can salvage anything from this trip."

II

The next meeting was two hundred and eighty hours later in the wardroom with all officers attending, including Captain Shawley and his Executive Officer.

"Captain, please report."

Shawley shook his head. "The major cities, or what once passed for them, are all in ruins. The place has been pretty well picked over. We hit the Manager's palace at Zarma, if you could call it that, and picked up a couple thousand coins and some hangings and artwork, very primitive stuff, I fear. Most of their coinage is debased, the few gold coins we found had more copper and silver than gold; the silver coins assayed out as mostly tin.

"No problems with the locals," he added. "The poor buggers are armed with matchlocks and swords. Most of them threw down their weapons the minute we landed. Not much mettle for battle against Star Lords, as they call us."

Walter Ovard looked as if he could hardly sit still he was so anxious. As soon as Shawley finished speaking, he rose up. "Commodore, there's wealth on Agramma, but it's not in the managers' palaces or the factors' manors. It's with the Church of Rome," he finished with satisfaction.

"Explain," Morland ordered.

"From what I could ascertain during my limited time dirtside, gathering up old stories and legends, Agramma was hit hard after the Federation Breakup. They were attacked more than once by space raiders and some of them used nukes. This pushed a border-line civilization and economy into complete chaos. The local church, which calls itself the Church of Rome—possibly an offshoot of the old Terran Roman Catholic Church—became the only organization left to maintain what was left of the former civilization. Whether by plan or happenstance, the Church has helped keep barbarism alive on Agramma by outlawing technology and science.

"Everyone here is very superstitious and it wouldn't be hard to establish ourselves as overlords and rule the planet. But first, we'd have to destroy the churches and the hold that the priests have over the people."

"That's not why we're here, Walter. If these poor bastards have allowed this Church of Rome to make their lives miserable, it's not our duty to set things straight. What I want to know is whether there's anything worth stealing here?"

There was a chorus of agreement from the other officers.

Ovard smiled. "Yes. This is where it gets good. The bishops and the priests have been collecting their tithes and dispensations through the centuries until they own about half the land and almost all of the precious metals. And, not all the locals are happy about it. Most of these people live in abysmal poverty, while the priests live like nobles in abbeys that are more like palaces than churchly offices. If there's anything worth looting on this planet, it's the abbeys and bishoprics."

Morland nodded cynically. He remembered reading about the Catholic Church during the Dark Ages back on Terra when they concentrated most of Europe's wealth in the Church's coffers. He couldn't do much to redress history, but he could change things here and now on Agramma.

"Good work. Men you know what to hit and where to go now. The priests have been collecting their tithes for us for a long time; they just didn't know it. It's our duty to relieve them of their worldly profits."

That got a laugh from the assembled Space Vikings.

"What do we do about the priests?" Laz Rivera asked.

"Kill them if they get in the way!"

"The abbeys are well-guarded, sir," Ovard added.

Shawley chortled. "Not against Space Vikings."

Next the new Chief Engineer gave his report. "Sir, the mines at Pennor have all been abandoned. I don't believe they've been worked since the Twelfth Century, Atomic Era. From the ore trailings I saw, this was one of the richest gadolinium mines in the Federation! It's going to take us some time to mine the ore and get some working ore processors up and running, but it's going to pay off in a big way."

"Good," Morland said. "However, this not some smash-and-grab raid. Ladbrok, it's going to be your job to organize some of the locals. Ovard will help you select them; I'm sure he's already got some ideas."

He looked over at the Assistant Historian who was already smiling to himself.

"I want you to locate some of the more ambitious locals and teach them the rudiments of mining and ore processing. You'll probably need to build some kind of permanent encampment. I want it strong enough that the local church doesn't come roaring back the moment we leave."

Ladbrok nodded.

Morland continued, "The mines are in the lesser populated northern area of the third continent, which the locals call Homeland. Destroy all the abbeys, churches, rectories and other religious buildings within a two hundred mile radius—"

"Wait a minute!" Shawley interjected.

"After they've been thoroughly looted, of course," Ladbrok added with a courtly bow.

"Good man," Shawley said.

"I'll make sure that Ovard picks only those natives who are either nonbelievers or who have been so trod upon by the Church that they will never submit to its authority again. I'd also like to get a few volunteers from both ships, men who are ready to retire and are looking forward to settling down, to run the mines and processing plants we leave behind."

On most Space Viking ships there was never a problem finding crewmen and ground fighters willing to leave the ship and settle down dirtside. Some were Space Vikings who'd either grown soft or tired of raiding and incessant warfare. Often times, it was the newest crewmates, who hadn't experienced the violence and mayhem associated with Viking raids, that wanted out. He'd almost quit himself after his first raid aboard the *Prince of Thieves*, after they'd hit Deirdre and sacked her major cities with a horrific amount of collateral bloodshed and damage.

"Chief, how much time will you need to get the gadolinium processing machinery and refineries set up and in operation?"

The Chief Engineer paused in thought for a few moments, then said, "Two to three thousand hours should do it, sir. Five thousand if you want to take more than a few pounds of gadolinium back with us."

"I do, make it five thousand hours. There'll be a bonus in it for you if you can do it in four thousand. Is that enough time for you, Ladbrok?"

"With some help, I can have the mines reopened and running, and a new town built as well." He smiled wolfishly. "In fifty years, my men will be running the entire planet."

When they returned to Agramma four thousand hours later, they had a big celebration in the main room with the crewmembers of both ships. In jewels, gold and silver looted from the Church, they had taken almost four hundred million Sword-World stellars worth of booty. They also had some two hundred pounds of refined gadolinium in their holds. It wasn't their greatest haul, but they'd done very well considering that their loot had been taken off a world most Space Vikings would have avoided like the plague. Since the half dozen worlds they had visited in the interim had provided little more than chicken stealing that was certainly something to celebrate.

Once everyone had recovered sufficiently the next day, Historian Walter Ovard reviewed the remaining planets he considered good candidates for another base. Ovard was anxious to continue because only one of the planets he'd put forth as objectives had proved worth raiding on this voyage. Morland agreed. He didn't see any reason to stop until all their holds were full or until they found a likely base world. Vann Stenger and the *Faerie Queene* had remained behind and by now there should be at least one, and maybe even two interplanetary ships, in service so he felt that Poictesme was adequately protected. The discussion was short because most people were nursing hangovers from the previous night's celebration.

They decided to hyperjump to the nearest likely world, only one hundred and ten hours away, which was called Sarpanitum.

SARPANITUᏁ

I

During his stay on Agramma, Historian Walter Ovard had sent a pinnace back to Sarpanitum for more observation, since during the original scouting mission it had shown potential as a possible base world. When they arrived at Octavio's System, the pinnace commander Ensign Pavla Lancaster and her assistant historian came aboard the *Skull Splitter* to participate in the discussion of how and where to conduct their raids.

"Good evening, everyone," Ensign Lancaster said, although to Morland it was a few hours before noon. "You've arrived just in time."

This cryptic statement was explained during her briefing. Sarpanitum was just weeks away from the beginning of a major war that would engulf all of the nearly eight hundred million people on the planet.

Sarpanitum had four major continents, Ashnan, Kabata, Nishun and Lahar, with names dating back to the Federation. The Ashnan and Kabata continents were under one government, a communist dictatorship. They were making preparations to invade the Nishun and Lahar continents. The Nishun Union of Independent Nations was a parliamentary democracy, led by an elected official called a consul, while the Lahar government was ruled by a hereditary king.

Morland had encountered several so-called communist governments on other worlds, and, typically, they were false fronts for pernicious dictatorships. The one thing they all had in common was that they left their subjects downtrodden and miserable; their talk of equality and brotherhood was nothing but meaningless cant. The parasites at the top lived in luxury, while the brotherhood-of-man remained mired in poverty. However, what made communism worse than most totalitarian systems, was that the people lost not only their wealth but were brainwashed with an insidious ideology. As a political system, communism combined the worst elements of both a corrupt plutocracy and a venal theocracy.

There had been several communist dictatorships back on Terra before humankind went into interstellar space, and most historians blamed them for World War III. He figured that no matter how many casualties the resulting takeover cost, it would still be a boon for the inhabitants of Sarpanitum.

There were two spaceports on Sarpanitum, a large one located on the Kabata continent, at Emesh City, and a tiny one on Uttu Island off the east coast of Nishun continent. The facility on Uttu Island had been cannibalized, but probes showed that most of the installations at the Emesh spaceport remained intact.

"Unlike most Federation colonies, a large city never developed around Emesh spaceport," the Assistant Historian noted. "From surviving Federation records, it appears that Sarpanitum was one of the last worlds settled before the Interstellar Wars. The spaceport is located in Emesh City, which at its peak contained no more than seventy to eighty thousand inhabitants. It's fairly isolated from the more populated areas of the planet and there are only a few thousand people living there now—most in a neighboring town which they call Emeshton."

"With so few settlers, how did the population grow so large?" Morland asked.

"It's the climate; all four continents are in the temperate zone," the historian said. "There's very little planetary inclination and the weather and rainfall are moderate year-round. It's as close to Eden-like as any planet I've ever seen."

As Ensign Lancaster and the historian filled them in on the background and possible targets on Sarpanitum, everyone was astonished.

"How did you get such detailed information without being detected?" Reese Duggan asked.

"The Union of Independent Nations and the Lahar nations are very advanced in terms of computer and communications technology," Lancaster said. "We've been able to listen in on their transmissions, and even tap into some of their info-banks, without being detected. Though the technology of Ashnan is behind them in those areas, they greatly outnumber their enemies and their military technology is just about the same. Like most totalitarian regimes, most of their excess capital is spent on weapons systems.

"The government controlling Ashnan calls itself the Communist Republic of Sarpanitum or the CRS. The communists have spent the last century conquering all of the nations on their continent. The Communist Republic had invaded Kabata around five G.S. years ago. A lot of Kabatans, especially those with money, fled to the Nishun continent ahead of the communist armies. The Nishun Union of Independent Nations made a determined effort to spirit as many eminent scientists out of Kabata as they could. Now the CRS wants to invade Nishun; they've become the scapegoats for the Communist Republic's failed economic policies. The Lahar Kingdom got involved because they have a mutual aid pact against any Communist Republic aggression."

It was obvious to Morland that Ensign Lancaster wanted them to be the good guys and intervene on the side of the Nishun Union of Independent Nations. *They're still young and idealistic. When they've been around for a while, they'll realize that it's not our job to save people and governments from themselves. Our only goal is to make a profit. If, while in the course of doing that, we can help the downtrodden; it's all to the good.*

"This is all very interesting," Rivera said, "Emesh spaceport looks as though it has potential, and might even make a nice base. But why should we get involved in their war?"

The historian smiled. "Because the communists have systematically hauled most of the valuables they've stolen, during the last couple of centuries, to their capital, Hamilton City. And they've been busy little worker bees. Hamilton City was named after a famous Neo-Marxist theoretician, Albert Orr Hamilton, who claimed that the communist failure on Terra was brought about when the Soviet Union and Chinese Communist Governments joined the Imperialist Terran Federation. It was his proposition that—"

"I could give a Freyan fig about their dogma. I just wanna know where they keep their valuables?" Shawley interjected.

The historian nodded. "In answer to your question, Captain, most of Sarpanitum's historical treasures and valuables are hidden in underground vaults deep underneath the Commissariat Building. The Commissariat is the central headquarters and the ruling chamber of the People's Deputies and headquarters of the First Citizen of the CRS."

"Now that's the kind of answer I like," Captain Shawley said, with a grin.

Rivera didn't look convinced. "Why not wait until the war starts and let them fight it out. We can loot the capital city once all their troops are committed to the war."

Morland nodded his approval.

"One of the reasons we were sent to study this world was to see if it would make a good base world," Lancaster said earnestly. "We both agree Sarpanitum would make an excellent base of operations. It has an intact spaceport and numerous industrial installations, as well as a large educated population base."

Rivera shook his head.

Morland understood his pessimism. They had seen many planets that looked promising from orbit only to be disappointed once they were on the ground.

"The communist government will never work with us," Lancaster continued. "From what we've observed, we believe both the Kingdom of Lahar and Nishun Union of Independent Nations would welcome us and make good allies. Because of their technical knowledge, they will be easier to train in advanced technologies. And they'll make much better allies, if they haven't been devastated by war with the CRS."

The historian nodded his head in agreement with all of her points.

Pavla Lancaster then provided them with detailed estimates of the amount of loot on the Ashnan continent, including locations and the best ways to obtain it, with some rather unorthodox suggestions.

Morland was impressed with her planning and suggestions. Ensign Lancaster, no, Junior Officer Lancaster—possibly Senior Officer Lancaster in the future—was obviously capable of big things.

After hearing her plan, Shawley was worried. "This could be a dangerous maneuver, Commodore. I don't think we should use the *Skull Splitter* on something this risky. Wouldn't a pinnace work just as well?"

Lancaster handed Shawley a small report. "We've done all the calculations, Captain. A pinnace isn't anywhere big enough; it has to be a warship."

They all looked at one another in wonderment. No one aboard had ever heard of anyone using such a tactic.

"We'll check your calculations again," Morland said. "If they prove to be accurate, the *Skull Splitter* will lead the attack."

That provoked an instant reaction from everyone. "We can't lose you, David," Shawley cried. "Let me take the *Grim Reaper II* in first."

The other officers added their agreement.

Morland waved them all off. "I've made my decision. Let's all study Ensign Lancaster's plan and meet at the same time tomorrow. *If* her calculations are sound, I'll lead the attack. I'll also go over the pertinent information about whether or not this world is suitable as our base."

He forced himself to dampen his enthusiasm. So far, everything about this planet and the spaceport sounded good, but he'd been disappointed before. Still, the location was ideal; it was only two hundred hours from Poictesme and just over four hundred hours from Vishnu. They were a little more than a thousand hours from Odin, so they could also trade there without too much difficulty. They were almost two thousand hours from Marduk, which would minimize their chances of running into Imperial ships.

There was silence for a moment. "We should figure out the best time to attack as well," Shawley added. "These targets are pretty widely spaced."

Lancaster and her pet historian chimed in, "We have a suggestion about that."

II

The *Skull Splitter* rose up out of the river valley as it reached the edge of the city. The ship had skimmed the river for the last hundred miles in the early evening after the sun had set, doing its best to try and hide something that was too big to hide. Signals-and-detection were monitoring all radio stations but there was no indication that anyone had spotted them. If some poor sailor had seen them as they had whisked overhead, he'd probably thought their ship was a hallucination or the after-effect of his last binge.

The bridge crew stared petrified at their screens, now displaying ghostly infra-red images of the local scenery, in grim fascination. Their course was set, having been programmed into the computer, and the Commodore had ordered that only their normal-space astrogator could override it.

Morland ran a mental checklist, looking for possible errors in their plan, as he sat statue-like in the captain's chair. *This will go down in the annals of warfare either as a brilliant maneuver or the biggest cock-up ever.*

Gytha Valkanhayn, who was in charge of the pinnaces, was following right behind. After the *Skull Splitter* took out its target, the pinnaces would attack all of the identified troop barracks and military installations in Hamilton City with conventional warheads. If anything went wrong with the *Skull Splitter's* operation, Valkanhayn would head the rescue effort.

Other Ashnan cities weren't going to be as lucky as Hamilton. Marxburg, a large city three hundred miles to the southeast, was a major troop gathering point for the invasion and the temporary headquarters for three communist armies. As a result, several nuclear missiles from the *Grim Reaper II* were speeding toward it.

Besides Marxburg, the *Grim Reaper II* was also attacking two of the southern ports from which the invasion of the Lahar and Nishun continents was to be launched. Both ports, Elysian and Glorious Legacy, had artificial harbors since Ashnan's southern coast did not have any natural ports. Morland had been impressed with what he had seen of the two ports in the telescopic screen. Even using Sword-World equipment it would have taken a year or two to do such a monumental job. Of course, a contragravity-using civilization would never have needed to build ports for seagoing vessels.

However, both cities and their attendant navies would no longer exist in a few minutes as nuclear missiles were already on their way.

Lancaster and her team historian had discovered that the First Citizen of the Communist Republic of Sarpanitum, Tasso Anders—known as the Silver Fox for his gray hair and the way he outwitted his opponents— gave a weekly evening radio address from the Commissariat Building in Hamilton City. The Commissariat was the CRS headquarters and the largest building on Ashnan. The address was required listening for all citizens of the Communist Republic of Sarpanitum, which meant that most of the Party members would be concentrated around their radios and more vulnerable to a surprise attack.

As the *Skull Splitter* soared toward Hamilton, Anders' voice droned on in low volume in the background. Morland was glad that he could follow most of what he was hearing, although he was not remotely interested in the struggle of the proletariat and the need to work unceasingly for the state, the subject of today's propaganda broadcast. The important thing was that he was able to understand the local version of Lingua Terra, a necessity for the planetary base he had in mind.

Two of the *Pay Dirt's* pinnaces were attacking the major port city, Valpo, on the west coast of the Kabata continent. In the early evening air, their missiles fell down on the city like cascading fireworks. Valpo, was the third of four ports where the communist invasion fleet was gathering. Since Lancaster's intelligence had revealed that there was a great deal of resistance to CRS rule in Valpo, the pinnaces were using conventional missiles to attack the troop barracks in the city and to destroy the invasion fleet in order to minimize civilian casualties.

"We have left the ocean and are commencing attack," Shawley's Exec announced on the viewscreen. The *Grim Reaper's* Executive Officer was leading the rest of her pinnaces, which had traveled for hundreds of miles under the ocean, in a dawn attack against the final port occupied by the CRS invasion fleet, the twin cities of Ashur and Salvasar on the east coast of the Ashnan continent. They were located on a bay inside a large peninsula that jutted out of the coast with one city on the north side and the other on the south. The twin cities were the birthplace of the seven ancient nations of the Lansing Peninsula, which had been conquered by the Communist Republic of Sarpanitum several generations before.

The Lahar and Nishun continents had been settled by immigrants from these cities four or five hundred years ago. According to the historian the seven nations, and particularly the cities of Ashur and Salvasar, were regarded with great reverence by the citizens of the Lahar and Nishun. Because of this, Lancaster had recommended that they not be destroyed by nuclear weapons, even though they were full of CRS troops and government installations. Instead, they would be using Omega-ray and neutron bombs to kill the troops with radiation while preserving as much of the cities' structures as possible. This would have the unpleasant side effect of killing many of the civilians who lived there, but there was nothing to be done about that.

"Target now in sight," Rovard Harvan announced as they flew directly over Hamilton City. Suddenly the great dome of central Commissariat Building appeared on the viewscreens.

This is it! Morland activated the battle klaxon, calling everyone to full alert. The *Skull Splitter* began rapid deceleration; he hoped everyone aboard had followed orders and was strapped in tightly. If they hadn't, they were going to be sorry.

Suddenly, traveling at approximately fifteen to twenty miles an hour, the *Skull Splitter* slammed into the Commissariat Building. The bridge shuddered as if the ship had just taken a nuke amidships. Even though he was strapped to his chair, Morland hung on tightly to his armrests while the craft shuddered and buckled as it blasted its way through the huge domed building. The noise was like that of a moon grinding against its primary; it filled his ears, vibrated his bones to the marrow and made his back teeth hurt.

Then they were through and the ship began accelerating.

"All systems go," systems-and-detection declared.

Morland expelled a great breath he hadn't even been aware he'd been holding back. The crew was cheering and he noticed that Lancaster wore a relieved smile now that her plan had worked.

"Ground troops, you are good to go," Morland announced. It was nice to be back in the thick of things, rather than worrying about Gilgamesher plots and Mardukan retaliation attacks that waited in the wings....

Ladbrok's response came a few seconds later, "Underway, sir."

The treasure vaults of the CRS were directly under the Commissariat Building so the biggest problem they had faced when planning the attack was how to break into them safely and quickly. Destroying the building with conventional explosives would have caused it to collapse on top of the vaults and they would have had to waste time digging them out. Leaving the building intact, meant they would have been attacked by all of the troops garrisoned in the building while they looted it.

They had briefly debated dropping Omega-ray bombs nearby in hope of killing everyone in the building; however, the blast might have caused a shock wave that could have leveled the building—not to mention the delay while they waited for the radiation levels to drop.

Once it was determined that the ship and crew would survive the impact, Morland had decided to follow Lancaster's plan, using the *Skull Splitter* like some gigantic air-born bulldozer to shove the Commissariat Building off its foundations. The timing of their attack had the added benefit of killing almost everyone inside, which included most of the senior Communist Party members and top officials who were attending the First Citizen's address.

As they rose back up above the city, Morland used the telescopic screen to view the demolished building. A small mountain of rubble was being rapidly cleared away by contragravity grapplers and loaders. Most of the building's superstructure, that portion which had survived the collision, had been shoved completely off its foundations by the *Skull Splitter's* impact.

"All reports indicate the initial attacks have gone as planned," Rivera announced. "Valkanhayn has taken out all known troop barracks and she is bombing the remaining government offices."

The *Skull Splitter's* ground troops had set-up high-intensity lights to illuminate the foundation site and all approaches leading to it. Their excavation team covered the mound like a hive of hungry army ants. So far, no opposition had appeared. Only a few handfuls of dazed civilians had been observed and they were doing their best to flee the area as fast as possible.

Shawley's grinning face appeared on the viewscreen. "We've made contact with several resistance groups. One we weren't even aware of used a powerful transmitter to broadcast news about our attack against the communist government. We're coordinating with them for places to land our troops. I can tell they aren't quite certain of our motives, but they seem willing to work with anyone who will help them oust the CRS."

"Once the other nations find out what we're doing, do you think they might try to intervene?" Rivera asked. "After all, they might not like the Communist Republic, but they might hate off-worlders who mess in their affairs even more."

Lancaster shook her head. "Their militaries are in defensive mode, waiting for the communist invasion, which we've just aborted. It would take them months to mount a counterattack, even if they wanted to—which I doubt."

Morland looked at the screens. The action below was winding down. "Tell Valkanhayn to load up the pinnaces when she's done. We're going to be leaving in an hour. Tell the *Grim Reaper II* to return from Valpo by then and load the remaining plunder and provide all the support necessary for our ground troops. Now let's move to the next phase: "Rovard, send a message to King Altos of the Kingdom of Lahar and tell him I would like to meet with him."

"Aye, aye, sir."

III

As he approached the palace, Morland could see soldiers spread out unobtrusively on the terrace. They had chosen to meet at the palace because it was the only place close to the capital city of Port Chatham large enough to land the *Skull Splitter*. The normal-space astrogator had set the *Skull Splitter* down carefully, but she'd still knocked down numerous trees in the park surrounding the King's palace, but; at least, they'd missed the gardens which looked lovely from the air.

On the bridge, Morland used the telescopic screen to look through the window into the King's private chamber. He could see signs of tension on some of his bodyguards' faces, but none on King Altos'—at least, on the viewscreen. Altos was staring through the large window at the gigantic warship, which dwarfed the King's palace, trying hard not to let his emotions show. That was congruent with the intelligence data that Lancaster had obtained.

Twelve years ago, when many of his own countryman and elected officials had counseled neutrality and accommodation with the Communist Republic of Sarpanitum, Prince Altos, had objected. Against his father's counsel, Altos had made a series of speeches galvanizing public opinion in support of an alliance with the Nishun Union of Independent Nations in order to thwart the Communist Republic's expansion.

Shortly thereafter, Prince Altos had dropped out of the University of Lahar, against the wishes of his new wife and father, in order to enter the kingdom's top military academy. After graduation he had been commissioned into the Royal Army. His father had abdicated, so that his son would not be involved in the fighting, and Altos had become King of Lahar at the age of twenty-four.

Their meeting had been set for early afternoon at Port Chatham. Morland, who'd been up all night, didn't want a long session. However, it was of great importance to their mission that he convey their intentions to the Lahar and Nishun governments in person, rather than letting them stew over their attack on Ashnan and come to the wrong conclusion. It would be easy for them to misinterpret their attack as a typical Space Viking raid against the entire planet, not just the Communist Republic.

Morland had decided the best way to present their intentions was to do this through a meeting with the King of Lahar, rather than a host of government officials from Nishun. The Nishun governments—based on the numerous messages they had sent to the Sword-Worlders—appeared to be insulted that they, the more powerful of the two entities, had not been consulted first.

The delay provided Morland with an opportunity to talk to Ladbrok about how the excavation of the vaults was proceeding. The reports about the large amount of wealth hidden in the vaults of the CRS were not an exaggeration; indeed, if anything they were understated. His troops had been emptying the vaults out steadily ever since the attack and Lord Ladbrok reported they weren't even close to getting reaching the bottom.

Morland took an aircar from his ship to the palace. When he stepped from the aircar onto the terrace, Sergeant-Major Burris announced on the car's external audio system: "Presenting Prince David Morland of Poictesme, Commodore and Commander-in-Chief of the Poictesme Space Navy and commander of the expedition to Sarpanitum."

An elderly man in a military uniform stepped forward, announcing: "May I present His Majesty Altos I of the Kingdom of Lahar and the unincorporated Territories of Lahar."

The King stepped forward and they shook hands. "By what title should I address you, Prince Morland?"

"Commodore is the one I'm most comfortable with, Your Highness."

Altos introduced him to several of his advisors and military officers. Morland made no attempt to remember any of their names. He was only going to deal with the King and let Altos deal with his own internal politics as he saw fit.

"Your Highness, I want to assure you that my associates and I mean no harm to the Kingdom of Lahar or any of the Nishun continent's governments or peoples."

"Obviously, that sentiment doesn't extend to the territories held by the Communist Republic of Sarpanitum," King Altos noted. "Do you intend to continue to press your attack against them?"

"Your Highness, hostilities have come to an end," Morland said, detailing the full scope of his flotilla's attacks on the CRS and their results. "The Communist Republic of Sarpanitum has ceased to exist as a real power on the continent of Ashnan, or on the world of Sarpanitum."

When he finished that pronouncement, he saw a variety of emotions play across the faces of the men around the King. The middle-aged military men seemed skeptical, with several looking disappointed. Perhaps they regretted that the confrontation with the CRS they had been planning for all their adult lives had just been summarily dismissed. On the other hand, the younger officers and older men looked happy, some exultant. It would have been them or their children who would have done all the dying in a war against the CRS.

King Altos was one of those who managed to simultaneously display both joy and skepticism. He asked Morland detailed questions about the attacks on CRS facilities as they strolled onto the terrace. Morland was always happy to stretch his legs in the open air after being confined to a ship for hundreds of hours. Confirming the historian's analysis, the king was greatly relieved to find that the twin cities of Salvasar and Ashur had not been destroyed.

"Our ancestors came from Ashur City over two centuries ago," he said, explaining how his family had come to be the rulers of the Kingdom of Lahar, after fleeing communists and how they had colonized the continent of Lahar. "Many of the refugees were well-educated and schooled in technical sciences. There were many merchants and professional men who knew they would not live long after the communist takeover. Our people have flourished despite the colder weather found here in Lahar.

"It gives me great pleasure to learn you have spared the ancient cities. However, I cannot help but wonder what your intentions for Sarpanitum are now that you have defeated the Communist Republic?"

Morland smiled, having expected this question. "Your Majesty, it is our intention to stay here on Sarpanitum. Our instruments and surveys have indicated that much of the old spaceport on Kabata continent is intact and, since the spaceport is unused, I am planning to convert it into a base for my flotilla. From that base we will trade with the nearby worlds of the Old Federation."

He thought it better not to mention that they would attack and raid those worlds as well. "Of course," Morland continued, "I wish to open trading relations with Lahar and the Nishun Union of Independent Nations as well."

"What about your holdings on Poictesme? Are we to become part of your demesne?"

Morland shook his head. "We have no desire to rule this world. Our only goal is to set up a trading base from which we can travel to nearby worlds."

Altos appeared skeptical. "Can you give us a guarantee that we will retain our freedom?"

Morland shook his head. "No, but I can give you my word that we will not attack any free nation on either Lahar or Nishun unless attacked first."

The King was pondering those words when Morland received an urgent call from signals: "Commodore, incoming call from the *Grim Reaper II*; the Captain said it was important."

He excused himself and returned to the aircar. Shawley's grinning face appeared on the screen. "I'm afraid we need the *Skull Splitter* back in Hamilton City."

Morland was puzzled, since everything had been going smoothly when he left the ship to meet the king. "What is the trouble?"

"It's no trouble," Shawley laughed. "We've just run out of room."

"What do you mean, 'run out of room'?"

"All the storerooms and cargo bays on the *Grim Reaper II* are packed all the way up to the gunwales."

"Well, just start filling up the pinnaces."

"David, that's what I'm tryin' to tell you. Everything's full: all the storerooms, holds, vacant rooms and cargo bays on the *Grim Reaper II* as well as those of all the pinnaces. And we still haven't seen the end of the vaults. I've never seen this much gold and jewelry in my life," Shawley said, with awe in his voice. "It's like the legendary Fort Nox on Terra!"

Morland sent the *Skull Splitter* off to Hamilton, leaving one of the pinnaces behind. As he walked back up the terrace to resume his meeting with the king, he tried to adjust to the fact that he was now rich—filthy rich. After a moment of exhilaration he turned his thoughts back to his mission here. There was still a lot to accomplish before this deal was finalized.

"Any trouble?" the King asked, as he rejoined him.

"I just needed to transfer some personnel around," he said smoothly. There was no need to let King Altos, or anyone else on Sarpanitum, know that they were looting the Commissariat's. They would find out soon enough.

"We were discussing trade," the King said, resuming their conversation. "I am curious to know what you want from us. Since I can certainly think of a great many things that you have that we would be interested in." He turned to look as the enormous globe of the *Skull Splitter* slowly rose into the sky, looking more like a rising moon than an interstellar ship.

"Actually I would like to buy some of your land," Morland stated.

The King's jaw all but dropped to the ground.

One of the reasons Ovard had originally targeted Sarpanitum was that the old records on Poictesme had shown there had been a large neodymium mine on the planet, located on the North continent. Since neodymium's special magnetic properties were essential for Abbot lift-and-drive engines but not much else, it was no longer mined on Sarpanitum. From the old records Ovard had uncovered on Odin, Sarpanitum, just before the collapse of the Old Federation, had been one of the largest sources of neodymium in this sector of space and it once had been the world's largest source of income.

Morland explained that the area he was interested in, due to its remote location, would be ideal for their own industrial park. He didn't mention the neodymium to the king, since it could well lead to problems. Altos wasn't stupid; once he found out about the ore, he might want to mine and refine the neodymium himself for interstellar trade. Of course, he wouldn't come to realize its value—since most of the planet's Federation era records had been lost during the Interstellar Wars—until it was too late.

Fortunately for Morland, the king was mostly concerned about the size of the mining settlement even though the mine was located in the far north of the continent well away from any city or rural settlement. Morland promised King Altos that there would not be any permanent settlement once the installation was up and running, just a few caretakers, since the industrial park would be largely automated. That produced another look of awe as he went into the basics of robotic technology.

"We have a great deal to learn from you," King Altos said. "We haven't had any off-planet visitors since the Big War."

This answered another of Morland's questions; he had been wondering if Sarpanitum had ever been visited by Gilgameshers, interstellar merchants or other Space Vikings. It was good to know they hadn't, since the locals wouldn't have any preconceptions about Space Vikings to overcome. Knowledge that had proved a hindrance on other worlds as Sword-Worlders did not have a good reputation.

"I am puzzled," the King said, "as to how you will pay us. Obviously you don't have any of our sols."

The locals still referred to their money as sols, from the Old Federation sol. They apparently hadn't lost everything over the eight centuries since the Federation's collapse.

"I propose we pay you in gold, Your Highness," Morland said, "One hundred thousand gold stellars, or ounces of gold." Gold was very valuable on the Lahar and Nishun continents. They had only a few sources of it, since most of the gold mines were located on the other continents. He wasn't about to let the King know that the price of gold would probably drop drastically now that the Space Vikings were going to be spending a good portion of the communist's stolen hoard.

The King appeared pleased and, after discussing it briefly with his advisors, he agreed to the purchase price. Morland said he would have someone deliver the gold and sign any necessary papers the following day as he shook hands and made his way to the waiting pinnace. By then his energy was beginning to fade, as the events of the day and his loss of sleep were catching up to him.

IV

The spaceport, when examined the next day, turned out to be larger than anyone had estimated, due to a man-made lake bordering its western edge that covered over a third of its area.

"We have crews in the lake looking for cracks and whatever drains have been plugged," Rivera said. He was relaxing and eating a sandwich when Morland entered the bridge.

"You look like you got a good rest," Morland said, as he gave his breakfast order to a robot server.

"Once I saw that King Altos' soldiers weren't going to shoot you, I went to bed," Rivera joked. "I figured someone had to be up early to get things organized."

Morland sipped cautiously at the hot coffee while eating his breakfast and reading a report Rivera had handed him.

"Any reaction from Emeshton?" Morland asked. Emeshton was a small town a few miles west of the spaceport that consisted of small buildings that appeared to have been constructed in the last century or so.

The old city adjacent to the spaceport itself was mostly deserted with only a few hermits and scavengers living there now. Walter Ovard had estimated that it had once housed fifty to eighty thousand people. A lot of the old buildings were in ruins or torn down. It was at the end of a railway that led north, and then west around the mountains to Valpo.

"What was the old city called, again?"

Ovard looked up from a tattered book he was reading. "The original settlers called it Emesh City, Commodore. Most of the terrain and continental names come from the Babylonian myth-cycle which the planet was named after. Emesh was built decades after the planet was settled as part of the Federation military buildup during the System States War. The small spaceport on the island was the original spaceport. It was small because when Sarpanitum was settled the Federation no longer allowed chartered worlds so there was no one to invest in a large modern spaceport. Emesh is geographically isolated; its sole attraction was the spaceport. After the fall of the Federation and the loss of interstellar trade, Emesh City slid into a quick decline."

"Well, now that we're here, it's going to thrive again," Morland said.

The old city of Emesh was on the southern and eastern sides of the spaceport. To the west of Emeshton, the terrain rose in a series of rolling hills to some mid-sized mountains. A river flowed out of the middle of the mountains, roared down a string of spectacular waterfalls, where it formed a lake between the spaceport and the new city. It then wound around the spaceport and ran right through the ruins of Emesh City. The terrain was scrub desert except for the greenery along the river and the irrigated fields next to the new town.

"Any reaction from Emeshton?" he asked again.

Rivera answered, "Yes. About an hour ago they set up a table in the middle of the largest open square in town. They have a white flag on either end of the table, seven people sitting behind the table, and several empty chairs facing them. There's no sign of any troops and it would be a difficult place to stage an ambush."

Morland only nodded because his attention was on the latest log entries.

Even with the *Skull Splitter* and *Grim Reaper II* fully loaded, considerable gold and other valuables still remained in the vaults below Hamilton City. The ground crews had covered the vaults up with rubble and posted guards so none of the Ashnans could loot them. The total amount of plunder taken was staggering—just over three billion and seven-hundred million stellars. Almost a hundred times what they had made on Agramma; the total accumulated loot on this voyage was around four billion stellars.

We've just completed the greatest single raid in Space Viking history! he thought, as he set the report aside and grinned at Rivera. "Good work all around. Wake up Burris and have him meet me at the combat-car in forty-five minutes."

Rivera chuckled. "Burris has been up for over an hour. He's checking the combat-car out right now."

"Laz you should have wakened me," Morland said, as he gulped his coffee faster to wake up. "I shouldn't be sleeping in while my crew is working."

"You needed the sleep," Rivera said brusquely. "It wouldn't do to have our leader stumbling around half-awake. The locals might think you're a drunk, like DeBorder used to be." He turned to the communication screen. "I'll call Gytha. She wanted to go with you."

He brightened. "Good. She did a good job of eliminating the opposition in Hamilton City."

"Yes. However, I don't expect she'll be with us for long. It seems that Gytha has decided that young officer, Pavla Lancaster, is her replacement. Gytha's been talking about marrying Ladbrok and returning to Poictesme. They were both up well before I was and Gytha seems to be training Lancaster on just about all her former duties as signals-and-detection officer."

Not a bad idea, he thought swallowing his breakfast, refilling his coffee cup and rising to his feet. Gytha would be hard to replace as his Second Officer. Harvan was still green, but he preferred to make officer replacements from among his own crew.

Lancaster had only been on a few voyages as a junior officer when she joined the *Pay Dirt* on Excalibur. When she'd asked to be transferred to the *Skull Splitter*, he'd already noted she had the makings of a good senior officer and had okayed her request. She wasn't experienced enough to replace Valkanhayn as Second Officer, but she'd probably make a good fit as Fifth Officer in signals-and-detection. He would have liked to promote Reginald Mathes to Second, but Reg preferred his weapons station and did not want to be promoted.

The problem he faced was that they would have at least one, possibly two interplanetary ships, ready to launch by the time they returned to Poictesme and he was quickly running out of qualified officers: Laz Rivera, who would have made an excellent captain, didn't want the promotion. And Gytha was talking marriage and babies.

Half a dozen former ships' officers had joined up on Hoth, he'd have to spend some time interviewing and going over their records when they got back to their temporary headquarters on Poictesme.

The Emeshton greeting committee, town council or whatever it was, had heard news about the attacks on Valpo on their radios. They assured Morland they were happy to be out from under communist rule and they seemed to mean it. Emeshton was obviously a provincial backwater as far as the CRS had been concerned; there was only one CRS representative in town, a political officer whom the locals had placed under house arrest.

"We have no place for Comrade Zalts, Prince Morland," said one of the older men. "He won't live to see another sunrise if he stays here."

"We will take him back to our ship. He might prove to be a useful source of information."

Morland asked them to appoint one person as liaison between the town and the Sword-Worlders. They all turned and looked at the youngest man there, who appeared to be in his late thirties. He was a little shorter than average, stocky, with jet black hair and blue eyes, which was an unusual combination on the Sword-Worlds.

Hachmed Perkins was his name. When Morland asked his title, the group said they had not been allowed local elections under the communists.

Morland told them they could hold elections or choose their

government however they wished. After a brief huddle the group informed him that Mayor Perkins would now represent the town.

They were just beginning to discuss forming work crews to aid in the cleanup of the spaceport when several people exclaimed and pointed. "What's that?"

When he turned around he saw a large whirlpool of swirling water on the lake. Someone on his crew had apparently unplugged the drain. Soon he would see just how big his new spaceport was going to be.

V

About two hundred hours later, Morland opened formal relations with the Nishun continental government, officially known as the Union of Independent Nations. He had met Consul Joao Molambo, a man in his early sixties who was partway through his third five-year term. Molambo had even provided him troops to assist in the pacification of the Kabata and the capture of communist apparatchiks, collaborators and Party members. The pacification had been accomplished with few problems, since most of the CRS troops in the Kabatan continent had been concentrated in Valpo for the planned invasion. Many had died in the subsequent bombardment.

They had also begun training the Kabatan locals in Sword-World technologies. Those with degrees and technical training were being encouraged to migrate to Emesh City and work for the Kabatan Free Territories, or the New Base Venture as the Sword-Worlders called it in private. Some of the locals, primarily recruited from Valpo, were being trained as a military force with the idea that his own militia could replace the Union troops whom Morland didn't trust a hundred percent.

It was always better to use your own janissaries.

For now, they were ignoring Ashnan, the eastern continent. Based on what they could discern from radio chatter, it sounded as though various politicians and military strong men were seizing control of parts of the continent now that formal communist rule was at an end. There were pockets of communist resistance, but they didn't appear to be threats to Morland's base world venture so he decided to put off dealing with them until sometime in the future.

When Vann Stenger arrived at Sarpanitum with the *Faerie Queene* a few hundred hours later, it took all of Morland's will power not to jump down his throat for leaving Poictesme. Vann, however, had anticipated his complaints.

On a secure link, Vann said, "David, I know you wanted me to stay on patrol in the Tri-System, but Giffard Zhorgay launched two interplanetary ships and I didn't see any real need to stick around. If the Imperials arrived with a flotilla large enough to kill two interplanetary warships, with all their missiles and ship defenses, there isn't much the *Faerie Queene* could do to stop them."

While fuming inside, Morland was forced to concede that Vann had a point. While he might hold the title of Commodore, his only claim to command among the venture's Space Vikings was personal loyalty and his successful track record for profitable raids. Any of his captains were free to leave anytime they wanted, as long as they agreed to make proper restitution for the cost of their ships. All that was holding them back was loyalty and friendship. One more reason he desperately needed a base world and officers who owed their fidelity to something larger than one man.

He also needed to find a proper title for Giffard Zhorgay, who was no longer the *Skull Splitter's* Chief Engineer, but a planetary ruler—even if the planet was a lifeless world, no larger than most moons. Zhorgay was a loyal crewman and Sword-Worlder with few ambitions other than to build ships, so he didn't have to worry about him going independent. Count Zhorgay had a nice sound to it; Koshchei wasn't large or important enough for a princedom.

All the available officers at the Emesh spaceport gathered at the rehabbed Interworld Building to hear Stenger's account of his latest trip with *Faerie Queene*, a short swing by the local trading worlds to look for signs of Imperial warships. "We didn't see any signs that the Mardukans had returned to Rhiannon," Stenger was saying. "We did a night ops and interrogated several of the natives. I left some passive detectors on their two moons so we can examine them to see if anyone visits in the future. It's too good a manufacturing site to give up."

Morland agreed. "For now, we'll stay away from any dealings on Rhiannon until this situation with the Mardukan Empire is concluded. Still, it's good to know that we have detectors there to check on whenever one of our ships is in the area."

Although they still had plenty of plutonium from their raid on Tashmetum, they would need a great deal more over the next few years if Morland's plan to turn Sarpanitum into an industrial base were to come to fruition. The only radioactives on the planet were a few old and depleted uranium mines, no reactors had survived the intervening years. Sarpanitum must have imported their plutonium back in the Old Federation days. On the next ship to Poictesme, he would have orders for Zhorgay to dismantle two of the breeder reactors they had found on Koshchei and have them shipped to Sarpanitum. That should be done in under a thousand hours.

Since they were only two hundred hours apart, trade had begun between Poictesme and Sarpanitum. It was being carried out irregularly at the moment because they only had the two-hundred foot pinnaces available to carry freight. At one of the Koshchei shipyards Morland had sent orders to Zhorgay to have a crew convert the largest of the interplanetary passenger ships, they had found abandoned in the shipyards, into a hyperspace freighter. The one closest to being complete was a small ship, only a thousand feet in width, but it could be rehabbed much faster than any new ship they'd have to build from scratch. It would take men off the next warship, but they needed a dedicated freighter to put his Sarpanitum development plans into action.

"We had some trouble with the robotic equipment on Rhiannon and had to repair it," Stenger was saying. "We sure could have used your dad, David."

Morland replied that his parents would be arriving on the next pinnace from Poictesme. It had taken only one winter in Litchfield on Poictesme for his mother to become unhappy. Litchfield was in the middle of the continent so its winters were very cold; she was accustomed to Joyeuse's more moderate climate. When he'd written to his parents that Emesh City was in a warm dry desert, his mother had sounded eager to move. His dad was willing because he could live happily anywhere so long as he was teaching and repairing robotic equipment. His sister Zandra and her son Richard, who had arrived on the most recent pinnace, had told him that their parents would be along on the next ship, after his dad's current teaching session was wrapped up. Having his family with him would make Sarpanitum feel more like home.

Navid, Parviz's son, was growing up. He'd just hit puberty and his voice was breaking. Morland wondered how Janna was doing and for the first time in a long while felt a stab of regret. *Maybe I should have stayed on Nissaba and found a way to make our relationship work.*

His attention was drawn back to the present when Vann Stenger made an announcement. "Here's the moment you've all been waiting for." He paused to draw two bottles out of a bag he was carrying. "The famous rum of Ammut."

Vann had refused to say what he thought of the taste, preferring to leave it for everyone to discover for themselves. That meant he thought it was either really good or really bad. Morland tasted his first sip and was impressed; Ammut rum had a tangy cinnamon taste and a warmth that started low in the belly and worked its way up.

Everyone was impressed by the rum to varying degrees, but it started the usual debate over the merits of other well-known spirits. Morland thought Poictesme melon-brandy was a little better but he didn't consider himself a connoisseur.

"That was just the white rum," Vann Stenger stated. "Now you have to try the dark rum." He poured a double-shot into each glass.

"Wow!" Reese Duggan exclaimed. "That's really great."

The others agreed. Even Laz Rivera, who wasn't much of a drinker, wanted more.

"The dark rum is stored in casks made from a native tree found only on Ammut," Vann Stenger explained. "It's the wood that gives it both color and flavor. I got these samples from the locals. They make it in small homemade stills, since all of the old distillery plants were abandoned centuries ago."

After making friends with the natives and exploring the area, Stenger had left a crew behind to fix up the least damaged distillery plant. "We'll have to bring some more people and equipment to Ammut if we expect to get any real production going. Most of the fields are overgrown and the natives won't be of much help."

"Sounds like you don't like the place," someone said.

"What's to like? The gravity is twelve percent over Galactic Standard, it's right on the equator, always hot and humid, the Neobarbs are primitive and the women are short, squat and unattractive. Plus, they've never seen anyone who looked like us and were scared witless by my appearance. I spent most of my time trying to keep the natives from scampering away."

Everyone laughed. Vann Stenger's tall slender frame, pale skin and thick shock of red hair were not unique on the Sword-Worlds, although they frequently were on other worlds. Morland knew that Vann had grown up in a mild climate on Joyeuse and heartily disliked hot, humid weather. He also preferred tall women, as Morland recalled from their many times together chasing women in Longinus Town.

PART TWO

GILGAMESH

High Maxwell XXIII tried to keep from jumping out of his seat as he went over the Oracle's latest projections. Instead he compulsively bounced his left leg off his right knee under his desk. *The Prayerful Worshipper's* tardiness was disturbing and the latest profiles were introducing instabilities and unknowns into the Oracle's data banks. Even worse, the Scion was supposed to be returning to Gilgamesh on that ship. The time had come for his eldest son to prepare for the next step in his succession as the next High Maxwell. He hadn't seen Conn in over a decade and they had much to discuss.

The Prayerful Worshipper should have been back from her visit to Poictesme over six hundred hours ago. Poictesme was eighteen-hundred light-years from Gilgamesh a hyperspace journey of some two and a half Galactic Standard months. *The Prayerful Worshipper* had never been late before, nor had her predecessors. He had some guesses, but no firm data, as to what might have delayed her return.

It was mandated by the Charter that each Maxwell Scion spend a decade living on the Homeworld so that he would know more of the universe than their secluded life in the Enclave. He had done the same some thirty years past. Living in Oracle House and fraternizing with the locals had been good training; he's learned much about people and how harsh life was on the downtrodden Homeworld.

It was also mandated in the Charter that every ten Galactic Standard years a ship was to visit Homeworld and return with information on any unusual visitors or events. Ever since the Exodus, over six centuries ago, these visits had unfolded like clockwork. Always, without fail, the ships returned reporting the same status quo. Now, all of a sudden, there was a problem—a missing ship. One with the Scion on board and on *his* watch!

The question running through his head was: *Why has this happened now, just as we're in the midst of a mission change? Are the events related?*

The High Maxwell made up his mind and hit the comm link to Programming. He used the red line and wasn't surprised when the Chief Programmer answered, his thin face strained with worry. "Sir, what can I do?"

"We've got a problem. I need to see you in my office."

The Programming warrens were located deep in Mount Liskamm so even with contragravity lifts it took almost five minutes for the Chief to make the trip to his office near the mountain peak. Merlin was well hidden, not just for defensive purpose, but because of the clandestine operation that rested underneath the entire façade of Gilgamesh. A scheme that only the Caretakers, a few thousand men and women, knew about. The rest of the world slumbered in ignorance, locked in fealty to the harsh god that ruled their lives.

During the Interstellar Wars, when the last bonds of the Federation had dissolved, Merlin had warned the Program Manager that soon war would come to Poictesme. Conn Maxwell's plan to save their world from ruin had worked too well. Poictesme had grown rich, making it a tempting target for raiders, aggressive neighbors and expansionists. To ensure Merlin's safety and the Mission, it was decided to move the big computer and its support staff to a world that would be safe from the holocaust that Merlin had predicted and was about to descend upon the Terran Federation.

After years of surveying the Federation's worlds, Merlin had picked Gilgamesh as the ideal location. Gilgamesh, like many worlds, had fallen on hard times during the Time of Troubles and was therefore not a target for plunder or conquest. Once a trading world, Gilgamesh was now isolated and decivilizing. According to the Oracle's calculations it was the perfect hiding place for the most advanced computer known to man, the former Big Brain of the Third Terran Force. There, Merlin would be safe and free to continue its plans to save humanity from itself.

Moving the heart of an entire world was not easy, even with Merlin's help. The Select had to be transported to Gilgamesh on the Exodus ships. This had taken almost twenty-five years. Those who remained on

Poictesme had been kept in the dark about the plan. Only a special few, the Caretakers, remained behind to keep their secret safe under the Arch-Archivist. It was his job to record events and prepare for their eventual return. A homecoming that could only happen when the next period of stability returned to the worlds of man. A postulate that was now, if no new counter variable arrived, on the verge of possibility.

Not a good time for the Caretaker ship to be missing.

As predicted by Merlin, shortly after the Great Exodus, Poictesme had been attacked by a neighboring world. In the mid-Twelfth Century Atomic Era, Osiris had sent a fleet to plunder Poictesme. When they were almost defeated by the Poictesme Navy, they had retaliated by nuking the capital city, Storisende, and bombing the surviving towns and countryside.

After that, no one needed to be convinced of Merlin's infallibility. Its one vulnerability, however, was a lack of information. To that end, they had taken the small fanatical religious cult of Yah the Almighty and made it the space-faring arm of Merlin, now called the Oracle. They'd used their technical expertise, backed by the Oracle's predictions, to overawe the locals. The Faithful were given ships, many of them the former merchant ships used in the exodus, to ply their trade with nearby worlds. They had been surprisingly successful and soon most of the former citizens embraced the cult, as the Oracle had predicted, making the believers of Yah the Almighty the most successful traders within the former Terran Federation.

But the Gilgameshers' duty was twofold: they were to trade with worlds throughout the former Federation and then return to Gilgamesh with all the data they collected about these worlds' economies, military might and technological capability. This data was dropped off at the main temple and sent to Mount Liskamm, where it was continually fed into the Oracle by over a thousand programmers and their support staff. Even with over three hundred trading ships, they were still hard-pressed to keep Merlin updated on the six thousand, seven-hundred and eighty-nine known worlds of the former Federation, not counting new entities like Sword-World cluster, or the Helm, as the Space Vikings called it. This data was integral to the Plan, the creation of a new stable and Universal State.

The door buzzer broke into his reverie about the magnitude of his work and he pressed the button that opened the portal.

Chief Vibart came in hesitantly. "What is it, Your Worshipful?"

"*The Prayerful Worshipper* is still overdue," he said. "Does the Oracle have an explanation?"

Vibart, who looked almost a decade older than his fifty years of age, shook his head. "Misadventure is all that comes up, sir."

"That's what I feared. Have we heard back from Kwannon yet?"

"Yes, High Maxwell. The ship we sent there after *The Prayerful Worshipper* was late and just reported in. From the information they obtained on Kwannon, *The Prayerful Worshipper* left as scheduled. Its next stop was Poictesme. That's the last anyone's heard from her."

"Then we have to assume the worst, she's either been captured or destroyed," the High Maxwell decided. "Chief, have there been any unusual activities or sightings in the Poictesme sector since *The Prayerful Worshipper* last visit a decade ago?"

Vibart said, "Yes, several Space Viking ships have been observed in that sector."

"Is that unusual? Space Viking ships roam much of the Old Federation."

"In this case, it is. Few Space Vikings travel that far into that part of the former Federation, mostly because of travel times. Plus, many of the worlds in the Terran Sector are decivilized or in ruins. However, due to the changes introduced by the new nexus, things are changing throughout the former Federation."

A century ago, the Oracle had predicted that the new locus of civilization would be Tanith and her League of Civilized Worlds. However, the League had stopped expanding fifty years ago and Tanith's current ruler, Rodrik Trask, was more interested in maintaining the status quo than in regenerating civilization. Now, Marduk had emerged as the new loci for the emergence of a galactic-wide civilization. The Oracle had predicted this a decade ago and only now, with the new Empire, were its predictions coming to fruition.

As per the Plan, it was the Caretakers duty to help any such state reach its true potential. So, the colony on Tanith had been shut down and moved to Marduk. The intelligence they were able to provide soon made them welcome allies. Emperor Lucas, unlike his forbearers, who were in thrall to the Trasks, was a leader with a grand vision, a plan to reunite humanity and raise her up again from barbarism under the rule of a Universal State. Of course, not everyone agreed with Lucas's vision so it was necessary for them to offer any and all support they could muster.

"What does the Oracle say?" the High Maxwell asked.

The Chief Programmer replied, "It calculated a number of possible outcomes. The highest probability was that *The Prayerful Worshipper* was ambushed by Space Vikings. The lowest probabilities were: an accident or the crew mutinied, both probabilities ranked below the .00001 percentile."

"Why would Space Vikings attack one of our ships, and specifically the only one that is not a trading vessel?"

The Chief said, "It could be they have questions about our mission, which means we inadvertently left some clue behind on Poictesme. Or more likely they were in desperate need of loot and attacked the ship assuming it was a regular trading vessel."

The High Maxwell frowned. "The barbarians are growing desperate, but I find it hard to believe they'd ambush one of our ships, especially this one."

The Chief shrugged. "Desperate times call for desperate measures."

"I don't believe the answer is that simple," the High Maxwell concluded. "I'm going to send out several ships to survey the area and learn the extent of the Space Viking's incursion into that sector."

"Why not send another ship to the Homeworld?"

"Because we don't want to attract any more attention to Poictesme than absolutely necessary. If indeed the Space Vikings are using Poictesme as a base of operations, a visit from another ship might well stoke their curiosity."

"I agree. However, won't they be expecting some kind of response from us?"

The High Maxwell nodded. "That's why they won't think anything is unusual when several of our ships suddenly appear in that sector."

SARPANITUᎷ II

I

Mayor Hachmed Perkins was one of the most plainspoken men Morland had ever met. He wondered if the Emeshton town fathers had appointed him as Mayor, not because they valued his leadership, but to act as a staked goat to test Morland's intentions. If so, the joke was on them. He had big plans for Perkins.

They were eating lunch together with his parents in the new Emesh spaceport cafeteria. It was part of a complex of old administration buildings that they had rehabbed right after taking over the spaceport. The crew had fixed up several of the buildings, along with repairing or replacing power, water and sewer lines, while installing the machinery and equipment they had brought from Koshchei.

Once Captain DeBorder returned from Tanith they would have the rest of the technicians and equipment they needed. *In about six months,* Morland thought, *we'll have a fully functional spaceport.*

His father, mother and sister had joined them at lunch; his parents had recently arrived from Poictesme on one of the pinnaces that were traveling back and forth between the two worlds. He was trying to make up for lost time by spending as much time as possible with his family, now that they were all in the same place.

"Too many of our townsfolk are shiftless," Mayor Perkins sputtered through a mouthful of food. "They've lost their appetite for learning and they don't want to work. Many of the refugees are even worse. They just want to be told what to do and where to go without thinking. Too many years under communist rule. All this new equipment you're trying to teach them about, they ought to be on that like flies on...a corpse." he paused again to see if he'd offended Morland.

Morland tried hard not to laugh. "I fear, you're right."

While Hachmed Perkins was rough around the edges, he'd proved to be a real asset for Morland. He was a font of information about Kabatan continent and politics, as well as their former communist masters. His crews from Emeshton had already cleaned up most of the spaceport and he had the mental flexibility to learn new ideas and techniques. Now he was trying to find homes for the second wave of refugees who had started showing up a few weeks ago.

Perkins was right, though; most of the refugees who were pouring into Emesh City and Emeshton from other parts of the Kabata had very little initiative. While communist rule had fallen lightly on Emeshton and been resisted in Valpo, the rest of the continent had been under the Communist Republic's control for decades and it showed. Morland was reminded of one of Otto Harkaman's comments about communist workers—"we pretend to work, while they pretend to pay us"—as one of Harkaman's many reasons for not using those planets as base worlds.

According to Perkins, Valpo had fallen to the CRS about eight years ago. "Once Valpo surrendered, we decided we couldn't hold out anymore," he said.

What Perkins left out, which Morland had learned from one of the other townspeople in Emeshton, was that Perkin's wife had been killed in the fighting, leaving him to raise two daughters.

"Fortunately," Perkins continued, "as long as we kept the iron ore flowing the communist bloodsuckers weren't too interested in bothering us."

Iron ore was Emeshton's principal export, followed by a certain herbal tea leaf that was native to the area. The area around Emesh was mostly desert and harsh scrub land, but crops grew well if irrigated. There was an extensive irrigation system that made use of the power generated by the many waterfalls as the Arras River made its way down to the plains beside the spaceport.

"These newcomers are like Arras flood waters, they are drowning Emeshton," Perkins said, his voice rising. "We're running out of room. The refugees are staying in some of the old warehouses now, but they need a lot of rehab. Maybe you can find places for them here in the city. We don't have the materials or labor to build new buildings. If it wasn't for your generosity in sending food, most would be starving."

Emesh City was quickly becoming the new de facto capital of Sarpanitum and the entire area was having growing pains. Both the Union and the Kingdom of Lahar had sent delegations to Emesh and along with them had come businessmen, bankers and others who were anxious to trade and interact with the Sword-Worlders. People displaced by the conquest of the Communist Republic had also followed, hoping to find work—or more likely charity.

Although they'd been there almost a year, the assimilation of the Sword-Worlders into the everyday life of Sarpanitum was another work in progress. Morland was unable to find any similar historical analogues to their experience on Sarpanitum. In the four hundred and some years since the Space Vikings had first entered the Old Federation, most Space Viking base worlds had begun as primitive Neobarbarian worlds. Sarpanitum was a Civ-Level 7 planet with gasoline engines, early automobiles, airplanes, telephones, motion pictures and radio.

"We're fixing up the old buildings here as fast as we can," Morland said. "I'll have Laz Rivera work with you to determine who can be put where."

"Thanks, Prince David, that will take a lot of pressure off the town. Maybe people will stop pestering me so I can get some sleep at night."

He'd given up on telling people that he wasn't a prince, people needed a symbol of authority and they were going to have one. And if it wasn't him, it would be somebody else.

"I also hate to keep bothering you for a lift and it's a long walk around the lake," Perkins said slyly.

Morland laughed. "I think we can put a couple of troop carriers at your disposal."

"Great," Perkins said, turning his attention back to his food.

One of the things Morland liked about Hachmed Perkins was that he didn't waste any time getting to the point.

"This food's pretty good," Perkins said, changing the subject. "A lot better than that carniculture, ah, stuff you usually feed me when I visit."

They all agreed with that and Morland's father asked why.

"We found a fabulous local cook," Morland said. "I heard she was picked up when some of the troops went out foraging for supplies."

They had heard from recent refugees that the ruling elite of the CRS had a private retreat in the mountains in a southern part of Ashnan. He had sent a few ground squads to see if there was any valuable loot, figuring that even if there wasn't, the retreat probably contained a cache of some supplies they could use. They had found both valuables and storehouses full of foodstuffs and supplies. Whatever else you could say about them, one thing was certain: the communist leaders had never suffered from any of the same shortages their subjects had.

The cook had brought herself to the attention of the troops by calming the local villagers, who had panicked when the Space Viking combat-cars had first appeared. She had also insisted on being taken along, stating that she was the greatest chef on two continents and that she should be cooking for the new rulers of Sarpanitum.

"Yes, their cook's been a great help to us," his sister said. "Randa's identified a lot of local spices and foods and has already come up with some excellent suggestions on how they can be combined with ours."

"Randa?" Morland asked.

"Randa Sayana is her name," his sister said.

"I've probably seen her around but you should point her out to me so I can properly thank her. I haven't eaten this well since we left Joyeuse."

His sister gave him that smile he had long recognized that meant he was in for a surprise. "You haven't seen her yet, have you?"

As he pondered his sister's words, his mother pointed over his and Zandra's shoulders. "There she is now."

Morland turned and stared, hearing his sister's laugh in his ear. Randa Sayana had entered the room leading a line of troopers, each carrying a box of supplies. As she passed each table in the cafeteria, almost every male head in the room swiveled to follow her progress. She was a full-figured woman with long hair that framed her face like raven wings and had the stage presence of a Tri-D actress.

Zandra stood and motioned for her to join them at their table. "Randa, you haven't had a chance yet to meet my father, Percy Morland, and my brother David."

He stood up and shook hands with a woman a little younger than he was, stammering a greeting and giving her compliments on her cooking.

Suddenly his sister's look and the comments he had heard made sense. Along with her curves Randa was almost as tall as he was, with broad shoulders, a firm grip, and, as he quickly found out, a commanding personality. This was obviously one woman who had not been beaten down by communist rule. They visited briefly until his mother elbowed his father for staring.

"Pick up those boxes and get moving!" Randa barked at the men standing behind her who had relaxed and set them down.

"Nice to meet you, Commodore Morland," she called over her shoulder as she walked away, the eyes of every man in the room following her.

Fortunately Morland was saved from any further comments from the women in his family by an announcement over the loudspeaker: "Commodore Morland to the command center."

Other announcements followed, calling the other senior officers. Happy to make an escape, he excused himself and left.

II

The other officers were waiting when Morland arrived at the command center. Reese Duggan, the *Skull Splitter's* Hyperspace Astrogator, pointed to a screen on which the signals-and-detection officer of one of the two pinnaces in orbit around Sarpanitum's single moon was waiting.

"Commodore," he announced. "We have detected three emerging spacecraft approximately five light-minutes from the planet. They have all made the agreed upon signal."

"Three ships?" Rivera said, licking his lips thoughtfully.

"More allies?" Duggan suggested optimistically.

DeBorder and the Pay Dirt, I hope, Morland thought. They only had one ship, the *Skull Splitter*, in-system.

A few minutes later the officer reported the ships had emerged just over a light-second away. The screen chimed and Javen DeBorder's face smiled down at them. "Hello, everyone," taking in all the people who crowded around the screen. "Once again I'm happy to report a successful voyage."

"Who are your friends?" Morland asked.

DeBorder looked down, tapped a button and an unfamiliar face appeared on the screen. "I'd like to introduce Ivar Nash, captain of the merchantman *Zama*, out of Tanith. The *Zama* was sent here by King Rodrik, who is offering to invest in our base world venture."

Morland introduced himself and the others to Captain Nash.

Captain DeBorder's smile grew even larger. "My other friend needs no introduction. Gentlemen, may I present the new Captain of the *Gift Horse*," as he tapped another button.

The smiling face of Tylor Ragnarsans appeared on the screen.

It turned out that from the moment he first heard about the abandoned spaceship on Aditya, Tylor Ragnarsans had dreamt of nothing else but re-outfitting her and getting her away from the Adityans. Aditya was a Neobarbarian planet that Morglay had conquered and colonized centuries ago and was later deserted during one of the dynastic wars on Morglay. On a raiding trip, DeBorder had visited Aditya and discovered an abandoned spaceship in the middle of a city fallen into ruin. The ship was still intact and venerated by the locals as some sort of totem or shrine.

Tylor hadn't mentioned his plans to anyone because he did not have enough money to hire a crew nor did he want to borrow any funds from anyone else. Or, worse, have them steal his idea.

As much as Tylor wanted his own command, he had seen what the stress of owing money had done to Javen DeBorder. After the Nissaba, Lyonnesse and Tashmetum raids had provided him with enough stellars to pay the bonuses necessary to attract a good crew and get a ship up and running, he had approached DeBorder with his plan.

DeBorder had been enthusiastic and said he would transport Ragnarsans and a crew to Aditya. Ragnarsans had not mentioned his plan to either Morland or Stenger. He had told DeBorder that he wanted to surprise them.

Morland heard most of the story as the *Pay Dirt, Gift Horse,* and *Zama* descended to the surface of Sarpanitum and landed at Emesh spaceport. He suspected that Ragnarsans had kept his plan under wraps because he'd felt slighted that the first interstellar ship out of Koshchei had gone to Captain Shawley rather than to him. He wasn't sure just what his reaction would have been to Ragnarsans' plan if he'd known about it beforehand.

Morland's relationship with the other Space Viking captains and officers was somewhat tenuous. Only those directly under his command aboard the *Skull Splitter* were bound to him by contract and law. The others were not oath-sworn, nor did he own their loyalty. They were more a band of brothers with him serving as the patriarch. However, if he were to give them orders they strongly opposed, it was quite possible they would space-out and leave him holding the planet by himself.

So far, things had worked in Morland's favor because many of them had become friends and blood brothers. Still, as his command grew larger, these ties would begin to fray and lessen. Maybe it was time for him to give some thought to becoming the planetary ruler and making more formal arrangements with his fellow Space Vikings.

As Tylor told it, the abandoned spaceship had been grounded on Aditya, some sixty years earlier, when its Dillingham engines had failed. From the ship's logs, it appeared that the Space Viking crew, after several misadventures and profitless raids, had been on their last legs before landing on Aditya. There the crew found themselves stranded, without the proper equipment to repair the lift-and-drive engines, and unable to leave.

Aditya had fallen to a Civ-Level 4 and the only local machinery available was water or wind-driven mills. It hadn't helped their repair efforts that the local steel was of dismal quality. Since the Time of Troubles, Aditya had decivilized into a number of competing city-states, with no one city in control. The crew had quickly gone native, using their superior knowledge to supplant some of the local rulers.

When DeBorder and Ragnarsans had landed, they'd found few traces—other than some familial names—of the former Space Viking crew. They had quickly determined the ship's problem, then had traveled from Aditya to Xochitl where they had purchased a new drive. Once the Abbot engines were repaired, Ragnarsans had accompanied the *Pay Dirt* to Tanith where he'd had the ship serviced. While at Tanith, he changed the blazonry to a horse rearing over a globe. Tylor had accepted DeBorder's quirky suggestion for the new ship's name, *Gift Horse*, because it appealed to his own sense of humor.

More than anything, Morland realized, Ragnarsans wanted to prove that he could be a successful ship captain as well as anyone else.

"How hard was it getting the *Gift Horse* aloft after it was idle for so long?" Morland asked.

"It wasn't too difficult. Once we isolated the problem it was just a matter of replacing the Dillingham engines, after that it was mostly doing a cleanup and making some cosmetic repairs to the interior. The Adityans didn't bother anybody, they only screamed at us when we were outside. The ship had assumed some kind of special status with them. No one dared approach the ship—apparently it was taboo. Probably some bugaboo started by the original crew who wanted to keep the locals out of the ship and off-limits in case help arrived.

"I recruited several engineers and technicians on Xochitl and an experienced executive officer on Tanith who helped," Ragnarsans said, grinning from the communication screen.

Morland met up with the rest of his officers at his office in the command center, after the ships landed at Emesh spaceport. The *Zama's* Executive Officer was Nial Rymund. He had served with Rymund on the *Prince of Thieves*, his first ship, and remembered him fondly. He knew one of the other officers as well, Joris Kirbey, who had been an officer on the *Pay Dirt* when they raided Horus and Nissaba, but who had left the ship when it returned to Tanith several years ago. Kirbey had to be kicking himself because he'd missed out on a small fortune in shares. He was now back serving on the *Pay Dirt*.

After introductions were finished, they caught up on the latest Space Viking gossip. Two Mardukan ships had found the Space Viking ship, *Curse of Cagn*, raiding Chantico within the Mardukan Empire's new territory and blown her to smithereens. "They were not shy about advertising it, either," DeBorder concluded.

"I'm glad we decided to do our best to avoid the Empire," Morland said.

"A wise decision, Commodore," Rymund added. "I expect a lot of Space Vikings will follow you here, once word gets out about how successful you've been. The alternative is to go in the opposite direction."

"What do you mean?" Morland asked.

"Six Space Viking ships, based on Jagannath and led by Virgil Jaksan, Captain of the *Hero's Blade*, raided Gram. They didn't hit the whole planet, just raided a couple of big cities," Redmond said. He mentioned several cities, including Newhaven, where Morland's ancestors had originally settled before leaving for Joyeuse during the Troubles on Gram.

"Some of the ships took serious damage, but they all returned intact with lots of loot. There was already talk among the Space Vikings on Xochitl, where I first heard the news, that other Sword-Worlds could be raided but with some obvious exceptions. Prince Barrington warned everyone that he would treat a raid on Haulteclere as a raid on Xochitl, and hunt down the perpetrators. And no one in their right mind would attack Excalibur."

Morland nodded. Excalibur was not only the first Sword-World, but the most prosperous and best defended. It would be a tough nut to crack. While he'd long ago made up his mind never to return to the Sword-Worlds, he still found the news sobering. It reminded him of a prediction he'd read by Otto Harkaman about how the Space Vikings would eventually return home to loot the worlds they had once left. To anyone who had visited the Sword-World Helm recently, it wasn't all that surprising; some of the Sword-Worlds had decivilized to the point where they had become tempting targets.

DeBorder had some other news. "We heard on Xochitl that King Alwyn is dead. Apparently there was another rebellion against him and this one succeeded."

"What about the Queen and Alwyn's children?" Morland asked.

DeBorder shrugged his shoulders. "No one knows for sure. The rumor mill says they're all dead, but there's no proof. Nor was there any news on who is the current king, or claimant, of Joyeuse. No one on Xochitl knows anything about the current political situation there."

"What did you do with our stellar transfer?" Morland asked.

"I certainly wasn't about to transfer fifty million stellars worth of banknotes from the Bank of Tanith to the Royal Trust of Joyeuse without knowing who they were going to," DeBorder said somewhat defensively.

"I'm glad to hear it," Morland replied.

"Nor did I want to violate Sword-World law. We don't know whether or not the other investors in the New Base Venture are alive or dead. Or even if the new king—if there even is one—has any claim to Alwyn's share. So I deposited the money in the Bank of Tanith on Xochitl. Then I asked some old friends, when they find out, to send word back to us about what the political situation is on Joyeuse. It may take a while since there hasn't been any traffic from Joyeuse for over a G.S. year. When they learn what's going on, they'll send the news out on the next outbound ship for Tanith."

"So the banknotes on deposit at the Bank of Tanith are still in our name?" Morland asked.

"Yes, we can send the banknotes to Joyeuse whenever we sort out who's who and who's really in charge of the partnership."

"An excellent decision, Javen," Morland reassured him.

DeBorder preened. "Thank you, David. I thought the decision through by asking myself, what would the Commodore do?"

"I must say, you did exactly what I would have done. Now, we'll wait until we hear back from Joyeuse before we calculate shares and disperse the money among our two crews and officers."

King Alwyn had claimed ownership of the *Skull Splitter* based on his inheritance of the Joyeuse kingship from his cousin, former King Sesar. The King had put up approximately half of the funds for the New Base Venture; the rest had come from twenty or so original investors. Now that Alwyn was deceased, Morland didn't know who all the surviving owners of the New Base Venture, Ltd. were or how many shares they held. The ownership charter was held on Joyeuse and subject to change when shares were sold or traded on the local stock exchange.

However, possession was always nine tenths of the law, and Morland wasn't going to disperse funds to a new king, who was basically a usurper or a regicide. Until they discovered the fate of the original investors and their percentage of ownership in the New Base Venture, the money would remain on deposit at the Bank of Tanith.

DeBorder had also brought a guest from Tanith along with him. Prince Manfred Trask, the fifth son of King Rodrik, or, as he informed everyone with a glint in his eye—the first son of the second wife. He was on the tall side, with a long face and the "hawk"-like Trask nose. He had come to Sarpanitum to act as unofficial ambassador between Tanith and Sarpanitum.

"Unofficially," he told Morland later in private over drinks, "my Father sent me here to learn from you."

Morland was flattered, and said so. But, with all his heirs, he could appreciate why King Rodrik might want to fob one off on a friend. What he really appreciated was all of the industrial machinery Rodrik had sent aboard the *Zama* as part of his investment.

Manfred replied amiably, "Father is grateful that you are continuing to trade with us when other civilized worlds are so much closer. We can use the business, as our off-world trade has declined even more since your last visit."

Morland nodded in sympathy. "I'm sorry to hear that. I feel fortunate to count your father among my friends."

"Father only wishes he had more friends with your loyalty," young Trask replied. "Too many of the men he had counted among his friends have turned their back on us."

Morland nodded in agreement. It must have hurt Rodrik deeply when the League of Civilized Worlds disbanded and most of the member worlds suddenly joined up with the Empire. Trask had known and worked with those leaders his entire life.

"With all the attacks on Space Vikings our shipyards sit almost empty," Manfred continued.

"Do you think this is because of Tanith's ties to the Sword-Worlds, Prince Trask?"

He grinned, "Just call me Manfred. Between my brothers, my stepbrothers and myself, there are more than enough princes on Tanith. I'd rather be a regular civilian here on Sarpanitum. But, in answer to your question: Father doesn't think it's an official response, just Marduk's way of encouraging their subject worlds to trade within their own sphere, rather than with outsiders. Since Father refused to join the Empire, diplomatic relations with the Empire have been frosty. Recently, we've seen some very unhappy independent merchants arriving at Rivington spaceport with full cargo holds and no one to sell them to. Soon, Tanith's only off-world trade will be for necessities and luxury items."

"I'm sorry to hear that," Morland said. "Trade blocs are impediments to free trade and can cause the rest of us independent worlds real difficulties."

Manfred said, "I agree, and so does my Father. There are rumors that the Odin Confederacy is setting up its own trade bloc to counter the Empire's. Meanwhile, the Mardukan Empire is growing by the parsecs."

When Manfred finished citing a dozen worlds that had joined the Empire since it was declared, Morland realized with a slight shock that it had been over two Galactic Standard years since he had last set foot on Tanith. A lot of things had taken place in the rest of the galaxy during that time.

"What about the Gilgameshers? On my last visit to Tanith, they had completely abandoned their colony. Have they returned?"

Manfred shook his head. "No. We haven't seen a Gilgamesh ship on Tanith since before your last visit. Which reminds me, Father told me to tell you that new Gilgamesher colonies have been spotted in the Empire. He thinks you were right: now they're acting as the eyes and ears of the Mardukans. It saddens him to think how the family has been duped by them for so long."

"I thought that was a good possibility. Now that the League is gone they've moved onto greener pastures."

Manfred frowned. "That's one way of putting it. It doesn't leave us with much, though…. Those son-of-a-bitches used us and discarded us as if we were trash."

Morland nodded in agreement. There was no way to pretty up that situation. "Let me tell you what we've uncovered. After our last visit to Tanith, we unexpectedly found a Gilgamesh ship at Litchfield Spaceport. When they spotted us, their ship immediately took off, firing missiles at some of our installations." He went on to describe their battle with the ship, its obliteration of some of their Litchfield holdings, the murder of the Lord-High Mayor and the self-destruction of the Gilgamesh ship.

"Phew!" Trask exclaimed, shaking his head in wonder. "This is one Gehenna of a mystery. You've got gilgies killing people *and* committing mass suicide. None of this makes any sense. I can hardly believe it, much less come up with an explanation."

"We're still seeing some Gilgameshers in this sector, but they're acting as if nothing had happened. It's back to business as usual. It just keeps getting stranger and stranger."

"I wish I could give you some answers, Commodore, but this is so out of character for them that I'm nonplussed."

"Me too, me too."

"There is another matter," Trask said. He seemed a little fidgety, reaching into his jacket several times and then withdrawing an empty hand.

He's probably been told not to smoke in my office, Morland decided, suggesting that they go out onto the deck.

Trask was grateful, and promptly lit-up a cigarette as soon as they got outside. They were at the top of an office building overlooking Emesh spaceport that Morland had taken over as his headquarters. It wasn't the largest building, but the deck provided a panoramic view of the spaceport, the old city of Emesh, Emeshton and the mountains beyond.

"What a beautiful place. So many possibilities, I envy you," Trask sighed. "It must have been like this for my great-grandfather Lucas when he first came to Tanith."

He puffed nervously on his cigarette before saying, "My father has received discrete inquiries from the Empire as to whether we know the whereabouts of a ship named *Skull Splitter*, captained by one Captain David Morland formerly of Joyeuse."

Morland felt rocked to the core, as shaken as if there'd been an earthquake. The Empire was leaving no stone unturned. "DeBorder didn't mention this."

"Probably, because he doesn't know," Trask replied. "As far as we know, the ambassador only asked this question of my father. Father told the Imperial Ambassador that you had been on Tanith before leaving for Marduk, but that he knew nothing further about your whereabouts. He didn't mention your most recent, or DeBorder's, visit. The Ambassador mentioned that they had traced you to Odin—"

"Did the Ambassador say why they were looking for the *Skull Splitter?*" Morland asked.

"No. My father had informed me about your encounter with the *Challenger* at Rhiannon, so I suspect it has to do with Captain Vandarvant."

Morland nodded. "He promised revenge and he meant it." Word of their whereabouts would inevitably get out. Even if Javen and his crew had been quiet, there had been scores of retiring crewmen who'd stayed behind on Xochitl. Most would be happy to brag about how they had beaten an Imperial ship in a fair ship-to-ship battle. The story would eventually find its way back to Marduk.

"Next time you see him, please thank your father for me for not answering the Ambassador's questions about our whereabouts."

"We don't owe the Empire a damn thing," Trask said forcefully. "We were one of the founders of the League of Civilized Worlds. My great grandfather saved the Mardukan royal family over a century ago. If it wasn't for Lucas Trask, there wouldn't be any Bentrik Royal family, or a Mardukan Empire. What really angers my father is that they didn't even consult with us before they declared their so-called empire."

Suddenly Morland realized that King Rodrik hadn't just been nostalgic about the dissolution of the League of Civilized Worlds when they'd talked. Tanith had once been an important world, even out of proportion to her population, wealth and location. Marduk's declaration of empire had returned Tanith to the backwater she had once been and was about to be again. With the remaining Space Vikings bypassing Tanith to raid farther and farther into the reaches of the Old Federation, Tanith would soon find herself even more isolated and impoverished.

"The Imperials don't know where you are at the moment. And I don't want to suggest the entire Empire's looking for you," Trask said, "however, you are clearly important to one of the factions advising the Emperor."

Manfred went on to explain the factions at the Mardukan Court which were each putting forth a different strategy for expanding the Empire's reach. To the most aggressive faction, the civilized worlds of the galaxy were the only important ones; they wanted all of Marduk's attention focused on bringing them into the Empire in order to eliminate any possible competing sovereignties, such as Odin or Aton. If they could bring them in without much violence, as in the case of Baldur, that was fine. Otherwise, they were quite willing to intimidate or even invade the civilized worlds to annex them into the Empire. To this militant faction, the defeat of an Empire ship by a mere Space Viking ship diminished the aura of military invincibility that they wished the Empire to project.

Another faction took a much longer view. They were content to have the civilized worlds join of their own accord; they didn't think any effort should be spent on forcing them into the Empire. They believed that the world-by-world conquest of all the Neobarbarian worlds was the solution. Even if it took generations, eventually the Mardukan Empire would encompass so many worlds—with so much concentrated economic power from trade between Imperial worlds—that no civilized planet could afford not to be a part of the Empire.

The third faction was even less violent. They favored the peaceful assimilation of worlds via trade only. Their strategy was simply an outgrowth of the policy of the former League of Civilized Worlds, which had been more of a trade association and alliance than a political association.

"What strategy does Emperor Lucas favor?" Morland asked.

Trask grinned. "Officially, he hasn't come out in favor of any of them. However, the Mardukans have conquered a number of Neobarbarian worlds recently—Baphomet, Hachiman, Malbecco, Neith, and Schacabac—and there have been plenty of trade initiatives" mentioning other examples. "However, the Empire hasn't attempted to takeover any more civilized worlds since Baldur. Although, we have heard rumors that the Mardukan Navy has a very visible presence in the vicinity of Isis."

"So the Emperor's leaning toward peaceful conquest," Morland said sarcastically.

Trask chuckled, lighting another cigarette and leaning on the balcony to look out over the spaceport. "I think Lucas the First is leaning toward whichever policy works best."

The Empire will be here sooner or later—most likely sooner, thought Morland. *We'd better be damn well ready for them, too.*

III

Those preparations gained greater urgency a year later when a freighter just in from Poictesme reported that a Mardukan Naval ship had visited the planet asking about Space Viking ships in general, and the *Skull Splitter* in particular.

"What about our ships?"

"They stayed hidden behind the planets and moons of the system," Captain Ivar Nash replied.

Morland laughed. "There are enough planets and moons in the Tri-System to confuse even the best computer and astrogator."

"Yorick handled them perfectly," Nash said.

Morland was always amused and gratified by Yorick Ladbrok's knack for making friends with anyone and everyone. Even though Ladbrok was the *de facto* ruler of Poictesme, everyone who interacted with him called him by his first name.

Apparently when the call from the Imperial ship had come in, Ladbrok had delayed taking it. He had someone put a communication screen in a shabby old room, dressed himself outlandishly, and played the part of an ignorant Neobarbarian prince to the hilt.

"Yorick told them he had traded with a number of ships, but none with the name of *Skull Splitter*. Next he asked what a Mardukan Empire was. Then his wife came into the room, so big that *she* looked ready to give birth right then and there. *She* let rip a string of curses and insults to the Mardukan captain for not paying proper respect to Poictesme's ruler. The Imperial left very flustered and frustrated," Nash finished laughing.

Despite his anxiety over this latest development, Morland had a silent chuckle when the captain had referred to Gytha Valkanhayn only as "she." The more reserved Valkanhayn was on a first-name basis with only a few people, unlike her husband.

"Were you around long enough for the birth of their child?" he asked.

"Yes, a healthy baby boy," Captain Nash replied. "They've named him Teodor, after Yorick's late father."

The news that Ladbrok's father had been killed with former King Alwyn on Joyeuse had hit Ladbrok hard. Based on what they'd learned from returning captains, no single noble on Joyeuse had been able to amass enough power to declare himself king. There were skirmishes going on between the various noble houses, warlords and mercenaries. The political situation was bordering on anarchy. The possibility of a Space Viking attack should have been enough to encourage stability, if for nothing else than to defend itself. Morland was just glad he was safely out of the Joyeuse morass.

On the bright side, it left no one with a plausible claim to ownership of the *Skull Splitter*, which meant that Morland and his crew owned the money he had been holding in the Bank of Tanith. He'd have the shares distributed at the next yearly payout.

Turning his attention back to the freighter captain he asked if there was any other news. "There's been another raid on the Sword-Worlds. I heard on Tanith that the *Manticore, Princess Erika* and *War Hammer* looted Durendal," he said.

"Besides beer, what's worth raiding on Durendal?" Morland asked. For the past century, Durendal had been the site of a seesawing dynastic war between two political factions. Determined not to lose to one another, both sides had launched numerous nuclear attacks against each other, resulting in a world blasted back into barbarism.

"Actually," Captain Nash said. "They brought mining equipment and excavated the known sites of old bank and treasury vaults. Though some of the areas were so destroyed nothing was left, they salvaged plenty of gold and silver."

That, he thought, *is a damn good idea!* He could think of a few places where that technique might work for him. "At least they were digging below ground where they wouldn't have to face that wind."

Nash laughed, since Durendal was best known for the unceasing wind that blew across the main inhabited continent. The Captain rose, reaching into a shoulder bag and drawing out a data tab. "Yorick asked me to give this to you when our business was done. He asked that you play it as soon as possible."

That didn't sound good. Thanking the freighter Captain for his information, Morland sat down to review the recording about the Mardukans' visit. They'd been lucky this time: no ships had been en route between Koshchei and Poictesme, when the Imperial ship had entered the system. If one had, the Empire might have discovered their shipyards on Koshchei and appropriated them on the spot.

"As per your plan," Ladbrok reported, "the interplanetary ships were well hidden, hiding their signatures behind some of the local moons as previously determined. The Mardukans came in expecting to see a Neobarb world and that's what they saw. Of course, this may have been a scouting mission and the Imperials may return in the future. If they do, they will be woefully under prepared."

Although they were in the process of moving some of the industrial installations from Koshchei to Sarpanitum as fast as they could, they were still dependent on Koshchei for machinery they didn't have on Sarpanitum. And, if the Empire ever found out what else he was doing on Koshchei, his future plans would suffer a severe blow. Despite Ladbrok's assurances, they were not yet prepared to hold off an Imperial squadron.

This visit to Poictesme was another sign of the Empire's aggressive expansionism. They had recently taken over a Neobarbarian planet called Belphegor at the edge of claimed Imperial space, and were constructing a major navy base at the old spaceport. Although it was over eight hundred hours from Sarpanitum, Belphegor was only six hundred hours from Poictesme. It was also less than two hundred hours from Rhiannon, which Morland didn't think was a coincidence. Stenger had been back to Rhiannon once in the past year, and the sensors he had left had shown four visits from other ships during that time.

He couldn't be certain that they were Imperial ships that were visiting

Rhiannon, but he wasn't about to take any chances. He resolved not to return there with less than three ships. He also tried to diversify their sources of fissionables. As historian Alex Feraday had predicted, they had no luck making friends with Tashmetum. So far, every attempt to trade with them had been met with outright hostility. Morland had given up on trading with Tashmetum, but he still held out hope for Mara, which had a single planetary government with which to negotiate. Although they hadn't actually traded anything yet, Mara had been willing to talk with them.

He had dispatched Vann Stenger and the *Faerie Queene* to do the negotiating; Vann had presented himself as an independent trader from Poictesme. It wouldn't pay to let the Marians know they were negotiating with the Space Vikings that had raided them. They had dangled the bait of contragravity, which he believed would eventually reel the Marians in.

There had been no such problems trading with Lyonnesse. Premier Cohen had welcomed them back. Though not yet a unified world, Lyonnesse had proved to be a good trading partner. They did all their trading through Albion since the other nations distrusted their intentions.

At least there were some worlds where they could trade. At one time he had worried that Space Vikings or independent traders would show up at Sarpanitum to sell their loot or to trade before Emesh spaceport would be ready to accommodate them. The spaceport had been fully functional for almost a year and still no outsiders, other than freighters from Tanith, had landed. Morland was grateful that Javen DeBorder, Anse Shawley and Tylor Ragnarsans had continued to trade with him when they could go anywhere in the galaxy. He might have to send one of them on a trip to some of the other Space Viking base planets to spread the word about Sarpanitum.

In the meantime, they would continue to trade with as many of the Neobarbarian worlds in their sector that were profitable trading partners. Among those worlds was Nissaba. He had renewed his acquaintance with Princess Janna on a short trading trip a few G.S. months ago. With Padishah Parviz's assistance they had cleaned up the old spaceport in the center of the continent and stationed some personnel there, including two of the historians who had fallen in love with their horses. The King had also assisted them in looting some of the remaining Vahistas' castles, which made the visit very lucrative. Since Nissaba had several continents that were uninhabited, he planned to use them as dumping grounds for Sarpanitum malcontents.

Given the refugee crisis that was developing on Ashnan, he might have to act sooner than he anticipated. The breakdown of the communist government's central authority in the Ashnan and the battles between various strongmen for control of territory had created a continuing stream of refugees. Some of them had crossed to Kabata on one of the remaining engineering marvels of the CRS, a thirty-three miles long bridge that linked the continents of Ashnan and Kabata at their closest point.

The bridge, and the railroad that crossed it, ran directly to the Correa river valley, which was the most agriculturally productive part of the Kabata. The valley, which had gone from animal powered farming to mechanical equipment only within the last decade, was already being disrupted by the introduction of Sword-World contragravity. The flood of refugees was making a bad situation worse.

Having more contragravity equipment than experienced personnel, his people had been trying to teach the valley inhabitants new techniques, but had met with only limited success. It seemed that prior to the Space Viking invasion most of the educated and ambitious people living in the Correa Valley had either joined the CRS or moved to Valpo. Those left behind had most of their initiative hammered out of them by their former communist masters. He was beginning to think that it might be best for all concerned that those Correans, who couldn't or wouldn't learn the new agricultural techniques they were offering, be moved off-world. On Nissaba there was plenty of open land and the Correans' current practices would still be more advanced than those of the locals. There wasn't enough surplus food to feed them through another winter, not with thousands of displaced Ashnans arriving daily.

They had gone through most of the stockpiled foodstuffs last winter.

He'd thought that the influx of immigrants would settle down after the first year, but refugees were still streaming into Space Viking occupied areas, some looking for work, most looking for handouts. The displaced population needed to be dealt with soon or when winter came they'd be faced with mass starvation.

However, at the moment Morland was not in a position to transport hundreds of thousands of displaced persons to Nissaba—at least, not yet.

Some help had arrived when the allied nations of the Federation of Independent Nations and the Kingdom of Lahar offered to occupy the Lansing Peninsula. Distressed by the increasing state of anarchy throughout the Ashnan continent, and wanting to prevent it from moving into Kabata, they proposed an army of occupation. Morland had offered to pay their soldiers' salaries and provide barracks to house them. It saved him from having to tie down his own limited military resources; it would also help the locals make their own transition from wartime to peacetime economy easier, as well.

Morland was pleased that they had sought his permission before taking any action, since that was tacit acknowledgement that he was ruler of the planet.

Newly minted Lieutenant Lancaster pointed out that their navies did not have any ships capable of transporting the tens of thousands of troops necessary for such an operation. He had agreed and supplied the contragravity lifts necessary to transport their troops to the Great Bay of the Lansing peninsula, along with his local military forces. Sarpanitum was proving to be fertile ground for the recruitment of armies.

After a gruesome cleanup operation, where they removed the dead bodies and rubble from partially destroyed cities of Ashur and Salvasar, the troops had spread out through the peninsula without too much opposition. The only resistance came from a few surviving hardline communist troops, who were easily defeated by the larger and better supplied invasion forces. It was impossible for a non-contragravity force, like the communist guerillas, to hold a line against troops that could be easily transported to the rear. As word gradually spread that the Lansing peninsula was under the control of a stable interim government, tens of thousands of refugees headed for the area.

However, the allies ended up having even more problems on the Lansing peninsula than he had in the Correa Valley. Besides a population that lacked initiative, there were tens of thousands of former communist officials still alive on the peninsula. Though some had adjusted to the new government, many were actively working against it, either through agitation and protests or out-and-out rebellion.

Morland did his best to stay out of the occupation, but if things got any worse he would have to get involved. The problem, as he saw it, was that the allies were simply too accommodating with the former government officials and Communist Party members. If they had firmly taken charge and shot the first few troublemakers, they would have had fewer problems in the long run.

Morland might have his base world, but there was still a lot of work left before it became the stable base he'd planned on. And, it would have to be soon; time was not their ally, not with the Empire breathing down his neck.

GILGAMESH II

"I'm sorry, High Maxwell," Marshal Sayles said, "all the available evidence, which we've gathered in the last ten thousand hours, points to a Space Viking colony on Poictesme. None of our ships have approached the Homeworld directly since we don't want to lose another ship or attract undue attention. However, several of the traders we deal with have visited Poictesme and they have reported that Homeworld is now under the control of a Space Viking leader, they call Prince David Morland. They also mentioned observing significant industrial development both in Litchfield and elsewhere on the planet. It also appears that the barbarians are using the Koshchei shipyards to build up their navy. They don't encourage visitors, but money talks."

The High Maxwell tried to control the frustration he felt building up inside. "The situation on Poictesme has been stable for half a millennium. Why is it changing now, Chief Vibart? Is there some new variable or flux in the historical matrix?"

The Chief Programmer shrugged. "The emergence of a new order is typically a time of chaos and disorder leading to the next epoch of civilization. These events are numerous and beyond the scope of any human mind to comprehend or control. As soon as the new Order was identified, the Oracle has been pondering its ascendance and its effects on the other variables leading to the next epoch of Terro-Human history. It was the Oracle who commanded us to vacate the former League of Civilized Worlds and break off our alliance with the Trasks.

"According to the Oracle, the Trask line plays only an incidental role in the emergence of the matrix. Their work as catalyst of the new order is over. The historical movement has gone to the next phase and they are mostly irrelevant. The Bentrik line they nurtured and preserved will be the apex of the new epoch."

"Is there any connection between the takeover of the Homeworld by the barbarians and the new phase?" the High Maxwell asked.

"I have questioned the Oracle on this matter, Your Worshipful," said the Chief Programmer. "It sees no significant correlation between the rise of a new Empire and the events on Poictesme. It sees the Space Viking settlement as a predicted response to Imperial expansion. Now that Marduk has claimed a five hundred light-year boundary, this has significantly impacted the barbarians usual raiding and trading operations. The Mardukans have been destroying Space Viking ships and base worlds both inside their proclaimed boundary and outside of it. Therefore, it's not unexpected that some of the more ambitious and intelligent Space Vikings would seek new areas of operation, moving them closer to the Terran Sector and our own sphere of influence."

The High Maxwell nodded, although he had a feeling that the Oracle had overlooked some important variable, such as the importance of the Homeworld to the Caretakers. The Caretakers, the only inhabitants of Gilgamesh who knew the Origin Story and served the Oracle, had a special place in their hearts for the Homeworld. He knew that the Space Viking's presence on Poictesme disturbed him greatly, more than he could explain rationally, even beyond the death of his son. He was certain that it affected many of the Caretakers likewise.

The Space Viking barbarians were desecrating a sacred spot. "You realize, as word of their takeover of Homeworld has spread, there is a sense of growing unease among the Caretaker class. What does the Oracle have to say about this?"

The Chief Programmer shook his head with a withering look. "Superstitious rubbish. Poictesme's importance to the Plan ended the day that Merlin was transported off-world. The Oracle deals with facts and data, not feelings and emotional suppositions."

This may well be its greatest weakness, the High Maxwell thought. *Isn't there an ancient programming rubric that goes: Rubbish in and rubbish out. Maybe we've grown too dependent upon both the Oracle and its programmers.* To say such a thing aloud, even for the head of state and linear descendent of Conn Maxwell, would result in severe punishment, banishment or even death.

I'd better change the subject before I say something I'll regret. He turned to Marshal Sayles. "What kind of military threat are we facing in the Gartner Tri-System?"

The Marshal sighed. "A significant one, Your Worshipful. According to our intelligence, the barbarians have at least one or two Space Viking ships in-system at all times, plus—as of our latest intelligence—they have four to six interplanetary fortress ships emplaced throughout the Gartner Tri-System. It would take a large fleet to clean out this nest of vipers."

"Have they attacked any more of our ships?" the High Maxwell asked.

"No, Your Worshipful. They have interrogated some of our trading partners, but they have made no direct contact since *The Prayerful Worshipper* was destroyed. The barbarians have left our trading ships and our people alone."

"So we're at a stalemate," the High Maxwell said. "The Space Vikings don't dare risk taking any more of our ships due to the threat of war. We can't retake the Homeworld for fear of disturbing the coming together of the matrix."

"See, it is as the Oracle predicted," Chief Programmer Vibart said. "The Viking Prince David is no more anxious for war than we are."

"I don't want war, I want justice," the High Maxwell proclaimed. "A ship for a ship! Their Prince for my son! And I want those vermin off our Homeworld."

The Chief Programmer shook his head. "Terro-Human civilization is at a pivotal historical point in its transformation into the next historical epoch. The Time of Troubles is coming to an end and the new Empire is coalescing into the Universal State; our operatives tell us that there are three major factions within the new Imperial government, each vying for the Emperor's favor. Lucas the First is aware of their machinations and is playing them off against each other like a puppet master.

"According to the Oracle, it is imperative that we do nothing to upset the emerging matrix. It's code name for the Emperor is the Spider King."

"How will terminating a bunch of Space Viking barbarians affect the burgeoning matrix?" the High Maxwell asked. It ate at him that a mere barbarian had such importance that the most powerful man in the Terro-Human worlds had to withhold his vengeance.

"The Oracle does not give explanations for its decisions. It takes in data and makes the highest probability decision regarding the implementation of the Plan. It says that the Space Viking leader, David Morland, is a "heroic figure in an age that has no heroes" and that killing him would have unforeseeable consequences. He has developed close ties with the Trasks, and his allies and underlings would not take his death well. The probability of success for the new matrix is in the order of .67773, which as you know is very high. It drops to .34962 if Morland is killed or removed by our hand."

The High Maxwell reared back in shock. "These probabilities are astoundingly high. Unique, even. I accede to the Oracle's wishes."

"A wise decision, High Maxwell. A very wise decision."

VISHNU

The Darveld System's primary was an old G3 yellow sun with fourteen planets, with Vishnu being the only one within the habitable zone. There were three gas giants and several metal rich but uninhabitable planets. The system itself was busy with mining and cargo ships both coming from and going to Vishnu. Due to the dense traffic, incoming out-system ships were prohibited from arriving any closer than 3 AUs from the primary.

Vishnu was a large world, some ten thousand miles in diameter, but it was a low density planet with a gravity of 1.13 Galactic Standard. Because there was little planetary inclination, most of the super continent of Rama had a moderate temperature and was hospitable to most Terran life forms. Vishnu was also the most populated world in the former Federation with a population of over ten billion, four times the population of Terra before World War III.

Of the early Federation colonies, only a few had managed to survive the Interstellar Wars without incident. The Vishnuians were proud that their world had been under the same government for over fifteen hundred years and looked down upon younger civilizations, which included almost every planet in the former Federation except Odin, Aton, Baldur, Isis, Osiris and a half dozen other civilized worlds. They believed their world to be the only *truly* civilized planet in Terro-Human occupied space.

Morland didn't agree: he found Vishnuian culture overly conservative and moribund. Everyone wore gray tunics with colored stripes at the edges which displayed status and social class. Those who didn't follow the culture mavens were considered outcasts and treated accordingly. The one fact that always stuck out prominently in Morland's mind was that they had more mental institutions per citizen on Vishnu than any other world in the Old Federation. He wasn't sure if it was due to the pressures to conform or the stress due to overpopulation and overcrowding. All he knew for certain was that he never wanted to live there and the air smelled like that of a spaceship relying on recycled air for ten thousand hours.

Its major trade advantage for Morland was that Vishnu happened to be the closest civilized world to Poictesme that was outside the Mardukan sphere of influence. Marduk, which had a major revolt and change of government some hundred years earlier, was no longer considered by Vishnuians to be a truly civilized world, since it could no longer trace its lineage back to the former Terran Federation. Overall, they were aghast about the new Mardukan Empire and saw them as pretenders.

When the *Skull Splitter* had first landed several years ago, the Space Viking crew had attracted a lot of attention, as several centuries had passed since there had been a Space Viking ship landing on Vishnu. Now, Morland wished they'd presented themselves as merchants. Fortunately, there was little contact, other than diplomatic, between Vishnu and Marduk, but that could change as the Empire expanded.

It had been over a year since his last visit to Vishnu. Morland took one of the pinnaces down to the surface with his First Officer and two squads of ground fighters under the command of Sergeant-Major Xavier Burris. Normally, he would have landed the *Skull Splitter* (which now displayed the name *Nebula*, the name he used for trading runs) at the spaceport, but they were in the middle of a trade-and-raid run and he didn't want to run afoul of the local authorities. There were a lot of proscribed trade items on Vishnu, especially weapons and surveillance items.

The pinnace, following a predetermined course provided by the spaceport computer, moved smoothly through ever increasing traffic. As they descended, Morland looked out the viewscreen marveling at the thousands of towers and spires that were packed so closely together they looked like trees in some otherworldly metal forest. The tens of thousands of aircars and other craft traveled over, above and around the contragravity buildings like birds in ever changing flocks.

The huge hexagonal New Durban Spaceport, which had docks for thirty-six spacecraft, was almost full, seating dozens of large spacecraft, many of them traders by appearance, and two Vishnu Naval ships. All around the spaceport were the ground hugging buildings, the warehouses, machine factories, storage units, small business and squat apartment buildings and tenements called Lowtown.

With the Mardukans looking for him, Morland wanted to keep a low profile and thanked his good fortune for being able to switch names of his ship with the flick of a switch. An innovation which he'd had installed during his first visit to Tanith.

He was surprised at the tension and barely restrained hostility that greeted him when he went through customs at New Durban Spaceport. The customs officials were mostly interested in contraband. He and Vin Qual had a profitable line of trade in Sarpanitum silks and fine spirits, Poictesme melon-brandy, Nissaba pomegranate wine, Baldur honey-rum, Lyonnesse champagne and Ammut sugar-plum rum. The last thing he wanted to do was jeopardize their operation by smuggling.

Instead of doing any sightseeing, Morland took an airtaxi directly to Vin Qual's office, which was located in Lowtown, one of the least prestigious neighborhoods of New Durban. Nadira, Vin's secretary, whose grace and animation could even make a gray tunic look lively, was there to greet him. "Welcome, David. I hope they didn't put you through too much bother at customs."

"No, just wasted a few hours. Is Qual in?"

"Yes, let me get him. Will we have time for dinner?"

He smiled. "Of course, and maybe dancing later."

Nadira's eyes lit up. She used her intercom to talk with her boss, "He says to go right in, David."

Vin Qual was still sitting at the same old battered metal desk, although the shelves around him were now filled with samples of exotic off-world spirits that Morland had provided on his previous visits. He rose up, smiling, and they shook hands in the old manner.

"I'm surprised to see you here, David. Usually it's Vann Stenger making the milk runs."

"I need to get out of the office every once in a while. Running a planet is an ongoing headache!"

Vin laughed. "And one I'll thankfully never know."

"So, how's business?" Morland asked.

"Very good. The liquor clubs are raving about your latest discovery, the Ammut sugar-plum rum. I can sell as much as you bring me for top price. And more of the Asgard vodka, if you can find it."

"I'll try. DeBorder picked up that last batch on Tanith. Asgard is now under Mardukan rule so we have to go through a middle man." He gave Vin the bill of lading for the current shipment, then they discussed Off-World Imports' growing business.

"If sales keep expanding, I'm going to have to rent another warehouse," Vin complained. "I have to be careful not to expand our operations too quickly. To do so would give our competitors an opportunity to have us investigated."

Morland still found Vishnu perplexing; it was a world where if you did too well, without the *right connections*, you were suspected of criminal activity. Guilty until proven innocent. He wondered how Vin put up with it. *I guess it all comes down to what you're used to. Qual would probably view the Sword-Worlds as some sort of feudal anarchy run amuck.*

"So I take it our products are doing well?" Morland asked.

"We sell everything you give us. Actually, I have to hoard most of it and parcel it out to the city's many liquor clubs. I have to keep my margins down or I'll be prosecuted for racketeering. Fortunately, most of the spirits you provide are not available elsewhere, like the Nissaba pomegranate wine or the Poictesme melon-brandy, so some of the club masters have been quietly smoothing the way for our expansion."

"Politics as usual," Morland said shaking his head.

"You'd be surprised at how many important civil leaders are members of the clubs," Vin said. "The City Mayor is head of the Pure Spirits Club. He's also one of our biggest boosters and has been a big help in obtaining permits and lifting sales restrictions, helping with things that might take as long as generations without his aid. Of course, that means giving the Pure Spirits Club first pick of any new shipments." He went on to detail some of the other problems his import company, Off-World Imports, was having due to its rapid growth.

When Vin had wound down, Morland asked, "What do you know about the Gilgameshers? I understand they've had a colony here on Vishnu for a long time." He quickly gave Vin a rundown on the Gilgamesh murders and the ship suicide on Poictesme to explain his interest.

Vin paused for a moment, then said, "The first Gilgamesh ship visited here in the Fourteenth Century A.E. This was right after the Interstellar wars and at a time when interstellar trade had dwindled down to nothing, even here. Initially, the Gilgameshers were roundly welcomed both because of the goods they carried and their novelty. If they were arriving today, they wouldn't even be given a landing permit. But things were different, even on Vishnu, during those troubled times.

"About a century or so later the Gilgameshers created a small colony, albeit a semi-permanent one. The authorities refuse to grant them permanent immigration status; instead they can only stay for ten G.S. years. Therefore, every decade the Gilgameshers rotate their traders. As long as they don't put down roots or bring their families with them, the authorities are mollified.

"Despite this roadblock, the Gilgameshers have become one of the major trading arms of Vishnu. Many of the old line firms have had contracts with the Gilgameshers going back centuries and it's almost impossible for a young firm, like ourselves, to trade with them. This is why, until you arrived, we did most of our off-world purchasing from small tramp freighters who were too small or insignificant to be noticed by the bigger companies."

"So you don't think it would be worth my time to visit the colony and try to talk with someone in charge?" Morland asked.

Vin covered his mouth with his hand. "Excuse me, but the idea of talking with the Gilgameshers is so ridiculous that it's almost beyond comprehension. They live in a gated community in Lowtown, not far from here. They do not meet without outsiders unless it has to do with business. Besides, what would our Gilgameshers have to do with an event that occurred on Poictesme?"

"I don't know. It's a mystery that's been festering under my hide like a trapped tick."

Vin nodded affably. "Last time he was here, Vann was asking about the Mardukans."

"Yes, he probably told you about our run-in with the Mardukan warship."

"He did. The Mardukans have recently changed ambassadors and are making quite a stir in the capital's diplomatic circles. They're spending lots of money and making the rounds of the best parties and cultural events."

"Have they been asking about Space Vikings?"

Vin shook his head. "No. Not that I've heard. It appears the Mardukans are trying to buy influence in our government. They haven't made any public overtures about Vishnu joining their empire, but I'm sure it's been bantered around in high circles. They haven't had much success, and probably won't, since Marduk is not highly regarded here."

That made sense to Morland. The new ambassador was probably from the Mardukan group that wanted to win over the other civilized worlds non-violently. He doubted they'd have had much contact with Vandarvant's circle, which was a relief.

Still, it made sense for him to keep a low profile from now on.

P⊕ICTESME III

I

There had been many improvements to Litchfield since Morland had last been on Poictesme for the wedding of Gytha Valkanhayn and Yorick Ladbrok almost two G.S. years ago. The population had grown and more of the older buildings were either rehabilitated or had been demolished. Contragravity vehicles were everywhere. At the same time he noticed a cloud of smoke announcing the departure of one of the railroad trains; apparently some of the old ways still continued to linger on.

The obvious improvement in people's lives was good to see. He'd have to keep that in mind when dealing with the refugee crisis back on Sarpanitum next time he heard complaints about all the changes taking place. There was a quote about how difficult change was: "Good things in the long run are often hard in the short run," but he couldn't remember the author. Maybe it was from Shakespeare, as so many of the best quotes were.

Duke Yorick Ladbrok stood up to greet him as he entered his new office on top of the Allied Storage Building. The first thing he noticed about Ladbok's office was how well-decorated it was, with quality furniture and wall hangings. Much of it was Space Viking plunder, but it was well integrated, like the silver night-mask from Agni, next to a vibrantly colored war shield from Nissaba. Overall, it was much more elegant than his own office on Sarpanitum. Maybe he ought to have Randa try her hand, as she had suggested: "to make this place a fitting reflection of its owner."

Count Giffard Zhorgay, his former Chief Engineer, was seated in a large leather chair. The recording that Ladbrok had sent to Sarpanitum indicated that they were having problems with the new ship under construction on Koshchei. They had asked him to come to Poictesme to discuss it. Leaving Laz Rivera in charge at Emesh City, he had departed for Poictesme as soon as it could be arranged.

He'd even brought Randa with him, both for her company and for a sightseeing excursion since she'd never been off-planet before. They were spending a lot of time together and he was beginning to develop real feelings for her. Knowing that he had a full afternoon ahead, he'd left her in the hands of Gytha Valkanhayn who was going to give her a tour of the local shops in the Litchfield Mall.

After pleasantries had been exchanged, he asked them to describe the problems they were having with the project. Giffard Zhorgay described several difficulties, with an occasional interjection from Ladbrok, that all boiled down to one thing. They didn't have any plans to work off of.

Morland was a little frustrated. "Can't you just double the size of everything?"

"No, Commodore, the actual volume is more than doubled, and that affects almost every system," Zhorgay said, giving a few examples.

Morland began to see the problem and apologized. "Sorry for coming down on you, Giffard. I was unaware of all the issues involved."

"Neither was I until I really got into planning."

"What do you suggest? Can't you design—"

Count Zhorgay interrupted and shook his head, "That's the problem, Commodore. I'm a construction manager, not a designer. The people you brought from Tanith have never worked on this scale. We've all taken a few stabs at it, but we're just groping in the dark."

"Any suggestions?"

"If we could find a way to bring in Stafan Vinar from Excalibur, we might be able to put this project to bed," Zhorgay began.

Now it was Morland's turn to shake his head. They were not having much luck recruiting skilled workers from the Sword-Worlds anymore. A year ago, he'd sent Javen DeBorder to visit several of the remaining Space Viking base worlds, in between raids, to do some recruiting in person, but the *Pay Dirt* hadn't returned yet.

"Then the only alternative we have is for the *Skull Splitter* to stay on Koshchei to help us out," Zhorgay said.

"Why the *Skull Splitter?*" Morland asked.

"Because the *Skull Splitter* has the most advanced computer of any ship in the fleet."

Morland nodded. Before the wars of succession, Joyeuse had been the computer center of the Sword-Worlds, leading the way with innovative computer designs and construction. When the *Nebula* had been designed, no expense had been spared to give her the most up-to-date computer system possible. As a result, the *Skull Splitter* had the most advanced computer system of any warship in the Old Federation. The newer ships they were building on Koshchei were nowhere near as sophisticated.

"We need a larger, more powerful computer," Zhorgay continued, "in order to finalize the new design. None of the other available ship computers have enough computing power for what we need. All of the computers we've found on Koshchei are in ruins or are small and designed for specialized tasks."

Morland shook his head in frustration. "That's going to be a problem, gentlemen. If the *Skull Splitter* stays away from Sarpanitum for any length of time, it will be utterly defenseless if a Mardukan Imperial Naval ship happens to arrive. We can't count on the *Faerie Queene, Pay Dirt, Gift Horse,* or *Grim Reaper II* being present, since they're either doing patrol work on Poictesme or out raiding and trading."

Zhorgay threw his hands up in the air in frustration. Before he could say anything Ladbrok interrupted. "I think I may have a possible solution."

They both stared at Ladbrok, waiting for him to continue. "I put the word out about our problem, just in case someone would—"

"You what!" Morland exclaimed. "Yorick, we can't have any news about what we're doing leaking out, if the Empire ever found out what we are building—" He shuddered at the thought. Independent traders continued to stop off on Poictesme and it was almost impossible to maintain complete security. If they weren't careful, his plans would be all over the Old Federation.

Ladbrok held up a placating hand. "David, I just said we were looking for an advanced computer. I didn't say what for. I know that what's being done on Koshchei must remain our secret."

Morland sighed in relief.

Ladbrok continued. "I've discovered that you never know what people will bring with them to a new world. I thought it was worth asking."

"What did you find out?"

The Duke spoke into the intercom and a few moments later a lanky man with a bowl haircut entered the room. His name was Jeroon Clegg. He looked familiar to Morland but he didn't know why until Clegg said he had joined the *Skull Splitter*'s ground force soon after the Space Vikings landed on Poictesme.

"I remember you now," Morland stated. "You did very well. You were promoted to squad leader before the raid on Mara."

Clegg beamed with pride. "Yes, Commodore. When I returned to Poictesme, I learned that my father had died while I was gone and it was up to me to take over the family business, so I mustered out and returned home."

Clegg continued his narrative as they boarded an aircar and headed out into the area the locals called the Badlands. After Clegg had the family business running smoothly he had started going through boxes of old records and heirlooms stored in the back room of a warehouse. "The business has been in my family in one form or another for centuries, so there was a lot of junk in there. But I found a sealed package of what I recognized as data tapes, so I borrowed a reader and went through them."

Morland remembered that Clegg had been one of the people who had quickly adapted to Sword-World technologies; his section leader had been disappointed when he had left the ground troopers.

The aircar began to slow and descend. They were headed toward a small escarpment that looked like any other of the dozens they had passed until he noticed that there was a tunnel entrance in the side of the bluff.

"I was astonished at what I read on these tapes. Our oral histories are wrong about so many things," Clegg stated. "I was debating whether or not to let people know what I had found when I saw Yorick's message. Suddenly, I knew I had to take you there in person."

Morland looked around. They had landed within a few yards of the tunnel entrance. He could see that the entrance went back into the bluff for quite a ways but he could not see anything beyond that. "What is this?"

"From what I've uncovered, during Federation times this place had been known as Force Command Duplicate. A top secret installation from which the Terran Third Force Command had run their part of the war against the System States Alliance ten centuries ago."

"What makes it so important now?" Morland asked.

"Merlin," Clegg said, like a proud parent showing off his offspring.

"Merlin! I've heard talk about Merlin, but I always thought Merlin was some ancient ruler of Poictesme, a planetary president or something."

"That's what most people think," Clegg said, "except for those who still believe he was a god-like being. But Merlin wasn't any of those things. Merlin was a giant computer—the biggest ever made by the Federation!"

They stared at each other for a few moments. Zhorgay was the first to catch on. "A computer? For this installation here?"

"Yes."

"This is amazing," Ladbrok said. "It could give us the technical know-how to rival Marduk or even Odin!"

Morland's thoughts turned in another direction. "Is this computer still functioning? Can it do the job?"

"I don't know," Clegg replied. "It's been resting here for almost a millennium and there's been a lot of rust and deterioration. I don't know enough about computers to know if it can be salvaged."

Turning to Ladbrok and Zhorgay, Morland ordered, "Have all of our computer people in Litchfield drop whatever they're doing and come over here immediately. Also send some squads of ground fighters, I want this place secured!" To himself he wondered: *Was this the secret that the Gilgameshers had died to protect? I'd give anything to know what they were up to.*

While the two men returned to the aircar to send out his orders, he turned back to Clegg. "You've obviously explored this installation; why don't you give me a tour while we're waiting?"

"With pleasure, sir."

"If this works, you'll have done us a great service," Morland said as they walked toward the tunnel entrance. "As you are aware, I try to reward people for jobs well done. Is there anything in particular you would like?"

Morland had heard a variety of responses to this question when he had asked it over the years. But never the response he heard now.

"Sir, I would like to be captain of a ship."

II

They gathered in Ladbrok's new office to hear the final word on Merlin. The initial reports coming back from the computer specialists were disappointing.

"Will it do the job?" Morland asked.

"Oh no, sir," said one of the specialists on Count Zhorgay's staff. "From what we can tell, this computer hasn't been maintained for seven or eight centuries—maybe more. It was an advanced model for its day; apparently, it was used by the Federation's Terran Third Force Command to direct the war against the System States. Unfortunately, too many of the parts have deteriorated beyond repair and any replacements would have to be jury-rigged. Some of them are so far gone we'd need the original plans to replace them. It would take a miracle to get this old baby up and running."

"I would have to agree," said another specialist. "If we had detailed plans and the right machinery, we might be able to get it operating in a year or two. As it is…?" He threw out his hands in defeat.

"It would be a valuable exercise," one engineer stated. "Who knows how much computer technology was lost after the Collapse? There is much we could learn from studying this old computer."

Everyone in the room was quiet for a few seconds until an older woman spoke up. Morland couldn't remember whether she was one of the computer specialists or one of the historians, who had eagerly flocked to the meeting based on rumors of what was discovered.

"I'm afraid my colleagues are right, Commodore," she stated authoritatively. "This old computer is never going to amount to much. Even if this old machine still worked, it would have been slower than one of our modern computers. Computers always alternate between being able to compute massive amounts of data and being able to work very quickly. In the Old Federation large computers such as this one used machine language and were designed to be large data crunchers."

"Thank you," Morland said, wanting to cut off what he feared was a lecture on the history of computing machines. "I appreciate the effort all of you have put into this project on such short notice. I'll let you know, if I need further help."

After the room was vacated except for his command staff, Morland asked Giffard Zhorgay, "What is your estimate of how long you'll need my ship's computer?"

"I've gone over the design, Commodore. I estimate it will take between five and six G.S. months to complete the project thoroughly."

He frowned.

"I'm sorry, but that's the best estimate I can provide."

Morland nodded. "Then I guess I'll have to accept it."

He gestured to Ladbrok and Zhorgay to accompany him and left the room. Ladbrok looked a little apprehensive over what might happen in his office while he was gone.

"Well, that was a waste of time. Who was that woman, Giffard?" Morland asked.

"Ursulla Hovenden," Zhorgay replied. "She's one of the best computer specialists on my staff. She's not as knowledgeable as some of the others, but a lot more practical about what works, rather than what *could* work."

"Good, put her in charge of the computer end of the design project. Keep it as everyone's top priority. They can forget about that relic."

"I will," Zhorgay said. He looked a lot more relaxed now that he had the computer resources he needed to accomplish the project. "What about your idea that Merlin might be related to the Gilgamesh incident?"

Morland shook his head. "I'd thought maybe there was a connection until I learned that the computer was nothing more than a junk pile. I've beaten my brains for years trying to figure out this mystery and I'm no closer to a solution than I was when it first happened. The Gilgameshers aren't talking and they haven't made a return visit." He held his palms up.

Morland knew that the delay here would give him more time to spend with Randa, but he couldn't really enjoy it while there was too much unfinished work back on Sarpanitum. Things were running smoothly on Poictesme and he really wasn't needed here.

III

"I want to leave as soon as she's loaded." Morland said, as they prepared the *Skull Splitter* for its return. He was anxious to get back to Sarpanitum. This was the longest he had been gone since a brief trip to Vishnu over a year ago.

"What items do you want loaded, Captain?" Gifford Zhorgay asked. "Do you want those missile launchers we've been turning out or…?"

"Load all the missile launchers first, and then anything else there is room for on our list of needed machinery."

Gifford nodded and left.

Ladbrok looked like he would like to return to his office but politely asked, "Missile launchers?"

"Yes. I plan to install them on Sarpanitum's two moons. Hopefully we won't need them, but if the Empire or anyone else attacks I want to be prepared."

"Have the Mardukans come any closer to discovering our base world?" Ladbrok asked.

Morland shook his head. "Not yet, although we're living on borrowed time. At the moment, I'm more worried about finding crews that can operate the missile launchers and who are willing to serve on the moons. Both of the moons are small and very isolated. They are not comfortable environments. I suppose I could automate the launchers, but if an attacker caught on and jammed the communication links, they'd be worthless."

"I'm sure you'll find some volunteers on Sarpanitum, unless the economy has improved greatly since I've been there. I'm just glad the Mardukans haven't found us. Let's have a drink," Ladbrok said, gesturing back toward his office.

"Gytha has been using the interplanetary ships to train new crews and she's always looking for good recruits," the Duke said.

After they'd built six interplanetary warships, he'd directed Gifford to start rehabbing some freighters for hauling cargo. Business between the local worlds had really picked up. As soon as little Teodor was a year old, Gytha had demanded to captain one of them. Morland and her husband were happy to accede to her wishes; they both had been worried that she would want to captain a warship.

"Right now, Gytha's on her way back from Janicot with a ship full of chemical products and she's had pretty good success. She hasn't let our marriage or our little Teodor slow her down much."

Morland was disappointed he wouldn't see her or their son again before he left, but he couldn't wait another day for her return. He'd been stuck on Poictesme for over six months as it was. Finally, the design work was done and he was free to leave.

Ladbrok's communication screen chimed. "Sir, a message for you and Commodore Morland from Duchess Ladbrok."

Gytha was over a light-hour away from Poictesme so they couldn't carry on a two-way conversation. Morland suspected she just wanted to say hello and show off her son and he was right. Gytha's face displayed a broad smile, which was nice to see since she was rarely so expressive. The proud mother was clearly pleased to show off her son one more time. Morland thought Teodor looked like any other eighteen-month-old baby, but knowing mothers he came up with some compliments about his strong features. He knew she'd be going over their responses with a fine-toothed comb when their transmission reached her ship an hour later.

"Things are fine on Janicot now," Gytha was saying. "Our dear Countess had been a bit too dictatorial until I corrected"—her smile altered to one which would terrify most people—"the error of her ways. She apologized and I don't think we will be receiving any more complaints from the personnel on Janicot."

Morland and Ladbrok laughed so hard they had to hit the pause button before they started up the screen again. The Countess was a refugee from Joyeuse, from one of the original New Base Venture investor families, who'd relocated to Poictesme. She was highhanded and overly proud of her birth status. Eventually, for the sake of peace in Litchfield, Duke Ladbrok had made her a planetary representative on Janicot. It was the sixth planet in the Poictesme system and a lifeless world with a witch's brew of atmospheric chemicals and rare metals. They had repaired the old dome city and now it had a small but thriving colony.

The Countess was well known for her domineering ways, but she had never had any success with Gytha, and in fact seemed to be a little scared of her, an emotion that Gytha was quite willing to use to her advantage.

Teodor made a sound they couldn't hear and Gytha grinned down at him. "Yes I'm talking to Daddy." She continued "Teodor and I miss you, Yorick, dear. While these ships are comfortable, it's not as nice as being at home."

While she continued her message to Ladbrok, something itched at the back of Morland's mind. When the screen went blank, it hit him! He slammed his drink down, causing Ladbrok to jump and most of the ice cubes to bounce out. "Yorick, how many interplanetary ships do you have?"

Startled by the question, Ladbrok stared at him for a moment. "We have six interplanetary warships in-system."

"No, I mean, how many total interplanetary ships do you have, including those old ones we found on Koshchei?"

Ladbrok thought for a few moments. "I think the total number was over three hundred. Many of them are in very bad shape, or just the hull struts were laid. There are probably around seventy or eighty that are worth fitting out."

"Then call Giffard, I want to make a few changes to the *Skull Splitter*'s cargo list."

SARPANITUM III

I

"My friends, I came to you over fourteen years ago as a man of war. I am happy that I am leaving as a man of peace. I wish to announce that I will not run for a fourth term next year. It's time for me to retire, and it's time for a younger generation to take up the task of forging a more prosperous Sarpanitum with our friends from the Sword-Worlds."

Gasps and screams met this announcement from Consul Joao Molambo. Since Morland had already been briefed by the Consul, when he came in the night before for his regular meeting with King Altos of Lahar, he wasn't surprised and focused on the crowd's reaction. Some people had broken into tears and collapsed, while others were crying "No" repeatedly.

By Sword-World standards the Sarpanitums were an emotional people. Morland had at first been taken aback by the singing and dancing that started every formal meeting in the Federation of Independent Nations, but he had grown to enjoy it. The arena, currently packed with over eighty thousand people, had been nearly crazed with joy when the Consul had leapt off his seat and joined the dancers as they finished their performance.

Molambo was a former dance instructor who had become famous for traveling the length and breadth of the Nishun to teach dance. Those same skills had served him well as he worked his way up from regional to national office, and ultimately to the consulship.

The arena was in Siyawela, the capital city, and Molambo's speech was the climax of the meeting of his party, the Peoples Party. Molambo had literally created the Peoples Party himself, taking it from a minor party to a major power, assembling it from chunks of the other two main parties, the Conservative and Workers Parties. King Altos and Morland had been invited to share in the festivities.

Morland rose to his feet as Molambo ended his speech by saying that elections would follow his retirement in six months.

Molambo had prevented the Union of Independent Nations from being attacked years earlier by the Communist Republic of Sarpanitum. Three years into his first term he had launched a surprise attack on the communist's base on Greenwich Island; the only island with a harbor between the Ashnan continent and the east coast of the Union of Independent Nations. This attack, spearheaded by a new weapon, a ship that carried many airplanes on it, had been a suicidal effort in which hundreds of planes had attacked, but only a few dozen came back.

But the surprise attack had worked, wrecking Greenwich Island as a forward base for the Communist Republic. This had forced the CRS to delay their attack for over a decade while they rebuilt their navy and conquered Valpo to provide another harbor from which to launch their next invasion.

"Some tea, your Highness?" Morland turned as the young woman served King Altos next to him, fumbling mentally for her name.

"Thank you, Sophia," Altos said.

That was her name, Sophia Kasule. She had recently completed her schooling and was working in Siyawela. The King had asked her to join them and she had eagerly accepted because she was working in public relations and wanted to make new contacts. He also suspected the King of Lahar was subtly trying to set him up with his niece.

Princess Sophia was also interested in the political process in general and had been asking Morland numerous questions about politics and governing on the Sword-Worlds whenever she got the chance. He answered the questions as best he could, not wanting to let on that he had never come within miles of any court function on Joyeuse, much less been part of any decision-making process.

Molambo entered the private box, shaking hands with everyone.

Morland noticed that most of the people in the room, the senior officials of the Peoples Party, did not seem as upset as the rank and file in the arena. From the scraps of conversations he overheard, it seemed that Molambo's announcement had already started speculation and political maneuvering regarding his successor.

"Consul," announced one elderly man, "History will regard you as the greatest leader of Sarpanitum since DaSilva."

Molambo shook his head modestly. Morland had first heard of Henry DaSilva when he attended a ceremony with Molambo and King Altos at the DaSilva Library. DaSilva had been a leader of Sarpanitum back in the Federation days. He had foreseen the fall of the Federation and constructed a secret library in an attempt to preserve knowledge. The library, located on the side of a hill on the Lansing Peninsula, had been designed to survive a nuclear attack. It had been set up so that it could convey information to readers of any technological level. Basic information had been shelved in the front of the library in picture books. More advanced information had been cached in the rear of the library, behind walls carefully constructed to look like native rock.

The discovery of the library had begun a renaissance in the primitive, gunpowder-using civilization that inhabited the peninsula at that time. Within a few decades newly constructed wooden ships, following the routes shown on ancient maps, had set out for the Nishun continent. The two natural harbors on the west coast of the Nishun Continent had been their first destination, followed by the three harbors on the west coast of Lahar. The settlers had not found any human settlements, other than occasional signs of temporary hunting camps, until subsequent generations pushed east over the mountains of the Nishun continent. There they found other descendants of the original colonists, living at the same Civ-Level they had shared.

DaSilva was looked upon by the Sarpanitums with almost as much adoration as the Space Vikings gave the revered Admiral Otto Harkaman.

"Prince David, do you think you will be regarded as highly as DaSilva is?" Sophia asked.

Morland shrugged, then turned the question back on Sophia. "And please be honest in your reply."

"I do," she said, "You've saved Nishun and Lahar from the Communist Republic invasion. I have read the histories of the Pre-Atomic era about the massacres committed by the communists as a way of winnowing the proletariat—or in objective terms, their opposition. First Citizen Sovran murdered hundreds of thousands of innocents during the conquest of Kabata. First Citizen Anders would have done the same thing here in Nishun and Lahar had your ship not arrived. We will never forget you, nor will history."

Morland reddened. His first impulse was to disillusion her, by saying that the only reason he *saved* Nishun was because it fit into his plans for a base world. However, he quickly realized that wouldn't be politic. Instead, he relaxed, and told her that histories often distorted or rewrote the past, Merlin on Poictesme being only one of his examples. She mentioned several similar examples from Sarpanitum's past. Their discussion continued on into the evening, uninterrupted by the political maneuvering that was going on all around them.

II

"You'll find him a good man to do business with," Manfred Trask said as the combat-car descended towards Valpo City.

"Mayor Perkins said the same thing," Morland replied. "He called Commissioner Salitros the unofficial mayor of Valpo and said he could enter a room with a dozen angry men and a few hours later have them all kissing each other on the cheeks."

Manfred Trask grinned. "I hope he can contain himself during *our* visit! I'm still having trouble getting accustomed to these barbarian customs."

"You should have seen the way some of the more ignorant citizens of Poictesme bow and scrape before that hunk of junk they call Merlin." Morland said, "Once word got out that we'd rediscovered it, they came from all over the continent. Still, I must admit I'd rather be just about anywhere than Valpo City, other than Nifflheim."

Morland didn't like spending time in Valpo. The city, located just south of the equator was hot, humid, polluted and chaotic. The unofficial mayor had insisted on meeting him on his own turf, rather than at the modern climate-controlled building the Sword-Worlders had constructed to handle their business in the city. Sword-Worlders, who prided themselves on their minimal government had nothing on Valpo, which had practically no government at all.

Valpo was a large natural harbor with many different bays. Those bays were separated by steep ridges of sheer rock. Each bay was in effect its own harbor and in many ways a separate state. There had always been a lot of rivalry between the various bays, which wasn't helped by the fact that they had been settled by separate groups at different times. Valpo had temporarily united to fight the communists, but once the communists had been thrown out, Valpo had quickly returned to its former anarchic ways.

"To the left," Trask directed Burris, their driver. "That open square tucked up against that big rock."

When he had envisioned setting up a base in the Old Federation, Morland hadn't thought much beyond breaking loose from the restrictions of his birth and the chaos of an unstable government on Joyeuse. Another part of his plan was to bring his family to a place where they could prosper and be safe. He had assumed their new base world would make a living the same way most Space Viking base planets did, trading with Space Vikings and independent traders as well as resupplying and repairing the damaged ships.

However, despite news of their lucrative raids only a few Space Viking ships had come to their base worlds to do business. DeBorder said it was because most Space Vikings' believed Sarpanitum was just too far away from the Sword-Worlds.

One positive factor was that Sarpanitum was starting to receive visits by independent traders, based on Odin, Aton and other civilized worlds, but the small amount of business they did with them was still dwarfed by their trade with Tanith. They'd also had their first Gilgamesher confrontation. Vann Stenger had been trading on Lyonnesse when the Gilgamesher ship *Fairtrader* returned to that planet. Vann had informed them that they could not trade with Lyonnesse any longer and escorted them out of the system. "For a moment, I thought they were going to fight. Instead, they departed from Lyonnesse without a word. Usually, Gilgameshers don't back down from a fight. Maybe someone in authority has placed us off-limits?"

No one had been able to answer that question, nor any of the others they had about the Gilgameshers.

The combat-car settled down, giving a slight bump as it went off contragravity. Morland felt a blast of heat and humidity as he stepped outside even though it was winter and he had set the meeting for morning when it would be cooler—or more accurately, less hot. Several men escorted them into a nearby building with his bodyguards at his side. Burris and two more guards remained with the combat-car.

The building was slightly cooler, being located in the shade of the large rock. As his sight adjusted to the interior of the building, Trask said "Commodore, may I present Commissioner Jura Salitros, leader of the community of Canela."

Morland found himself shaking hands with a short, slender man whose dark-brown hair was beginning to gray; he appeared anywhere from forty to seventy years of age.

"Honored to meet you, Commodore," Commissioner Salitros said. "I appreciate your willingness to confer with me in person."

"It is my pleasure," Morland said. "We are happy to do business with you." Which was one of the ironies of their present situation; they were making more money selling and buying goods on Sarpanitum, than they were bringing in from off-world trade. This Valpo City deal was a typical example: they had chosen a site on one of the ridgelines that was easily accessible by contragravity and where they could also build a road to provide access to the city for their new trade center. To that end, they'd brought in a mass-energy converter to provide power during the construction and to power the building afterward.

Previously, Valpo City had a patchy electric grid that was frequently down, especially in the evening. Most of city's power had been provided by burning coal or oil hauled into the city, which had created a permanent layer of gray fog. Some bright boy on the construction crew had cut a deal to sell extra power from the mass-energy converter to the grid. During the construction they had powered the converter with the rubble they generated. When that phase of construction was done and locals had spotted them hauling in material to power the converter, they had eagerly approached them with an alternative. They were willing to bring garbage to the site to feed the mass-energy converter and, in addition, pay for the electricity they needed to power the city.

Decades ago, they had just dumped their garbage in the harbor. Lately they had progressed as far as hauling it to the edge of the city to be buried. Canela was the largest borough of the city, spreading out into the open country beyond and the borough's largest source of income were the fees they received for taking in garbage from the rest of the city. If they could use it to feed the converter, so much the better.

"Commissioner Salitros is smart enough to bow to the changes our presence has brought," Trask had explained. "He wants to be independent of our converter, and buy his own mass-converter. He feels that besides the savings of not having to haul coal to his city, he can burn up all the old buried garbage and create more usable land for building new homes. The refugees coming into the area will have places to live and their numbers will increase his political power."

Manfred Trask had proved to have an uncanny eye for profitable opportunities and, as much as Trask said he was learning by working with him, Morland felt that he was getting the better part of the deal. Trask certainly wasn't suffering as he seemed to have a good time in Valpo, preferring its primitive vitality to Emesh City's more sedate pace.

"Commodore Morland, I've heard of your taste for fish," Commissioner

Salitros said, as they walked into his private office. "May I offer you some of our finest fish, caught locally just this morning?"

Morland suppressed a shudder at the thought of eating something caught in the harbor. None of the boroughs that made up Valpo City had sewage treatment; their sewers just ran straight to the harbor. He managed a smile. "Thank you, Commissioner Salitros, but I just had breakfast before I came here. How were you aware of my preferences?"

"We have read much about you, Commodore Morland, even though we receive the Emesh City newspapers sometime after they're published."

Morland chuckled to himself. He had become—indeed all of the Space Vikings had become—celebrities on Sarpanitum. The residents of both Lahar and Nishun still treated them like heroes for destroying the communists, whom they had feared for decades. Their newspapers constantly sought interviews with him and the other senior officers. So it wasn't surprising that some of his likes and dislikes were well known.

"Some of our famous peach-brandy then?"

Morland gingerly accepted, hoping there was enough alcohol in the drink to kill anything microscopic that had spawned in the water before distilling. It was surprisingly tasty and potent. *Another trade item for the Vishnu liquor clubs*, he noted.

"Very good, Commissioner," Morland said. "I'd like to order some of these for my own pantry and maybe for trade."

Commissioner Jura Salitros smiled. "Your Excellency, we have three distilleries in Valpo City. My own is the finest, of course. The wholesale cost is two thousand sols per case of twenty-four bottles."

Morland did some quick figuring. It was a hundred and eight sols to the stellar, which was roughly eighteen and a half stellars per case. They could sell them for ten times that on Vishnu, maybe more. "We can use ten thousand cases. How soon can you have them for me?"

Commissioner Salitros looked as if he'd just been spaced out off a hatch. "Ah, a very good question, Your Excellency. I will talk with my factor and get back with you."

He called Burris on his personal communicator. "We have concluded our business and he has delivered the first payment of gold. How does everything look out there?"

"Fine. Do you want me to come in to help you carry it out?"

"No," Morland replied. "Keep an eye out for any problems. We will be right out."

He thanked Commissioner Salitros and his associates. He hadn't brought a lifter so he had the two guards carry the boxes to the aircar. As they lifted off he asked him, "Manfred, did you get the probes planted?"

"Yes. You did a great job distracting them with that speech of yours. The hand motions, walking around and everything. No one saw a thing."

Nor were they likely to find the tell-tales, either. Waving his hands behind his back Trask had tossed them onto the ceiling and high up on the walls. They were small enough that you could barely see them with the human eye and their chameleon-like ability to change color meant they weren't likely to be spotted by anyone who wasn't looking for them.

"Good."

They had listening devices planted in dozens of sites around Valpo, as well as in the homes or offices of most of the major political players, including Salitros, and throughout the other nations of Sarpanitum. While everything they had observed seemed to show that Salitros had only good intentions toward them, Morland had seized this opportunity to plant probes in his main office. A wise ruler always tried to keep one step ahead of his underlings, if he wanted a long and prosperous rule. Morland intended to live to a ripe old age.

III

Morland was staring out over the railing on the terrace at his new home, momentarily relaxing and enjoying the view of the spaceport dozens of miles away. The spaceport was as full as he had ever seen it, with the *Faerie Queen, Gift Horse, Pay Dirt,* and an independent freighter currently at berth. A new ship, the *Jolly Roger,* had just arrived from Poictesme, was on in-system patrol along with the *Skull Splitter.*

This was the time of year he enjoyed the most; the early morning rains had stopped, the sun had come out and the air had a fresh clean smell. The westerly winds were strong enough to climb over the mountains and bring rain to Emesh, but only for a few months during the winter. This was why the spaceport builders had put an aqueduct through the mountains to bring water from the rain forest to the city.

He turned his head at the sounds of happy laughter coming from inside the house. Randa and his sister were having a good time in the kitchen. Randa had promised a special meal for the meeting and his sister was helping her prepare it. He also had her to thank for his gracious new living quarters. She was the best thing he'd discovered on Sarpanitum. Randa had brightened up his life, and it wasn't just her great cooking.

Tired of living in one of the rooms in the old barracks that the Sword-Worlders had fixed up at the spaceport, Randa had gathered her possessions and gone exploring. She had walked across one of the recently repaired pedestrian bridges that crossed the river and selected a small four-story building and moved in. After hiring laborers to rehab it, she'd hauled in food, water and furniture.

Randa's plan of action had ignited a property grab once other people saw what she'd accomplished. Most of the Space Vikings in the barracks decided they were entitled to a building of their own. He decided that was a good thing; it demonstrated that the Sword-Worlders were beginning to see Sarpanitum as their home, not just another base of operations.

He had put Laz Rivera in charge of surveying the city, determining which buildings could be easily rehabbed, and then assigning some of the smaller buildings to people who wanted housing instead of bonuses for job performance. They also repaired or replaced the old pedestrian bridges over the river. In one of the old buildings they had found a reference to some cliff dwellings; further explorations had discovered a score of large homes carved into the mountains west of the spaceport.

The largest of these cliff dwellings had a spectacular view of the waterfall as the river initially came out of the mountains. Everyone had expected Morland to take it for himself, but the house was close enough to the waterfall that a continuous dull roar penetrated the living space, and he was happy to give it to Laz Rivera who had fallen in love with the view. Instead he chose a place many miles away from the waterfall because it had a back door into a small narrow valley. He always liked to have more than one exit out of a place.

Randa is not only the prettiest woman on the planet, he decided, *but the smartest as well.* Maybe she wasn't as educated as Gytha Valkanhayn or his sister Zandra, but she had presence and real vitality. It was Randa's decision that he quit living in an office building next to their headquarters. She had told him flat out that if he wanted her to continue as his chef, he needed to live in quarters that better represented his planetary status.

Frankly, Morland wanted a lot more than Randa's cooking, but first she wanted the respectability of marriage. *Is she the right one?* he asked himself. *Maybe?* However, he didn't feel ready to commit to wedlock until he got to know her better. The last woman he'd had strong feelings for, Princess Janna, had rejected him because he wouldn't convert to her religion.

The door announcer chimed and the faces of Javen DeBorder, Vann Stenger and Will Haversham appeared in his security screen. Ragnarsans was running late.

The *Faerie Queen* and *Gift Horse* had returned from Rhiannon a few weeks ago, when they had detected a Mardukan Imperial ship, the *Queen Myrna*, in high-earth orbit over Rhiannon. Another Imperial ship had been detected lying in wait around one of her moons. When they had asked the Mardukans for permission to land for trading purposes, they had been told that Rhiannon was now a ward of the Empire and off-limits to non-Imperial merchants. The *Faerie Queen* and *Gift Horse* had been forced to jump into hyperspace without picking up any plutonium for the Dillingham drives.

It was clear that the Mardukan Imperial presence on the planet was permanent; once Morland had been informed of this development, a meeting had been called to plan their next move. They were running dangerously low on radioactive fuel and they needed better and more reliable sources if they were going to continue to expand.

One of the robot tenders poured Poictesme melon-brandy for everyone. Morland preferred to use robots whenever possible for security reasons.

The *Pay Dirt* had just returned from Quernbiter, where DeBorder had gone to visit old friends and to recruit more experienced Space Viking personnel for Sarpanitum. He had not been very successful. "We had several hundred recruits respond to our initial call," DeBorder was telling everyone, "But, once they found out how far away Sarpanitum was, a lot of them lost interest. After screening for the skills we needed, we brought only fifty-four men and women back with us."

That's not good at all, Morland thought. While the locals had proved quicker at learning the basics of operating Sword-World equipment than expected, he still needed highly skilled workers, especially for the shipyards. All of their contragravity equipment was now being constructed in Emesh City. He planned to expand into other manufacturing areas as well, which demanded more skilled laborers.

"Why are they so concerned about how far we are from the Sword-Worlds?" Stenger asked.

Will Haversham, the *Pay Dirt's* First Officer, shrugged. "They want to be able to leave easily if they're dissatisfied with working conditions or pay."

"We could offer them a free return trip after a year if they decide to leave," Morland said.

That started a heated discussion. In the Sword-Worlds, such an offer was unheard of. When you were hired for an off-world job, you were responsible for your own travel costs if you left the job earlier than you'd contracted for. The discussion was interrupted by the sound of the door announcer. Tylor Ragnarsans strolled in with his Executive Officer to greetings from everyone, while Morland poured drinks.

"What kept you?" Vann Stenger jokingly asked him.

Tylor shot Stenger a sour look.

Morland sometimes wondered how much longer Tylor was going to be with them. He didn't think Tylor would leave for another Space Viking base word since he was unlikely to get a better deal anywhere else. However, Morland was beginning to suspect that what Ragnarsans really wanted was to have his own base world. Lately, he had been asking a lot of questions of Rivera and Trask: Questions about the day-to-day details and costs of running a base. How business deals were structured and how people were trained and recruited.

Morland knew that if Ragnarsans left, he would be sorry to lose him.

"How many men and women did you recruit with shipboard experience?" Ragnarsans was asking DeBorder, who was repeating the story of what happened on Quernbiter.

Ragnarsans was having personnel problems of his own on the *Gift Horse*. While a superb leader on raids, he was restless and jumpy during the hyperspace flight times between planet falls, constantly second guessing his officers' decisions. In addition, he had a tendency to micromanage which was a constant source of irritation, causing all but the most patient or inexperienced officers to leave.

Morland had sent many of his younger officers, such as Pavla Lancaster and Arvin Morrison, on raids with the *Gift Horse* to further their experience. They had all asked to return to the *Skull Splitter* after one or two voyages. Ragnarsans had been an able officer on the *Skull Splitter* and *Faerie Queen*, because Morland and Vann Stenger had been able to smooth over his personality quirks.

Tylor was fortunate he had found Dane Rolph—who was calm, relaxed and a perfect complement to his captain—to be his First Officer. Rolph had been one of the Space Viking's stranded on Tanith. It was time he had another talk with Ragnarsans, after the meeting, and try to give him some pointers on how to run a ship's crew.

But at the moment, they had bigger fish to fry. "We need to focus on this big raid," Morland said. They were meeting to plan a raid on Tashmetum. Though they had finally made their first trade with Mara for plutonium, the Marians had proved so difficult to deal with that it was beginning to look like they would never establish a long term relationship. The Marians were determined to receive both contragravity and hyperspace technology in exchange for their fissionables. They wanted to build their own hyperships so they could adequately defend themselves from any future raids.

He could understand the Marians concerns and desire for independence, but they didn't have any idea of the skilled workers needed to produce what they wanted and he wasn't going to overpay them for their plutonium. Nor did he want another competing sovereignty with contragravity and hyperspace capability nearby. With Rhiannon now a ward of the Empire, they had to turn to other sources for nuclear fuel since they only had enough plutonium for another year or two at the rate they were growing.

"Are we going to hit the same places as the last raid?" Will Haversham asked. "I would expect that they would be better defended this time."

"We have some new intelligence on other targets," Morland said, passing out copies of maps with notations on them.

"This is impressive. How did you get this?" DeBorder asked after a few moments, pausing in his study of the maps to refill his glass.

"They were prepared by Feraday," Stenger said.

There were puzzled looks exchanged until Rivera asked, "Another one of our Ship's Assistant Historians?"

Morland filled them in on what Feraday had been up to. He was the historian who had surveyed Tashmetum as part of Historian Walter Ovard's examination of nearby star systems for raiding targets. Alex Feraday had been so taken with the world that after their attempts to trade had failed he asked to return for more reconnaissance.

On one of their trips to strip the industrial installations on the outer planets of the system, he had been dropped off dirtside. The pinnace had approached Tashmetum's surface at night in a rainstorm and traveled hundreds of miles underwater before stopping at a small deserted island in the middle of the biggest ocean. Feraday had then taken a one man air-cavalry mount and traveled to the heavily wooded area on the fringe of a major city and proceeded to create a new identity as a native.

Morland added. "He's established a cover as a graduate student at a university in a port city, so it's an area with a lot of people coming and going where strangers aren't unusual."

"How's he getting us the information?" Ragnarsans asked.

"He has a small transmitter," Morland said. "He broadcasts to the cavalry-mount, which stores it. Whenever one of our ships is in-system, they swing by and activate the cavalry mount's transmitter."

They reviewed the information, discussing the pros and cons of the various targets Feraday had suggested and determining the best way to loot them. Watching them, Morland couldn't help but feel envious. It seemed like a long time since he had experienced the excitement of a raid against a tough target.

Vann Stenger must have noticed his expression. "Why don't you bring the *Skull Splitter* and come with us, David?"

DeBorder immediately added his assent, as did Haversham. Rivera, Ragnarsans and Rolph were silent, although that wasn't unusual for Dane Rolph, who rarely spoke unless spoken to first.

Morland considered the idea for a moment, but a moment only. "No, someone needs to run things here. And Laz is always asking for help so I couldn't very well leave him." Everyone laughed at that. "Besides, while I miss raiding in some ways, this is where I want to be and what I want to do."

"It's also where you are needed the most," Rivera said. Everyone was silent, agreeing with him.

"Lunch time," Randa interrupted, coming in with a robot server carrying several trays with a variety of food on them.

Suddenly hungry, they hastily cleared the maps and notes out the way. "So this is your special treat," DeBorder said, teasing her. "It looks like ordinary curry carniculture to me."

It sure does, Morland thought, although he didn't recognize the yellow-colored sauce.

Deftly serving them, Randa teased them right back. "I guess you'll have to try it. We'll see whether your taste buds are too old to tell the difference."

There were a couple of laughs before everyone dug in.

"This is fantastic!" Morland exclaimed. "A symphony to my taste buds."

The others were just as fervent in their praise.

"What gives the curry that special taste?" DeBorder asked.

"It's a rare spice that grows only in certain mountainous areas. It supposedly came from Terra itself. It's called saffron."

They all dug in appreciably. "Sarpanitum saffron," Morland said. "We will have to find more of this."

Later, after the meal was finished and Randa was out of the room, DeBorder asked, "When are you going to make your consort an honest woman?"

Morland felt his face blush. "It's not like that. She doesn't want to take any further steps until we take it to the next level."

"Oh, like marriage," Ragnarsans said.

"It's not that simple…"

"Sure it is," DeBorder said. "Elevate yourself to Prince and make her your Princess. She's got the right stuff; the people will love her."

Ragnarsans nodded. "If you're not interested—"

Now he was turning red, but it wasn't from embarrassment. "We'll work it out ourselves with no meddling from outsiders."

The others took the cue and DeBorder wisely changed the subject, "How is the special project on Koshchei going, David?"

"Slowly," Morland said. "The plans are finished and construction has started. But we don't have nearly enough experienced workers. It could take over a decade at this rate."

"Well, I did recruit some experienced shipyard people," DeBorder said.

"Every skilled person helps," Morland said.

"How is this being financed?" Ragnarsans interrupted. "Did you dig up the rest of the communists' hoard?"

"No," Morland replied. "You remember that 'raid' on Durendal we heard about a while ago?" They all laughed; since there had been no one to fight on Durendal it didn't really deserve the term raid. "I passed the idea on to Ladbrok. He excavated all the banks and treasury vaults in the former capital city of Poictesme—Storisende, I believe it was called—that had been nuked. There was a great deal of gold and other valuables in the vaults." They all smiled appreciably. "That and my own considerable resources are the source of financing."

"Maybe we won't need it," DeBorder said. "When I arrived in-system, I saw a large number of interplanetary ships in orbit. If we get enough of those in-system, maybe we won't need any other help."

While listening to Gytha Valkanhayn Ladbrok's radio message on Poictesme, Morland had come up with a great idea. He had subsequently taken some of the many interplanetary ships on Koshchei, stripped them of any nonessential equipment, and converted them into missile platforms around Octavio's System. Instead of having to beg people to serve on missile launching stations on one of Sarpanitum's barren moons, he had an oversubscribed waiting list of people anxious to receive ship training. The interplanetary ships served both functions.

"Those ships are defensive only. Their Abbot lift-and-drive engines are Federation-era engines and won't go as fast as present day lift-and-drive engines," Morland said. "If someone attacks us I want to be able to go on the offensive as well."

"Things are progressing well, David," Vann Stenger said. "What's that old saying: Rome wasn't built in a day?"

Rome was one of the old empires on Terra. He didn't remember much about it other than it had been powerful and lasted a long time.

"I would feel a lot happier if we had more skilled workers," Morland stated. "The way we are going about recruiting them isn't working. We are going to have to try something different."

"What about the recruiters we've sent to Xochitl, Nergal, and Jagannath, as well as the Sword-Worlds?" Stenger asked. "Shouldn't we wait to see how well they do first?"

"We're running out of time," Morland replied. "The Empire isn't going to wait until we're ready before attacking." There wasn't much left for him to do on Sarpanitum that Rivera or someone else could do. It was time for him to take decisive action. "I'm going to go recruiting myself."

"David, we can't have you gone that long!" Laz Rivera exclaimed.

"I do not intend to be gone for very long," he replied. "Not more than a few G.S. months, I expect."

The others looked at each other in puzzlement. "Where can you recruit skilled personnel that close to Sarpanitum?" Ragnarsans asked.

"On Vishnu," he replied.

Ragnarsans shrugged. "Will the authorities even allow you to recruit their citizens?"

"I had Historian Ulrik Selner look into it and there's no law against emigration, just immigration. True, very few citizens ever leave Vishnu, but maybe that's because they don't have an opportunity to do so. I'm going to offer them free travel to Poictesme, as well as free passage back if they're not satisfied within the first G.S. years."

"Hmm," Laz Rivera said. "That might work...Vishnuian society is very stratified and I'm sure there are a number of citizens who feel as though their abilities are not appreciated or properly rewarded. As to whether or not they'll leave their homeworld, that's yet to be ascertained."

"It's worth a try, Laz. We sure aren't having much success recruiting on the Sword-Worlds these days."

"That's true," Ragnarsans said. "But that brings up another problem. Aren't we trying to keep a low profile now that we've got Vandarvant and the Mardukan Navy barking at our heels?"

"He's right, David," Rivera added.

"Maybe not," Morland replied. "All Vandarvant knows is that he was in a battle with a Space Viking captain named David Morland. He doesn't know where we're from, where we're based or anything else. If I arrive on an interstellar freighter and present myself as Prince David of Sarpanitum, who's to know?"

Rivera nodded. "You make a good point, David. Still, I'd like to go with you and act as your public face. No sense in advertising your presence on Vishnu; after all, there's a Mardukan ambassador there and probably some sort of Naval attaché or intelligence officer."

"Also a good point, Laz. I'll let you be the public face, while I work behind the scenes. Still, we're going to have to take a few risks in order to build the kind of fleet we're going to need to maintain our independence."

Everyone in the room nodded, but no one was smiling.

VISHNU II

I

The airtaxi dropped Morland and his two bodyguards off at Vin Qual's building and had departed before he realized that Vin had moved. There was a sign to that effect, giving Off-World Imports new address. Since it wasn't that far, he decided to walk to the new building. The shabby Lowtown neighborhood they passed through reminded him of the section of Wardshaven he'd lived in as a child before his parents had emigrated from Gram to Joyeuse.

It was the middle of the day and his clothing was non-descript, but he kept his hand on the pistol inside of his jacket. Off-worlders were tempting targets for stickups and robberies, although he doubted anyone would bother a big man with two bodyguards. Still, it paid to be cautious.

When he arrived at the warehouse, Morland knew he was in the right place when he saw the Off-World Imports sign above the new address. He hadn't been to Vishnu in over a year and nobody had told him that Vin Qual's business had moved to different quarters. Either it had just happened or the freighter captains had forgotten to mention it, probably the latter.

On the first floor, he found a large waiting room with many chairs, many of which were occupied. The building had that newly rehabilitated feel to it that he recognized from Poictesme and Sarpanitum. The receptionist was new and she refused to let Vin Qual know that he'd arrived.

"He's in a meeting," she said peevishly. "You'll just have to wait with everyone else," as she gestured toward the open chairs.

"How about Nadira? Could you let her know her friend David is here?"

After a few minutes Nadira came running out and threw herself into his arms, to the great amusement of the other people in the waiting room. Chattering happily she brought him back to her office, telling him the story of their recent move. "Thanks to you, David, the business has grown rapidly. We needed bigger quarters and this was the best place we could find."

"This is quite a neighborhood," Morland replied.

She frowned, saying, "Yes, but it's the only place we could find this close to the spaceport. Now that we have freighters of our own, we needed to be closer to the docks."

He wasn't certain what her new position was but she had plenty of time to update him on the company and her personal life, which she intimated would improve if he were around more. With business growing, Qual had purchased and rehabilitated two old freighters.

Morland had encouraged this expansion on his last visit. He didn't want to become overly dependent on King Rodrik of Tanith to move freight and he wanted to put his limited ship-building resources on Koshchei to work on something other than warships. In fact, that was one of the reasons he'd come to Vishnu.

After Nadira informed Vin Qual of his arrival, Qual hastily broke off his meeting to see him. "How are you, my friend?"

"I'm well," Morland said, using his hand to circumscribe the room, he added, "And it looks like you're doing well, too."

Qual nodded, blushing. "It's thanks to you, David. Our old quarters were just too small and I used some of the profits to purchase this building. You should have seen it before we rehabbed it. It was a wreck, but the only one available."

Morland knew that even in Lowtown the movers and shakers owned everything that didn't move. And they parceled out buildings like party favors to friends. It was a sign of Qual's increasing stature with the power structure of New Durban City that he was even *allowed* to buy a new building, no matter how decrepit.

Nadira came in with drinks, Poictesme melon-brandy for Morland and a soft drink for Qual. She gave Morland a flirtatious smile, then spun around and left with her gray tunic swirling around her long legs.

"So, what brings you to Vishnu, David?"

He took his eyes of Nadira's legs, saying, "I'm here to recruit skilled workers for our spaceyard on Poictesme."

"You're here to recruit people?" Qual asked somewhat incredulously.

Morland explained his problems recruiting highly skilled workers. "I had thought more skilled people would be emigrating from the Sword-Worlds to the Old Federation, but the numbers have not been what we've expected."

"Why is that, David?"

He took a sip of his brandy. "I think it's another sign that the Sword-Worlds are withdrawing, turning inward. Too many ships have been returning from the Old Federation with bad news. The Imperial attacks on Space Vikings and their base worlds have made their expeditions less profitable, many are even returning home to stay. It's a new game and the Space Vikings still want to play by the old rules."

Vin Qual nodded.

"I've had agents on every Space Viking base planet offering bonuses and even sent word back to the Sword-Worlds that we're looking for labor, but I'm not getting a lot of recruits. Even if I sent a ship to the Sword-Worlds today, it would be almost a G.S. year and a half before they returned. So, it's time for a change. What I've decided to do is recruit skilled personnel from Vishnu."

Vin drew back. "I'm not certain what kind of a response you'll receive, David. Our government here has never encouraged our citizens to travel to other worlds, and few Vishnuians have evidenced any interest in interstellar travel. People here like to think that Vishnu is a special place, better than other worlds. I'm almost unique on Vishnu in that I welcome dealings with off-worlders."

Morland knew from his previous visits to Vishnu that the society itself was very rigid and tradition-oriented. Still, he was betting that there were a substantial number of skilled workers who had no chance of advancing themselves in Vishnu society, due to their low birth, status or other circumstances. He was certain that some of these would be willing to take a chance at an opportunity to start a new life on another world.

"Even though off-world events are much more in the news lately, people are much more amused than interested," Qual added.

"I know that both Marduk and Odin sent ambassadors to Vishnu a few years ago to try to increase their influence," Morland said.

"True, but their presence had provided more in the way of entertainment than any real achievement. Both ambassadors are trying to reach trade agreements with the government and various import/export firms and are not getting anywhere."

Morland had run into the same problem himself before he met up with Qual. "Have you talked with the ambassadors, Vin?"

"Why would I do that?" asked a surprised Qual. "I don't run in those circles. I have enough problems just keeping up with our increased business. I don't need any more attention."

"Why not contact the ambassadors and see if you can drum up any interest?" Morland asked again. "It's about time we expanded our markets."

"Call an ambassador just like that?" Qual asked. He seemed positively frightened by the notion.

Morland spun his communication screen on the desk around. He had become familiar with how it operated while the *Zama* was descending to the planet. He and Laz Rivera had come in the freighter because he did not want anyone to risk someone at the spaceport connecting the *Skull Splitter* with Sarpanitum. He didn't think the Empire had spies watching for him on Vishnu, but he did not want to take any unnecessary chances, especially now with the new Mardukan ambassador on planet.

As Qual looked on in astonishment, he spoke with one of the Odin ambassador's secretaries and made an appointment for three days later, telling her he represented both a local and an off-world company.

"Now how about the Mardukan ambassador," Morland said,

punching in the code as Qual grew even more agitated. The secretary for the Mardukan ambassador, Edvard Jonson, was standoffish until Morland mentioned that he had an appointment with the Odin ambassador.

"How about that same evening?" the secretary asked.

"I am sorry but I have other plans," Morland said, increasing Qual's nervousness. Since Qual had already invited him to dinner at his home that evening, he was telling the truth. "How about the following day?"

It appeared the Ambassador's calendar was full until Morland mentioned he would be leaving the day after. That wasn't true but Morland was curious as to how much of a rivalry there was between the two worlds.

After a few moments the secretary returned. "Prince David, would you be interested in joining the Ambassador at a social dinner as his guest the evening after your appointment with the Odin Ambassador?"

He would and said so, asking if he could bring a guest. As Vin's pallor became even more ashen, he was informed that what he asked was perfectly acceptable.

"Now I have a date with Ambassador Edvard Jonson," he said. "See how easy that was?"

Sweating and stuttering, Qual sputtered, "I can't go to dinner with the ambassador! I'm just a small business owner, or I was until I met *you*. There's no one in my family lineage, not even distant ancestors, of noble blood."

Morland debated about telling him that he was the son of a technical school teacher and robot-repair mechanic, but decided that would not help quell his anxiety. "Perhaps Nadira will accompany me."

Relief washed over Qual's face. "Yes, that's good. She likes you, she talks about you a lot, and she's much better at these social affairs than I am. Yes, please take her."

"Good. Now, there's another matter: Laz Rivera and I have prepared several advertisements for broadcast on your telenews system. Could you recommend the best channels to put them on?"

II

Morland sipped at the Vishnu version of coffee, doing his best to wake up. Nadira was unusually quiet as she piloted her aircar toward company headquarters. He wondered if she was aware of what he had discussed with Vin's wife. He grinned to himself. It had been a wild few days.

The visit with the Odin Ambassador had been a disappointment. He had identified himself as Prince David of Sarpanitum and said he would like to explore a trading agreement. The Ambassador saw him only for a few minutes before passing him off to an aide.

"I thought I was here to discuss trading arrangements with a civilized world," he said as he showed Morland to the door. "I don't deal with Neobarbarians. Talk to someone on my staff."

Morland had been only mildly annoyed by this response since the Ambassador's attitude was the same one he had grown up with on the Sword-Worlds. If you didn't have hyperdrive and contragravity, your planet was considered a barbarian world no matter how socially civilized you were. Apparently even if you obtained those things, as Sarpanitum had, you were still a Neobarb world to some *people*.

The Odin Ambassador's aide wasn't helpful at all. He didn't recognize the name of Off-World Imports and wasn't interested in doing business with it, promptly passing him off to another staff member, obviously much lower down the rung. This staffer at least knew of Vin and was friendly, although he clearly didn't have the portfolio to set up any kind of trading agreement. The whole affair reminded Morland of his first visit to Vishnu, when he had spent day after day of wasted effort trying to find someone willing to do business with him.

Dinner later that evening at Vin's home had been pleasant, as he was finally able to meet Vin's wife, Vantha, who was Nadira's older cousin.

After dinner Vantha had pulled him aside to tell him that Nadira was much more interested in him than he'd thought, and was talking about following him back to Sarpanitum with anyone else he could recruit.

His instantaneous negative reaction to this news had surprised him, and he spent the rest of the evening pondering why. Nadira was attractive, pleasant and a good companion. Though he'd had some good times with her, he had no deep attachment to her—and he certainly didn't want her trailing after him to Sarpanitum!

Nadira appeared to be interested in him personally, rather than for his wealth and status. It certainly was a leap of faith for her, raised on Vishnu, to even consider leaving her home. *So, why am I so opposed to having her return to Sarpanitum with me?*

The answer shocked him: Nadira was not the kind of woman he could visualize being a ruler's wife. He had long resisted his officer's requests, both on Poictesme and on Sarpanitum, to take a title more befitting his status such as prince or king. Being called Prince David on this trip, even by crew members in on the deception, had made him a little more accepting of the idea. Maybe, after all these years of being in charge, he was finally comfortable with the notion that someone born as a commoner on the Sword-Worlds was not out-of-line by proclaiming himself a prince or a king on an Old Federation world.

Regardless, he could not see Nadira as his future wife. Now with Randa, it was easy to visualize her as a princess—or even queen.

The dinner party at the Mardukan ambassador's residence was quite different from his experience with the Odin diplomatic corps. Ambassador Edvard Jonson was openly friendly, and had treated Morland and Nadira no differently than his other guests, most of whom were Vishnuian nobility, big business owners, prominent politicians, or some combination of the above. By this point their off-world labor advertisements had been running for several days and were the talk of the town.

The Vishnuians were another story entirely, since they were openly scornful of his recruiting efforts.

"Ridiculous idea!" mocked one of the nobility. "Only the dregs of society would ever be interested in leaving Vishnu. They would be departing from the graves of their ancestors—forever."

"You'll get nothing but malcontents," another said.

"Agitators interested only in more pay and less work," insisted one of the businessmen. "You'll be lucky to have a handful of men show up, and none of them will be worth anything."

Morland was curious himself as to what kind of response his recruiting ads would get. His telenews advertisements had directed people to Off-World Imports on the following morning which was the beginning of Vishnu's weekend. He merely stated that he hoped for good results and left it at that.

Unfortunately, the Vishnuians treatment of Nadira was just as uncharitable. The women at the party, once they determined her social status through detailed questioning, treated her like a social pariah. Several of the businessmen made snide remarks about Vin growing too big for his britches. Morland could see Nadira was struggling to keep her composure during the questioning which at times had the feel of an interrogation.

Ambassador Edvard Jonson frequently interrupted this questioning, asking general questions about Sarpanitum and what Morland was looking for to trade. The Ambassador was impressed when Morland told him the population of Sarpanitum was over eight hundred million people, noting that was more people than there were on most worlds in the Old Federation.

The Vishnuians, whose planet had over a dozen times that many inhabitants, snickered at the Ambassador's comment—probably because their population had been stable for centuries. Others asked Morland how they developed space travel on their own, implying that as a Neobarbarian world they must somehow be cheating to have gained interstellar space flight.

Morland lied, stating that his father had traded with Gilgameshers for hyperspace technology and the training to use it. That got everyone off the subject of Sarpanitum as they aired their feelings about Gilgameshers, which were even more negative than those of the Sword-Worlders—if possible.

I wonder if there's any world in the Federation where Gilgameshers are accepted for themselves.

As the party broke up into small groups, Morland was cornered by one of the Ambassador's staff who asked a number of detailed questions and seemed to be very interested in a trade agreement. He told the Assistant Secretary that he would contact them after discussing their questions with Vin Qual. At that point he decided there had been enough talk for one night and rescued Nadira, who was seated with a group of Vishnuian women who were busy taking turns sniping at one another rather than her.

Ambassador Jonson made a point of coming over to him on their way out and saying that he hoped they could reach an agreement. He thought that was a good sign.

"David!" Nadira exclaimed, grabbing at him, jolting him out of his reverie and causing him to spill some hot coffee on his pants. "Look! Look at that."

He jumped when the coffee burned his legs, then craned his head to look out the aircar window, trying to see what she was so excited about. The aircar turned slightly and he saw a line of people waiting along the side of the building. So they'd had a decent turnout after all. Then with a shock he realized he wasn't looking at the front of the building but the back.

The line of Vishnuian applicants wrapped all the way around the building and it was still—he checked his chronometer hastily—ten minutes before the doors were even going to open.

He hastily called the *Zama*. "Ivar, we're going to need more people here," he stated, describing the situation.

"We've already been contacted, Prince David," Captain Nash said. "I'll have additional equipment and personnel there in a few minutes."

Morland greeted a young officer at the door of the building. "Quite a crowd we have here. How have they behaved?"

"Very well, Commodore," he replied. "No fighting or cutting in line or anything like that. Can't say I like the look of this neighborhood though."

"Fortunately it is a little too early for the criminal element to be up," he replied, looking around warily. "Once the additional personnel arrive, send the ship back to the *Zama* and ask to have a squad of troopers sent here. That should help everyone in line feel secure and keep the jackals at bay."

The equipment, which was additional veridicators, arrived and was quickly put into operation. The veridicators proved to be essential as some of the applicants had exaggerated their skills; an even smaller number lied outright. The majority of the applicants proved to be just what he was looking for, skilled workers with years of experience who found advancement blocked in their current job for a variety of reasons, many of them having to do with their with poor social status and low-caste birth.

Even better, hundreds of them had ship-building skills.

What was even more astonishing was the number of Vishnuians who had come from the rural areas, even though his advertisements had been running for only a few days. There were no liars and only a few exaggerators among this group. They had all come for the same thing—an opportunity to own their own land.

He had a fresh group of personnel brought in from the *Zama* at noon, along with some food and drink to deliver to the people in line. They also started weeding out everyone in line who could come back the following morning. Those that couldn't come the next day stayed in line; it was early evening before they were finished.

"Incredible!" he said to Laz Rivera who had been with him the whole day. "Your ads were a great success. We have over seven hundred qualified recruits, everything from shipwrights, master engineers and manufacturing technicians to robo-equipment operators and highly experienced agricultural workers."

"Don't forget the hundreds more who are coming back tomorrow," Rivera said tiredly.

"I won't," he replied, just as exhausted. Turning to another crew member, he ordered, "Call Captain Nash and tell him not to bother picking up any other cargo. His freighter just got turned into a passenger ship."

GILGAMESH III

"At last," the High Maxwell cried, "we know where Morland and his band of pirates are based!"

"Yes, Your Worshipful," Marshal Sayles replied. "We just learned this from one of our ships returning from Vishnu. The Space Viking David Morland, who now calls himself the Prince of Sarpanitum, has been recruiting skilled laborers on Vishnu. One of our people was visiting with a local merchant when he saw a report about his meeting with the Odin Ambassador on his Tri-D screen. No one had ever thought to record local shows for information on our infamous Space Viking.

"It appears that Poictesme is not Morland's primary base, but a world named Sarpanitum. The Oracles' files show that one of our ships last visited Sarpanitum three hundred and twenty-six years ago. According to their survey, it was at Civ-Level 4 and not worth trading with since it had few trade goods of value and limited resources of fissionable ores and other rare earth elements."

The High Maxwell nodded in approval. "Send our brother a thousand nusols as a reward for his diligence." It had been a long wait, but worth it. *Now what do I do? I know the Chief Programmer would tell me to ask the Oracle, but I'm tired of having my every command second-guessed. It's time I exercised my authority without some naysayer of a programmer looking over my shoulder. My first solution would be to assemble an armada of Gilgamesh ships to deal with the pretender directly; however, that would violate so many rules set down by the Plan that my orders would be circumvented and my own life forfeited, even without a successor at hand.*

I must be more devious. Why not use the Mardukans to my advantage, since my next eldest son will soon be traveling there as part of his rite of passage.

"Does the Mardukan Ambassador know of Morland's presence on Vishnu?" the High Maxwell asked.

The Marshal shrugged his shoulders. "Ambassador Edvard Jonson is not part of the war faction on Marduk. He's a member of the trade faction, so he's probably unaware of the search for the Space Viking Morland. He probably only knows him as Prince David of Sarpanitum."

"When is the next trade ship leaving for Marduk?" the High Maxwell asked.

The Marshal checked his pocket reader, punched in his question. "There's a ship, the *Faithful Follower*, departing for Marduk in less than seven hundred hours."

"Good. My son, Rodney, is scheduled to depart for Marduk shortly. See that he's on that ship. That will leave us time to prepare a false invoice from Sarpanitum. I'll have my son give it to our head of operations on Marduk with a note from the Chief Dispatcher. He can see that it gets into the right hands."

The Marshal bowed. "It will be done."

PART THREE

SARPANITUM IV

I

"How well did you do?" David Morland asked.

"Eight hundred and seventy-nine new Vishnuian recruits," Vann Stenger replied. "Several hundred of them experienced in some aspect of manufacturing. We're still a popular destination even after a year. As it was, I turned down more applicants, who didn't have the skills we needed, than I accepted."

"We can use all of them," Morland replied.

"How are things going on Koshchei?"

Morland smiled; he had just returned from Koshchei less than a hundred hours ago. "Overall, better than we'd expected. These days our biggest problems have to do with cultural differences between the different workers and their adjustment to life on a barren and airless world. Many of the Sarpanitans laborers, who are the hardest workers, have been unable to adjust to life in the domes and have had to be relocated on Poictesme. Not surprisingly, it's the former communists who are working out best there; unfortunately, most are hampered by a lack of motivation and a poor work ethic. The Vishnuians are better adapted to living under claustrophobic conditions and have settled in quite well. Thank goodness everyone speaks Lingua Terra."

They were in Morland's office at Emesh Spaceport with Laz Rivera, sharing news after their respective trips. As always, whenever he returned from Yorick Ladbrok's office on Poictesme, Morland resolved to do a better job decorating his own office. *It is improving*, he thought, looking around as Vann poured drinks. Randa had replaced all of the Space Viking furniture, which typically consisted of unmatched pieces looted from a dozen different planets, with a local hand-carved desk and locally-made chairs, tables and couches. The only Space Viking item left in the office was the communication screen. The couches were along the wall in one corner, with footrests and end tables adjacent to them. And they had just hung one of Rivera's paintings on the wall.

There were over three thousand Vishnuians on Koshchei, with a thousand Sword-Worlders and Poictesmians, but only a few hundred Sarpanitans. The work was going so well that Yorick Ladbrok and Giffard Zhorgay were spending most of their time dealing with personnel clashes that varied from when breaks were taken during work to the strange smell of a neighbor's food during lunch.

Most of those quarrels were easily resolved. Those workers who were not able to adjust to working in domes on an airless planet were either put to work on Poictesme or brought to Sarpanitum, where they joined several hundred Vishnuians who were already working there. At Emesh City they would labor in a variety of areas, especially the shipyard where they had just begun work on the landing legs for the first ship to be built on Sarpanitum.

"Did you bring back any more interplanetary vessels?" Stenger asked. "I saw that there are now over a dozen in-system."

"Just another five-hundred-footer," Morland replied. "We only had two ships and had to evacuate about three hundred workers from Koshchei. In addition, there was a lot of machinery and equipment that I wanted to bring to Sarpanitum."

Vann nodded. One five-hundred foot ship just about filled the entire cargo hold of a two-thousand foot ship, leaving very little room for anything else, including the barracks used to hold the ship's complement of ground fighters. Normally, it would have been almost impossible to clear enough space between decks to hold a five hundred foot ship; however, they had the facilities at the Koshchei spaceyards to reconfigure the cargo decks, making space for the smaller vessels.

To transport the fifteen-hundred footer interplanetary ships from the Gartner Tri-System to Sarpanitum, they'd had to temporarily install Dillingham hyperspace engines. The Dillingham engines were roughly half the cost of the typical interstellar spaceship and had to be recalibrated every time they were moved from one ship to another, which was both time-consuming and expensive. They'd only done it for four ships before they decided they were better off using more of the five-hundred footers.

They had thirteen—no fourteen with their latest addition—interplanetary warships spaced throughout the Octavio System, serving as both missile platforms and training bases for future ships' crews. The bulk of the crews being trained now were Sarpanitans, which surprised Vann Stenger.

"Vann didn't think the locals were bright enough to be spacemen, did you?" Rivera grinned. "I wonder what a certain native would think if she heard that?"

Stenger grinned back, finishing his drink and rising out of his chair for a refill. He had started spending time with Randa and it was beginning to seriously annoy Morland, which Morland suspected was her intention. Vann had even asked for his "permission" to start seeing her; he had given it grudgingly, but it still rankled.

Randa was right; it was time to take their relationship to the next level.

"Don't put words in my mouth," Vann said in mock protest as he filled up his glass with his favorite Poictesme brandy. "I was just surprised because I've heard that the economies of Lahar and Nishun are booming and that there aren't enough qualified people to fill every job."

"That's true," Morland said. "Even the election of the socialists on Nishun has not slowed things down—yet."

After Joao Molambo's retirement, the Peoples Party had not taken his advice to nominate a younger man. Instead, they had nominated a long-time party stalwart, who was even older than Molambo. An uninspiring choice, he had failed to hold on to the people Molambo brought into the party. In an election where no one party achieved a majority, the Peoples

Party was forced from power as the left-leaning Workers Party worked with the radical Social Justice Party to form a coalition government.

While that had worried Morland somewhat, he was more concerned about the news reported by his spies and those probes he had managed to plant in the Union Assembly Hall in the capital, Siyawela. The Social Justice Party was secretly discussing pulling out of the Lansing peninsula and turning power back over to the locals. Some of them were motivated by the cries to bring their remaining troops home, while others thought the locals were ready for their own government.

It appeared the Social Justice Party contained a large number of communist sympathizers who were well aware that the retreat of the Union of Independent Nations would almost certainly bring the former communist officials to power on the Peninsula. Morland's primary concern was that his people were just beginning to develop several industrial sites on the Peninsula, which had turned out to be rich in mineral resources, including fissionable ores, and he didn't want any political disruptions.

"Did you recruit many teachers?" Morland asked.

"About sixty or seventy," Vann Stenger replied. "Just how many schools do you intend to start anyway?"

"While you were gone I opened new ones in New Napier, Kasrilapolis, and New Lansing."

The Sword-Worlders had started new schools because the facilities in Emesh City could not handle the demand for higher education. Literally thousands of people had come from all over Sarpanitum to Emesh City in order to learn Sword-World techniques and technology, and there was simply not enough room for them. Too many of the old buildings in the former capital had deteriorated from neglect and old age. While they had demolished the worst of them, his people didn't have time to build new ones. There were too many other critical projects, mostly concerned with defense, that were far more urgent.

Morland had opened new schools a year and a half ago in Siyawela on Nishun continent and at Port Chatham on Lahar, but that had not been enough to satisfy all the demand. New schools were also opening in Valpo and in the Correa river valley.

"Do you have any other news from Vishnu? How is Vin Qual?" Morland asked.

"He's fine except for some backlash due to his part in our emigration program. Apparently, it's caused a political reaction that's reached all the way up to the Vishnuian Grand Senate. No one in charge was prepared for the large number of citizens willing to leave Vishnu. Several new political parties have formed and are criticizing the powers that be. The government there is not used to dissent," Stenger said with a shrug.

They'd better get used to it, Morland thought scornfully. He had come under constant criticism from the new government in Nishun; they thought he should be giving away the Sword-World technologies for free to benefit the people of Sarpanitum. Meanwhile, the farmers in the Correa river valley objected to learning new farming techniques, then objected to being displaced by people who were willing to learn them. He had sent two shiploads of volunteers from the Correa Valley to Nissaba where they could practice their obsolete techniques until they starved to death.

Maybe it's time to speed up the practice and start sending the complainers as well.

He noticed Vann seemed to have more to say and gestured for him to continue.

"I brought along copies of a trade agreement with the Mardukan Empire for you to sign," Stenger said.

"That was fast," Laz Rivera remarked.

It certainly was. When he had left Vishnu almost a year ago, they had only a rough outline of an agreement with Marduk. He had expected that Vin Qual would work out the rest of the details. However, the freighter captains told him that Qual had resisted every chance to meet with the Ambassador or his staff. He was clearly uncomfortable dealing with diplomats. They had done some sending back and forth of proposals via the freighter captains but that was no way to conduct a negotiation. So he had sent Vann Stenger to try to restart the negotiations. Apparently Vann had done a lot more than restart them.

"Take a look at the prices in the agreement," Stenger said, obviously pleased with himself.

He did, expressing astonishment. "These are more than double Sword-World prices."

"Yes," Stenger said with a big smile. "They were anxious to negotiate and kept offering us better prices. Of course, the first rule of negotiations is that you turn down the initial proposal. The offers only got better over time."

He was surprised at first to see Sarpanitum saffron listed among the items on the proposed agreement. When he thought it through it made sense. The Mardukan Empire had a lot of ships. They might not spend as much time in space as Space Viking ships, but they would want anything that could improve carniculture rations. And saffron certainly did do that. It had been a hit from the first moment they had introduced it on Vishnu. The growing number of Imperial ships explained why gadolinium was the first item on the list.

"Gentlemen," Morland said, after he finished the document. "This agreement is going to make us very rich." Not that the previous years hadn't been profitable. Any of the principals in the New Base Venture could have long ago returned to the Sword-Worlds with enough money to buy a dukedom if they wished.

"Well done, Vann."

Vann Stenger rose and bowed. "I am happy to serve my Prince," he said with a mocking grin, as he refilled his glass.

"If I were a Prince I'd make you a Duke for this," Morland replied. He turned and looked sharply at Rivera, who was about to speak. Rivera was the strongest proponent of Morland declaring himself Prince, or even King of Sarpanitum.

Apparently changing his mind after the look, Rivera licked his lips. "How did Qual react to this agreement?"

"He was astonished. And pleased," Stenger added. "As any man who is going to be rich should be. However, nothing seemed to make that pretty office manager of his happy. She said she never wanted to see another Space

Viking as long as she lived."

He winced at the memory that brought back. Nadira had not taken it well when he told her that he would not take her back to Sarpanitum with him. He seemed to have bad luck when it came to women. One of the reasons he'd moved so slowly in his relationship with Randa. Although they saw each other all the time, especially since she was his chef for special events, none of their recent meetings had been in private.

Now with Vann in the picture and fewer distractions, it was time to make his move. He would pick out an engagement necklace for her after this meeting was over.

Misinterpreting his silence, Rivera said, "I don't understand why we're trading with the Empire on one hand and preparing to fight them on the other."

"According to what we have heard from Prince Trask," Morland said, "there are three or more political factions on Marduk in this new Empire of theirs. If we can appeal to the faction that wants to trade, maybe they can help us with the faction that wants to fight."

Rivera looked dubious. "My question is: How are we going to stay alive while we're appealing?"

For that question, Morland had no answer.

II

When the recording ended Morland felt a strong sense of satisfaction. The latest report from Nissaba indicated that everything was going well there. The colonists he had sent to Nissaba from the Correa Valley were now beginning to settle in one of the uninhabited continents. The positive reports they'd recorded should help him to persuade others to emigrate, freeing up more land for people who could put it to better use. Padishah Parviz and Princess Janna had sent their greeting; announcing that Parviz's eldest son had married and had a daughter that he named after his aunt.

If they had stayed on Nissaba and made it their base, it might have made sense to marry Janna. That would have cemented his alliance with the Padishah. He smiled at the thought. Though he had enjoyed his time with Janna, Nissaba was much more primitive than Sarpanitum, and had only about one tenth of its population. Nissaba's people were only now learning the basics of Sword-World technologies, while the Sarpanitans were learning how to crew hyperspace craft. Sarpanitum had been the right choice.

The spaceport at Emesh City continued to prosper. The first Space Viking ship, the *Black Hawk*—with the blazonry of a black bird of prey, holding a sword in its beak—had shown up a thousand hours ago. They had been raiding planets at a level slightly above that of Horus and had a mixed cargo of general merchandise. They needed minor ship repairs, ammunition, missile replacements and some shore leave; all of which Emesh was able to supply. Morland had overpaid for her cargo as a way of generating more business. The captain, who he did not know except by reputation, had been operating out of Jagannath , but had said that he would return to Sarpanitum.

"There are too many Space Vikings working the same sector of the Old Federation," the captain had told him. "They're staying clear of Mardukan space, picking the bones of a worked-over carcass. I heard Dagon was raided three times within the past year. I doubt there'll be any chickens left for a fourth."

He wasn't surprised; Dagon was a former Space Viking planet that hadn't functioned as a base since being sacked well over a century ago. Quite a few Space Viking base worlds had not passed the test of time— Dagon, Hoth, Skathi, even Melkarth had barely outlasted Sanchez. His two sons had run it into the ground after he died. Morland was determined that Sarpanitum would not suffer the same fate.

"With your base here," the captain had said, "I can trade with you, or even with Odin if I have to."

They gave the captain a list of their trade planets so wouldn't raid them. The captain left happy, noting that he had heard several other Space

Viking captains talking about visiting the Sarpanitum base and that he expected more to follow his lead. They traded most of the *Black Hawk's* cargo with Nissaba, Lyonnesse and Mara, while bringing back students from those planets to study Sword-World technologies.

The Marians all wanted to study hyperdrive. Morland encouraged them, thinking they might convince their government that building hyperships wasn't going to happen in a day, or even a decade.

Some students still came from Poictesme to study subjects that weren't taught at home, such as advanced robotics with his father. He had limited the enrollment at the University of Emesh to several thousand students to prevent them from overwhelming the city. As it was, the air was filled with dust from the construction of new buildings and roads as they struggled to keep up with the growing demand from all the newcomers and businessmen who were pouring in, hoping for a piece of the action.

The rum business continued to expand on Ammut as traders, both from Sarpanitum and independents, spread the product far beyond Vishnu. They had recruited a lot of people from Valpo City to assist the natives on Ammut since the heat and humidity of the prime rum-producing area didn't bother them, although they had to adjust to the heavier gravity like everyone else. Some of the Vishnuians had settled there as well, drawn by a chance to have their own land. Settlement on Ammut was limited due to the gravity, and they hadn't made much of an effort to train the natives in anything other than rum production.

Business was also growing on Sarpanitum. They were working furiously to expand saffron production, purchasing land in every climate zone that could support it. Fortunately the Kabata continent had the largest area of hot dry summers and rainy winters necessary for saffron growth, so Morland had purchased the bulk of the available land for saffron fields.

Factories and industrial plants had been established in all of the major cities of the Lahar and Nishun continents. They had also begun setting up industrial operations on the Lansing peninsula, trying to take advantage of its abundant mineral resources. They had initially been supported in this by the Kingdom of Lahar and the Union of Independent Nations, but six months after taking office the Union government pulled out of the peninsula. They claimed that their troops needed to come home and that the local inhabitants were ready to set up their own governments.

Warned by his various intelligence operations, Morland had been ready to step in and replace them, when King Altos had indicated to him that the kingdom did not have the manpower to go it alone. Ashnan, the former home of the Communist Republic of Sarpanitum, was the largest land mass on Sarpanitum; it had almost half of the planet's population and, as he was beginning to find out, plenty of resources. He intended that the Space Vikings should dominate it as much as they dominated Kabata. The army of locals they had been training, augmented by those Space Viking ground troops tired of raiding other worlds, moved into the peninsula to help maintain control.

The cities of Ashur and Salvasar were not any problem. Most of their inhabitants had been killed by the Omega ray bombs they had dropped when they invaded Sarpanitum. Both cities had many buildings that dated back to the Federation era. Other than a few with collapsium exteriors, most of the buildings were tear-downs. The other five nations along the Lansing peninsula were a different story. All of their cities had been constructed since the Federation fell, and consisted of numerous small buildings built close together with a rat's maze of paths and streets winding through them. Although governments had been established in the five nations by the soldiers of the Federation and the Kingdom of Lahar, the situation was unsettled with a lot of poverty and unrest.

Former communist officials were common in the five nations and many either held positions of authority in the new governments, or were taking advantage of the unrest by agitating the citizens to overthrow their rulers and set-up new communist governments. Three of the five nations seemed to be handling the unrest because their economies were improving. Two of the nations, Temuco and Sisulu, were not. He could ignore Temuco; it was the furthest away from Ashur and Salvasar and didn't have any resources Morland needed. Sisulu, with its capital of Bennetown located adjacent to a uranium mine he had reopened, could not be ignored, and he had concentrated most of his troops there and issued warnings to the communists not to disrupt the government or the economy. He hoped they would take his warning seriously.

III

A few months later another Space Viking ship showed up, although some Sword-Worlders questioned whether it qualified as a true Space Viking craft. The *Princess Erika* once had another name, but she had been renamed when her captain had fallen in love with a Neobarb princess of the same name on Mictlan. When her father refused permission for them to marry, the captain had arranged with the Princess to steal her away. When he arrived at the departure spot, he'd found the princess accompanied by over thirty female friends, relatives, and servants, whom she refused to leave behind. Putting that many young women on a Space Viking vessel produced the expected effect, and now, over twenty years later, the ship was famous for having so many children on board that they'd had to start a school.

Princess Erika was also famous for her part in the raid on Durendal, which Morland discovered was why she'd left the Tanith Sector for Sarpanitum.

"Some people on the various Space Viking base planets resent us for looting a Sword-World," Captain Dalgar said, after he had settled into a chair in Morland's office. "By Satan's Hellfire, Durendal was so run down it wouldn't make a good Neobarb world."

The captain looked as if he had some ancestors from Nergal. Besides his mahogany-colored skin his brown eyes had some of the reddish tint Nergalers were noted for. He was joined by his wife and two young men in their late teens who were obviously their sons since they had his dark brown skin and her blonde hair and blue eyes. "Now our own people refuse to trade with us."

Since the *Princess Erika* had not really raided a planet for years, its so-called raid of Durendal had been more of a scavenging operation that had turned into a problem, he explained.

"Why do they resent you?" Laz Rivera asked, who had joined them with a bottle of Poictesme melon-brandy. "You didn't destroy anything. What about the six ships that raided Gram? They sacked several cities."

"The captains of five of those ships have retired and sold their ships, and the new owners have renamed them," Captain Dalgar replied. "The other ship captain is a cousin of the King of Jagannath, so he doesn't have any problems trading on Jagannath."

"We trust that you will not show such prejudice," the former Princess Erika said in a hopeful voice. "We would like a place where we would be welcome and will be able to create a new home. We heard on Jagganath that you had established a base here and we wondered if you could use an additional trading ship."

Morland smiled back at her. Though she was two decades older than the woman whose face was blazoned upon the ship bearing her name, she was still beautiful. "Actually, I can think of another way I can use your skills," he said.

He described how he had used their example of digging up old bank vaults on Durendal to good effect on Poictesme. "We have some detailed records showing the locations of old banks, treasury vaults, and the like on planets we have found to be nearly destroyed. If you still have your mining equipment, I think we could reach a mutually satisfactory deal."

It turned out they did, although they had sold some and most of what was left needed repairs. They were very willing to reach a deal. He offered to service their ship for free and was surprised at what they found.

"The ship is clean and well maintained," Rivera stated. "But there are almost no weapons on it. There are no offensive missiles and only a few defensive ones. And only about half the people seem to have personal arms."

When he questioned Captain Dalgar about their lack of weapons, he received an awkward and embarrassed response.

"We sold off most of our offensive missiles for money in the past when things weren't going well," Dalgar said with a shrug. "With so many families onboard, we stopped getting involved on dangerous raids. That's why we brought the *Manticore* and *War Hammer* with us on the Durendal raid. If we met opposition there, we wanted to have some fighting ships to protect us."

And I felt poor before we set out on the New Base Venture, Morland thought sympathetically. "We're producing our own missiles and weapons here, so I can help restock your supplies. I will also send a company of ground troops along in case you encounter any resistance."

He resolved to send local troops from Sarpanitum that had recently finished training and needed experience along with a few good officers. The officers could also train any of the *Princess Erika's* crew who were willing. He put some of his staff to work examining their old records to determine which of the worlds they had visited would be the best candidates for vault mining operations.

IV

"So the Empire's a little distracted now," Manfred Trask concluded. He was newly returned from Tanith and was sipping his drink, with a cigarette in the other hand and his feet stretched out before him, on the deck outside of Morland's office. "I didn't realize how much I prized Ammut rum until I had to do without it. I was surprised to find we didn't have any back home."

"I'll send a few cases to your father on the next freighter," Morland said absently, preoccupied with the news Trask had just brought him. "So it's true. The Empire is now officially expanding beyond its five-hundred light-year boundary."

Trask nodded. "They recently sent a flotilla to conquer a Neobarbarian world named Manannán. They did so in their usual fashion, landing several ships and just taking over—no Neobarb world can muster a force capable of opposing them."

"Not many civilized worlds could, either. How's Aton taking it? I know Manannán was one of their trading partners."

"Not well, from what we've put together. Marduk has performed similar operations over a dozen times since they had declared themselves an Empire. However, Manannán was a trading partner of Aton's, which the Empire must have known."

"What's Aton going to do about it?" Morland asked.

"They already did it. Five months after the Mardukan takeover, six ships from Aton arrived at Manannán and forcibly ejected the occupying force. There was no bloodshed because the Imperial forces were seriously outnumbered and smart enough to leave before shots were fired.

"Now the Empire is in the midst of a diplomatic name calling contest, with Isis intervening on the side of Aton, no doubt threatened by Mardukan expansionism."

"Aren't we all threatened?" Morland asked. "The Empire's been poaching in this sector, as well." He told Trask all about the Rhiannon raid and the new Imperial base on Belphegor.

"I'm beginning to think the Empire has designs on all the worlds of the Old Federation."

"Do you think there will be an all-out war?" Morland asked.

"My father doesn't think so. He said that the Emperor has been very careful to avoid any war-like moves. He thinks the Emperor is afraid that if Marduk attacks Aton many of the other civilized worlds will join together against the Empire—especially Odin."

"If so, why did the Emperor authorize the invasion of Manannán?" Morland asked.

"We're not sure if he did," Trask replied. "Some extremists in the military expansionist faction of the government may have acted on their own. Our spies tell us that this faction is now suffering a loss of support because they were forced to back down over Manannán. Had Aton not taken action, things would be a lot different. From what we've heard, the Emperor is putting some restrictions on the Mardukan Navy which is where that faction is strongest."

That's good news, Morland thought. Maybe now he could worry less about the Empire finding and attacking Sarpanitum, and spend more time on rebuilding his base worlds. The extremist Naval faction was the one he feared, the one that called themselves the Space Viking Killers. Recently, he'd learned that the *Challenger* was one of the principal ships operating out of the Empire's new base at Belphegor.

"We've been keeping an eye on Belphegor," Morland said, "I sent one of our Poictesme freighters, the *Sansloy*, to Belphegor, ostensibly to trade but in reality to find out what it could about the base. Of course, the Mardukans sent them packing. We've talked with other merchant ships as well and they've noted that there were always about four or five Imperial Navy ships around Belphegor, either at the base or in orbit around one of the planets.

"The *Sansloy* also went to Rhiannon, and confirmed that two ships remain in-system there, too. They left right after observing the ships, not wanting to be identified."

"It sounds like the Empire's establishing its presence in this sector," Trask said.

Morland nodded in agreement. Fortunately they still had plenty of plutonium remaining from the last raid on Tashmetum by the *Faerie Queen*, *Pay Dirt*, and *Gift Horse*. They were also continuing to trade with Mara for plutonium, though each trade was accompanied by complaints about the unsatisfactory price. This appeared to be a planetary trait, as he had found when comparing notes with a captain from Aton who had traded with Mara in the past.

"Even a Gilgamesher would have trouble dealing with those Marians," the Aton captain had said, pronouncing his ultimate judgment on the world.

The Gilgameshers had continued to stay off Poictesme and were rarely seen in the vicinity of Sarpanitum, which was fine with Morland. He was no closer to unraveling the mystery of the Gilgamesher murder/suicide visit to Poictesme that he was the day it had happened.

They were continuing to develop their own fissionables on Sarpanitum, having found other sources of uranium on the Lansing Peninsula and had opened additional mines. Now there was a breeder reactor operating near the city of Bennetown, and another at Emesh City. He hoped that soon he wouldn't have to worry about new sources of fissionables.

The *Princess Erika* had also surprised him when they returned from Morrigu, where he had sent them to excavate bombed-out bank sites, by bringing uranium as well as gold and other valuables. Since they had heard about the shortage of fissionables on Sarpanitum, they had excavated an old uranium mine and refined enough ore that their storage holds were full.

Morland was pleased by their actions, since it indicated they were serious about being helpful partners. Now, the *Gift Horse* and *Grim Reaper II* were off to loot former bank vaults and safes. After all, there was no end of destroyed or decivilized worlds in the Old Federation and few of them were capable of fighting off their raiders.

V

As Morland was turning off the communication screen Randa came on to the terrace and sat in his lap. She nuzzled his ear before embracing him again. She'd been very affectionate since accepting his marriage proposal.

"Who was that?" she asked.

"Just another young lady who wants to visit me," Morland said. "I told her to come on up."

Randa gave him a suspicious glare. He had not realized until they began dating what kind of a reputation he and other Sword-Worlders had. When they first came to Lahar and Nishun they had been hailed as heroes for defeating the Communists. Like all heroes, there had been many women who had thrown themselves at the Space Vikings and they had been happy to return their affections. Pictures of them celebrating had been widely circulated in all of the Union and Lahar Kingdom newspapers. They thought they were reminding people of what they owed the Sword-Worlders, but he had discovered they had also created an image of them as womanizers. One that wasn't true in all cases.

"It's Pavla, she's just back from Joyeuse."

Randa smiled. Everyone liked Pavla Lancaster; she was an enthusiastic worker, more than willing to do any shipboard task asked of her.

The buzzer rang and he pushed the opener. Pavla Lancaster entered with a man about her age Morland didn't recognize. She gave the two of them a quick glance, resting her eyes on the large diamond that rested upon Randa's bosom. While in the Old Federation couples still wore engagement rings, on the Sword-Worlds they wore engagement necklaces.

After introducing Tomas DeLange as her husband, she said, "I met Tomas on Excalibur while I was visiting my mother. We knew each other from school, but lost track after I left Joyeuse."

Tomas smiled. "It was my fault since I left Excalibur to work on Tizona. I'm in the reclamation business."

Morland chortled. "You've come to the right place, then!"

Tomas smiled, saying, "So I heard. Eventually, I returned to Port Arthur for another job; the pickings on Tizona were getting sparse and our operation had closed down. I was happily surprised to find Pavla there; we reconnected as if only a few days had passed. When I learned she'd become a Space Viking living in the Old Federation, how could I resist!"

They all laughed.

"I am happy you returned, Pavla," Morland said. "You never know what's going to happen when someone visits their family; I would have hated to lose one of my promising young officers."

"Thank you, sir. However, my mother is best experienced in small doses. And I have my family with me now," she finished, snuggling up to her husband, who smiled back at her.

"But we're not the only ones with good news," she said, pointing at Randa's engagement necklace.

Morland felt himself reddening. "I thought it was time to settle down."

Randa didn't say a thing, but her smile said a thousand words.

"Well, congratulations Commodore, and you too Randa."

The ladies hugged.

"Did you get an opportunity to visit Joyeuse?" he asked. When Pavla had requested leave to visit her mother on Excalibur, Morland had asked if she'd make a side trip to Joyeuse, to find out what was going on there.

"There is still a lot of fighting between the different factions on Joyeuse," she told him. "Right now there are three different claimants to the throne. It made it easy for us to recruit skilled workers and good teachers. A lot of people are sick and tired of all the fighting. The economy is in real trouble and people are finding it hard to work in a city that's turned into a battlefield."

Morland was sorry to hear that. He'd grown up in Longinus and had a lot of happy memories of his childhood. "We can use all the skilled and educated people you can find."

"It's good that you've found a closer source of skilled people," Pavla said, referring to Vishnu. "Most of the other Space Viking base planets are either retrenching, because of the Mardukan raids, or being abandoned as the Space Viking overlords return to the Sword-Worlds. From what I heard on Excalibur and Joyeuse, Sarpanitum is farther away than most people are willing to travel. We wouldn't have gotten so many workers on Joyeuse if the political situation there wasn't so perilous. It would be different if they could see our world as we do."

'Our world.' Yes, Sarpanitum has become our world for many people, including myself, he thought, as Pavla asked Randa questions about herself and the upcoming wedding. He made a note to contact Rivera and have him offer Pavla one of the newly rehabbed houses as a bonus for her good work.

"Rivera will be very happy to have you back. He's always asking for more help. Vann says he is working on his magnum opus, but Laz is all hush-hush about it."

She laughed and said she would be happy to return. Then he told Pavla about her recruitment bonus, a home of her own, which made her even happier.

"Thank you, Commodore. I wasn't looking forward to setting up our new household in the old barracks."

VI

"So we're going to tear down the old building and start over," Morland said, describing their plans. The Sword-Worlders had adopted one of the Sarpanitum's more enjoyable customs, they were having a picnic lunch by the lake in a park between Emesh City and Emeshton.

"I am sure it will be the most successful restaurant in Emesh, to say nothing of all Sarpanitum," Vann Stenger said, as he devoured Randa's fried chicken.

David and Randa laughed happily about that. They planned to build a restaurant on the first floor with apartments on top that they could rent out to friends. The location, right on a wooded part of the river running through Emesh and a short walk from the visitor's barracks, was excellent. It was one of many businesses that were being opened up in the city as more Sword-Worlders began to regard Sarpanitum as their permanent home.

Of course, given the fame of Randa's cooking—the spaceport cafeteria was always bursting at the seams on the days she worked—any restaurant she operated would probably be successful, even if it were located in the middle of a desert.

"I've already loaded the *Faerie Queene* with trade goods for our voyage to Vishnu. What kind of recruits should I look for this time?"

"Right now, Vann, we need more teachers and agricultural workers.

Too many of the locals on Ashnan are unwilling to do farm labor and many of those that are willing do it badly. The communists destroyed the work ethic there. I'm at my wits end about what to do with those people. They want to be fed and sheltered, but don't want to work for it."

"I know you've sent a few shiploads of laborers from the Correa Valley to Nissaba. How's that working out?"

Morland shrugged. The first shipload DeBorder dropped on Almira continent, which was uninhabited, did poorly. When he returned three thousand hours later with three freighters full of settlers, about two-thirds of them had died. However, the survivors had set up hunting parties and their first few farms, but they refused to take on any more settlers. "Let them make do on their own, like we did!" was their cry. They threatened to kill the newcomers if DeBorder dropped them within their territory.

"So DeBorder set them down about two hundred miles away. They left a couple of technical advisors, three successful farmers and a blacksmith. The next time he returned with another five thousand exiles, they had their own settlement. This time they'd only lost about half of the original group.

"Since then, we've moved close to twenty thousand settlers onto Nissaba. But, really, we need to move ten times that many. We just don't have the shipping facilities to do it."

"At first, I thought it was cruel to leave them stranded there," Randa said. "Until I remembered what the communists used to do with anyone who objected to their policies."

Morland nodded. He'd visited a number of mass burial sites that were scattered throughout the former Communist Republic of Sarpanitum.

They were momentarily distracted by the landing of the freighter *Sansloy*, just in from Poictesme. The spherical ship looked like a silver balloon in the distance as it hovered over the spaceport. The spaceport wasn't too busy at the moment, with only the *Skull Splitter*, *Princess Erika* and several freighters from Vishnu and Tanith occupying berths.

The latest news about the Empire was that the crisis between Marduk and Aton seemed to be diminishing. While no one was apologizing, no one seemed to be threatening war anymore, either. Morland wasn't happy about that and said so.

"I know we all hoped for a war between Marduk and Aton," Vann Stenger said, pushing aside his emptied plate. He looked in the picnic basket as if hoping to find some more Poictesme melon-brandy inside, but there was none left. "That would have given us a decade or two before we showed up on the Empire's viewscreen."

"Exactly," Morland said. "Still, our preparations are going well." They currently had over twenty interplanetary ships in orbit around Sarpanitum, serving as both training craft and missile stations. Close to a thousand recruits had already graduated from training and were currently serving on various vessels. Some had opted to stay on Sarpanitum and had taken command of the missile ships and were training others, freeing up more of his experienced officers.

Some of the interplanetary ships would soon be back to their original use. The *Sansloy* was carrying industrial equipment from Poictesme for mining one of the Octavio System's airless planets. The trips to and from the planet Erva would provide additional training for prospective crews.

While he hadn't expected much from the Sarpanitum recruits, he'd been pleasantly surprised by many of them. Particularly those recruits who had been officers in the navies of the Union of Independent Nations and the Lahar Kingdom. Some even had a few interesting ideas about instructional drills and war-gaming. While many of their ideas did not translate well to space warfare, those that did had led to lively training exercises.

The *Skull Splitter* and *Faerie Queen* had already run a variety of drills with the missile ships, defending Sarpanitum against simulated attacks. He would have the *Pay Dirt, Jolly Roger* and *Gift Horse* do the same when they returned. He knew he could count on Tylor Ragnarsans to come up with plenty of suggestions and ideas.

"We're now better prepared for a visit from the Empire," Stenger continued, "than we are from our own communist rebels. Do you think it's going to come down to another war?"

That worried Morland, too, and he got up and began to pace around. "I think they want a confrontation. I suspect they think we'll back down before we take any decisive action. I've had some of the Lansing Peninsula agitators arrested and interrogated on veridicators. We've played their confessions on the telenews system, which led us to some of the saboteurs. Those we've caught have been publicly executed. There's less sabotage now, but I don't know whether it is because we're guarding our installations better or because we've killed most of the saboteurs. Still, the agitation and protests haven't slowed down."

Vann turned to Randa . "Any ideas?"

"Yes." She looked at both of them. "The leaders of this movement will never give up. Whether they are dedicated communists or just opportunists really doesn't matter. They want power. They've never forgiven you for taking it away from them. The only way to stabilize the area is to kill them all."

Morland smiled, putting his arm around Randa. "I love the way she cuts right to the heart of the matter."

"I got to know many of the Communist Party leaders," she said, "when I was forced to cook at state dinners for them. Most of them are pigs! They don't give a fig about ideology; all they want is power and more power—wealth, too."

Vann Stenger frowned. "We'll have to find them first before we can eliminate them. I know Morrison is working hard on that. What's he come up with?"

"Not enough," Morland said. He had placed Arvin Morrison in charge of their armed forces on the Lansing Peninsula. Besides being top flight at training troops, he was an ex-policeman with a good cop's sense for ferreting out leads. "He has found plenty of their leaders, but there seems to be an endless supply of them."

"There's not," Randa insisted. "A lot of the Party elite moved into the Lansing Peninsula because it was the industrial heart of the Ashnan continent. But the Party has always consisted of a select few on top with a large number of followers who were easily led and did what they were told, as long as they were fed and had a roof over their heads. If you kill off the leaders, you will end the rebellion."

She's absolutely right, Morland thought. People in some of the more populous areas of Ashnan had grumbled and criticized him for all the changes he had brought, but no one had rebelled in New Hamilton, maybe because most of the top communist leaders had died when the Commissariat Building was destroyed.

"So we've got to find all of the old Party elite," Stenger said. "There ought to be records somewhere."

When he didn't say anything, they both looked at him. "I recognize that expression," Stenger said. "What's your idea?"

"There have been a lot of rumors that they want to hold some sort of conference. I was trying to discourage it but…."

"Let them," Randa said.

The wedding festivities were a great success because so many people Morland had come to value as friends had been present. He had resisted Randa's attempts to draw him into planning the wedding ceremony, claiming that it was a Sword-World tradition that the groom only showed up on the wedding day and did what he was told.

With all of the ship captains and the leaders from their trading partners gathered together on Sarpanitum for the nuptials, they had been able to spend the time before the wedding mapping out plans for the future. Most importantly, they had formalized all of their various trade agreements into the Sarpanitum Trade Alliance, consisting of Sarpanitum, Poictesme, Ammut, Lyonnesse, and Nissaba. They also agreed to run a certain percentage of their trade through Vin's firm on Vishnu. As soon as they were back from their honeymoon, Captain Stenger would take the *Faerie Queen* and travel to Mara to try to persuade them to join the Trade Alliance.

Meanwhile, the newlyweds were going to honeymoon on Nissaba.

VII

Vann Stenger stood up from the desk and smiled as Morland walked into his office. "How was the honeymoon, David?"

Morland grinned back as they shook hands. "Wonderful. Randa had a great time; she claims that growing up she had never imagined a honeymoon like ours. She said it was like something out of the *Arabian Nights*."

"Did you have any problems with—dare I ask?—Princess Janna?" Vann asked with a smile.

He shook his head. "Water over the dam. Janna's remarried to one of the east coast princes and quite content. I will admit I was a little worried about complications when we settled on Nissaba as our honeymoon spot, but it worked out better than I could have imagined. Padishah Parviz treated me like a prodigal son—anything we wanted was ours to take. He even announced a citywide party to celebrate our wedding. Parviz was thankful for our help, and, of course, he was glad to have his son, Navid, back. Randa fell in love with the place and we couldn't have had finer hosts or a better time."

Vann nodded. "You're a very lucky man...."

"You're not still harboring a crush, old friend, are you?"

Vann shook his head, changing the subject. "We're having more problems with the Vishnu government. The last two ships we sent to Vishnu to recruit workers ran into problems. The local authorities constantly harassed them, trying to prevent them from meeting potential recruits."

"Did you lodge a formal complaint?"

"The government hasn't been the least bit interested in our complaints. They still don't officially recognize Sarpanitum as a civilized world. Our recruiting there has gone from merely embarrassing to the

Vishnu government to downright threatening. Despite their threats and harassment, we still were able to recruit over three hundred people, which was a tribute to how desperate some Vishnuians are to improve their lives."

"How about Vin Qual?" Morland asked. "He must be worried."

"Vin Qual's also experiencing problems. Several of the large trading firms are suggesting, not too subtly, that he should share his trading connections with them. They aren't happy to see a new firm succeed so rapidly; it threatens the status quo. Vishnu is even more socially conservative than we guessed. They've even gone so far as having the local government officials harass his office and warehouses."

"What's Vin doing about it?"

"He's stubbornly ignored them, using his friends in smaller firms whenever he has more business than he can handle. Still, he's worried that some government official might shut him down in order to placate one of their business cronies. He's asked that we put a moratorium on recruiting for a few years."

Morland nodded. "We don't want to lose him as a trading partner and friend. Besides, it doesn't sound like we're getting enough recruits these days to make much of a difference. Tell Vin we'll just stick to trade goods for the foreseeable future."

Vann Stenger nodded. "That's what Rivera suggested, too."

"I suppose you and Laz ran things better in my absence than I ever did."

More grins. "Actually Laz took as much time off as I would let him. If you have any complaints, you should direct them to me."

Morland sat down on one of the couches and let Vann fill him in on everything he'd missed while they were away. He wanted to have a drink but—while his personal clock told him it was several hours after dinnertime—it was only early afternoon Emesh time. He needed to follow his normal hours so he wouldn't have such a difficult time adjusting when he went back to work. A drink would probably knock him right out.

Randa had no such qualms; she had gone straight home to bed.

"While you were away, as we agreed, we dug up all of the remaining gold and other valuables from the vaults beneath the ruins of the Commissariat Building in New Hamilton. I sent two hundred million gold stellars to Yorick Ladbrok. The total haul was over seven hundred million stellars"

Morland whistled. "That's almost twice what we suspected. It'll more than take care of Ladbrok's costs." The Koshchei project had gone way over the projected costs. They had only needed a portion of the gold but he had decided they might as well dig it all up and store it now that they had a place to keep it. He recently founded the Bank of Sarpanitum and the gold would help back the notes they had issued. One of the immigrants that Pavla DeLange had brought back from Joyeuse had banking experience and had been appointed to run the bank.

King Rodrik had established a branch of the Bank of Tanith at Emesh City as well, which helped them because its credit was already established in the Sword-World Helm and on the Space Viking base planets, while theirs was not. Morland wasn't worried about spending their hoarded gold because they were rapidly replacing it as more Space Vikings and independent traders found their way to Sarpanitum. The *Princess Erika* was proving to be very successful at excavating wealth from the ruins of the Old Federation. She was currently on Parvati, one of the worlds they had raided years ago, digging up bank vaults and safes in more destroyed cities.

"What about the trade agreement with the Confederacy?" he asked.

"Their ambassador has come and gone. I sent him back with a counteroffer," Stenger said, as he concluded his update.

A diplomatic party from Odin had just left Sarpanitum, one of the things he had missed while on his honeymoon. Once Marduk had reached a trade agreement with them, Odin was determined to have one as well. Since Vin was still not willing to get involved in negotiations, they had sent proposals back and forth until Odin had followed it up with a diplomatic visit.

"Was the negotiator the Ambassador who wouldn't deal with Neobarb planets?" Morland asked, sarcastically.

Stenger chuckled. "No, but he sent his chief aide, so I guess we're more important now. He's decided that most of the terms in our counteroffer are acceptable. "

Reaching for a bottle of rum, Morland decided that the good news deserved a toast; adjusting back to Emesh time would have to wait.

VIII

Six Galactic Standard months after his honeymoon, Morland was interrupted one afternoon by one of his staff reminding him that Will Haversham had requested an appointment with him. He was intrigued, wondering what he wanted. While they settled themselves on two of the couches in his office, Haversham turned down his offer of a drink.

After the usual pleasantries, his First Officer asked, "Commodore, can I be frank here?"

"Of course, Will," he replied, wondering if there was some problem brewing with one of the other captains or with his crew. Haversham had really settled down since they had all become wealthy, but his drinking sometimes got out of hand.

"I would like to buy an estate from you."

Morland was astonished. Haversham was a very reserved man, whom he had never gotten to know very well. He had just assumed he was similar to DeBorder, who was rarely happy sitting still for long, and would probably remain a Space Viking until the day he died.

"It's always been my intention to retire when I had enough money set aside," Haversham said by way of explanation. "Once I became certain we were going to settle here, I sent for the woman I wanted to marry."

"You were engaged this whole time?" Morland said with surprise. It had been almost a decade since they left Joyeuse, which was a long time for a woman to wait. *She must be unusually patient.*

"Oh, certainly not. I actually dated Eva's older sister at one time before we left the Sword-Worlds, but she's married now. Eva comes from a good family back home—on Morglay," he added, reading Morland's expression as he tried to recall where Haversham was from. "She just arrived two days ago on the freighter from Tanith."

"Congratulations, Will," he said. There was very little available land left in the Correa Valley, and he had intended to save that for the locals. After several years of pushing hard for change and sending the worst of the resisters off-planet, some of the remaining locals had finally begun to use modern farming techniques. He wanted to be able to reward them as a way to encourage others. Then he got an idea. "Was there any particular acreage you wanted?" he asked.

Haversham said no and appeared to mean it.

"Then I'm not going to sell you an estate, I am going to grant you one. There will be a number of problems that come with it, but they are ones that I am sure you can solve."

Haversham leaned forward in his seat. "Tell me all about it."

Even though he had posted guard companies at either end of the bridge between the Ashnan continent and the Correa Valley, there were still refugees who were able to sneak past the guards and illegally enter Kabata. It wouldn't have bothered him if they weren't so disruptive, stealing food, mugging the locals and occasionally breaking and entering. He told all of this to Haversham, then described the land north of the bridge in Ashnan.

"That is the area I'm going to grant you," Morland concluded. "Organize it and put the locals to work so they don't have a reason to come south. You will need all that money you were going to pay me, because there are no Old Federation facilities or dwellings there. You'll have to build everything from scratch. Are you interested?"

"Of course, this is a grand opportunity," Haversham said. From his tone of voice, he meant it. "How much land are we talking about?"

"I'm going to start off with a grant of ten thousand acres. In a couple of years, after we see how well you've done with the original grant, we can discuss whether or not you need any more land."

Haversham smiled, accepting the implicit challenge.

"The deal is this: Whatever you improve, you keep. You can recruit anyone you want to help you. In regards to trading with the Ashnans, my only restrictions are no weapons or contragravity."

Haversham stood up. "I accept, Commodore, or should I say, Your Highness."

Morland reddened slightly. "You are starting to sound like Rivera and Stenger." Though the more the subject came up, the more accustomed to the idea he became. As they shook hands he asked, "If you don't mind my asking, why don't you want to return to Morglay, or any of the other Sword-Worlds? Morglay is pretty stable now."

Haversham shook his head. "Peace never lasts there more than a decade or two. Excalibur is the only truly stable Sword-World, and it's too crowded for me."

Morland nodded in agreement. The Sword-Worlds may have been their birth place, but better opportunities existed in the Old Federation, even with the Mardukan Empire around to complicate things.

"I have a final request," Haversham said, describing it.

"Another wedding sounds fine. I would be happy to officiate," Morland said with a wide smile. "Say," he added as Haversham turned to leave, "with so many of us getting married lately, when do you think it'll be DeBorder's turn?"

Haversham's usual reserve cracked for the first time. He howled with laughter, eventually bending over and shaking as tears rolled down his face. Morland didn't think it was that funny and decided that some of Haversham's exuberance was a delayed reaction to the stress he had felt while making his requests.

Morland resolved to invite him and his wife-to-be out for a social occasion sometime. Since Haversham was going to become a permanent resident of Sarpanitum, he should get to know him better.

That wasn't the end of what turned out to be a momentous day; more news arrived just as he was ready to join Randa for dinner.

"One of the freighter captains has just arrived, sir," said one of his couriers. "He's delivered what he says is an important message from Duke Ladbrok."

Randa, who was closer to the door, got up to receive the packet.

"What's it say?" he asked.

He heard the sound of Randa opening the message. "It says 'It's finished.'"

IX

"I can't wait to shut that guy up," said one of his men, making what Morland hoped would be the final adjustments to some instruments as the radio blared in the background. They had been working for several hours.

"What's it mean, this sacred homeland business they all keep going on and on about?" someone else said.

Pavla DeLange piped up. "They're mad over the Admiral granting that estate to Will Haversham. They consider that area to be the ancient homeland of their people."

Morland had been convinced by his captains to take the title of Admiral shortly after the *City of Emesh* was commissioned. He'd initially objected, until Senior Historian Selner had pointed out that King Lucas Trask I of Tanith had taken that rank when he only had three ships under his command. Morland had more than twice that many and the largest warship in history.

"They're communists," another man snorted. "How can they have a homeland when no one owns the land?"

Morland motioned for Pavla to back down, as she seemed about to get up to argue with the man. She had done a tremendous job the last few months as they strove to take advantage of the opportunity offered by the communists' convention. But she was over seven months pregnant with twins, and was supposed to be taking it easy.

"We'll have it ready in a few minutes, sir," the first man said.

"Good." He had been starting to wonder if he had made a mistake waiting for the final day of the five-day long conference. As he hoped, when they took no action the first few days, attendance had increased as people realized it was safe to attend. There was some chatter going on from all of the communication screens, mostly people complaining about the delay. He heard Arvin Morrison get on the screen and tell everyone to shut up since he was in command of all the ground troops. They had a right to be keyed up; they had been gearing up for this operation for over a month now.

Morland had pulled in every available ground trooper. He even brought in two thousand troops from Poictesme, along with everyone they had trained on Sarpanitum, which was another ten thousand fighters. The *Skull Splitter*, *Pay Dirt*, *Gift Horse* and *Faerie Queen* were fully loaded and could be here in minutes when he gave the word.

"Everything's finished and tested, sir," the chief technician said. "We can go whenever you say so."

"Pavla, send word to all ships that it's time get ready," he ordered. "Let me know when everyone is in position."

He looked around the bridge on the *City of Emesh*. It had taken them over three years on Koshchei to build this ship. It had cost much more than they had estimated, even when they had revised their estimate half a year into the project, but it was worth every centistellar.

They had set out to build a vessel twice the diameter of the typical two thousand foot globular ship typically constructed by Space Vikings, which would be roughly eight times the size. This was something that to everyone's knowledge had never been done. Previously, the largest ships had been the three thousand foot dreadnaughts of the System States War— and they were nowhere near this big. By the time the design was done and all of the ship's systems rescaled to fit the larger space, the ship was a little over forty-two hundred feet in diameter. He had wanted a ship that would give him an edge in a space battle and now he had one. The irony was that the *City of Emesh's* first battle was going to be in what amounted to a raid on his own world.

"Captains Vann Stenger, DeBorder, Ragnarsans and Rivera say they are in position," signals-and-detection reported.

Reginald Mathes started to reach for a prominent button.

"No," Morland said, standing up and walking over. "I should be the one to do it."

He pressed the button. Thousands of feet below them, bombs planted weeks ago went off, and the ancient arena in Bennetown, currently occupied by over thirty thousand communists, exploded.

"The operation seems to have been a complete success," Morland said, pouring drinks for everybody as they found seats among the couches and chairs in the room. They were in one of the lounges on the *City of Emesh*, having just completed their tour of the ship. There were still several items that hadn't been installed yet, such as bartending robots, so they had to pour drinks the old fashioned way. Even those who had helped with the original design of the ship were awed by the *City of Emesh's* size and everything she had aboard.

While the ship could still carry plenty of cargo, much of the space normally devoted to freight on a Space Viking ship had been turned over to weaponry. She had many times the missiles, both offensive and defensive, that a normal ship would have. *City of Emesh* also had a second layer of collapsium armor two hundred feet inside in to prevent missile impacts from damaging important systems. Plus she had deck space for a dozen pinnances, only six of which were currently occupied.

In an attempt to keep her existence secret, they were basing her on the other spaceport on Sarpanitum. This port, located on an island just off the east coast of the Nishun continent, had been the original port constructed to serve the world. It was a small port with barely enough docking space for the *City of Emesh* to land. However it was well away from Emesh spaceport and the prying eyes of independent traders and any other off-worlders who might be tempted to spy on her and sell the information to Marduk.

Morland just hoped that the *City of Emesh's* crew and those construction workers who had come here from Koshchei to help with the construction of the Sarpanitum ship would heed his request to keep their mouths shut.

"How many troops did you end up using?" Ragnarsans asked,

accepting a glass of Poictesme melon-brandy, his favorite.

"Over twenty thousand," Stenger said. "Practically everyone we've ever trained except the men on your ships," indicating Ragnarsans and DeBorder.

Morland switched from Poictesme brandy to Excalibur red-whiskey as he filled DeBorder's glass. Javen wasn't particular about his booze so there was no sense wasting the good stuff on him.

The explosions had collapsed the arena, killing almost everyone inside. After the detonation, the ground troops, using current intelligence and old records, had rounded up every suspected former communist leader and party member from the Lansing Peninsula to the remains of Marxburg. They had veridicated all of them. About half of those arrested had proved innocent of sabotage or agitation. However, they were often able to provide leads to others not on their lists, and by the time they were done over four thousand people had either confessed or refused to answer questions, which was the same as confessing in his mind.

The governing coalition of the Union of Independent Nations, particularly the Social Justice Party, had been vehement in its criticism of his actions, calling him the "Butcher of Bennetown." The Lahar Kingdom had been noticeable by its lack of any comment at all.

"When are you going to execute them, Admiral?" Ragnarsans asked, after hearing Stenger's description of their last month's activities.

"I am not going to execute anyone," Morland said, shocking the room into a series of outcries. Even Laz Rivera expressed his concern.

"No, I have not gone soft and I'm not at all concerned about the Union's criticisms," Morland explained patiently. "I am following the advice of my wife."

That statement provoked looks of confusion on DeBorder, Ragnarsans and on some of his other officer's faces.

"Then, what are you going to do with them?" Rivera asked.

"Remember my wife worked as a chef for most of the top communist officials, and she knows the Sarpanitum people better than any of us. It was her idea to exile all of them—and whichever of their families want to go with them—to Nissaba."

"Why Nissaba?" someone asked.

"We've already transferred almost a hundred thousand refugees from here to Almira continent. Nissaba has other unoccupied continents; after all, we wouldn't want to burden the earlier immigrants with these layabouts. We'll put them on the least attractive one, give them all of that old farming equipment that's lying around the Correa Valley and whatever Haversham has collected on his estate, and leave them to survive—or not—depending upon how willing they are to do hard work."

Ragnarsans shook his head. "That's a lot of effort and expense. They aren't worth it. I'd just shoot them all."

You can do that when you are running your own world, Morland thought, but he didn't say it out loud. "They're probably not worth rehabilitating, but it will show our people that we will use whatever force is necessary to preserve our rule, and that we can be magnanimous towards our enemies. I doubt if Sarpanitum will need a second demonstration."

While Randa had detested the parasites she'd been forced to work for, she had insisted that he be magnanimous toward the prisoners, saying that it would play well with her people. Having been to Nissaba, she knew that none of the people sent there would ever return. Particularly, without any spaceships....

"Besides," he continued, "it will also be a shakedown cruise for the *City of Emesh*. We are still figuring out how many crewmembers we need to run the ship. Given all the available space we can haul all of the communists there in one or two trips."

A couple of the officers looked as if they still disagreed, but they kept their objections to themselves. He suspected some of them still objected to the name he had given their new ship. Many people had wanted a more grandiose name, saying that *City of Emesh* sounded more like a passenger liner or freighter than a fighting ship. He had told them he had deliberately chosen an innocuous name. They were conditioned by their Space Viking past, where grandiose and prominent ship titles were common.

"There is another matter," Manfred Trask said. He had not participated in the debate, obviously waiting patiently for it to end. "When I came back from Tanith on the *Zama*, we stopped at Vishnu. Our mutual friend, Vin informed me of a problem."

It seemed that one of the large trading firms on Vishnu had gotten tired of verbal persuasion and sought other ways to share in Off-World Trading's good fortune. The Vishnuians had sent two ships to Ammut, one of them an armed merchantman, and boarded Vin's freighter, removing all the cargo.

"Vin's trading vessel had no missiles and no defensive weapons other than some personal weapons and a few dozen air-cavalry mounts at Tisel Island," he said, naming the island where the rum was produced. "There was no way they could resist. After the Vishnuians emptied his holds, they landed and took all the rum barrels on Tisel, too. Then they told the freighter captain that if Vin would not share his trade with them, the next time they would destroy his ship."

The news caused a minor uproar as everyone shouted questions or threats. Morland ran his hand through his hair and got up to pace around the room.

"What merchant ship?" Laz Rivera asked. "Who does she belong to?"

"That's a good question." Trask shook his head and said that the freighter captain didn't know.

Morland asked Rivera what he meant. "On Vishnu everyone has always told us that all the warships are under control of the government. So this was either a government ship or pirates…." He paused, "Where did they get it?"

Another good question.

One of DeBorder's officers was swearing, "We should raid Vishnu, teach those bastards a lesson!"

Everyone else scoffed at that. Space Vikings did not raid civilized worlds, not if they wanted to keep living.

Morland saw that they were all looking at him, waiting for him to decide what to do.

"Javen and Tylor, I know you've only been back for a few days but I'm wondering if I can prevail on you to make a quick trip."

They both said yes, and asked where they would be going.

"All of the jail facilities on the Lansing Peninsula are filled to bursting and we have to move those prisoners quickly," Morland said. "If the *Gift Horse, Pay Dirt, Skull Splitter* and *Faerie Queene* were used together, I think most of the prisoners could be hauled to Nissaba. It won't be a comfortable trip, but they'll get there alive."

Ragnarsans asked if all of their loot had been unloaded and their ships repaired. Since they had raided every planet on the list of worlds that Walter Ovard had scouted several years ago, Javen and Tylor had taken to revisiting some of the places they had previously raided. They had just returned from a lucrative raid on Eshmun, where they had netted close to half a billion stellars worth of loot, and their ships had the damage to prove it. This had been the *Pay Dirt's* first raid without Will Haversham as executive officer, and DeBorder had been concerned about how the ship would perform under its new exec. Apparently everything had gone all right.

They had asked Historian Walter Ovard if he would do some more scouting, but he was busy pursuing his life's dream. He had built a casino in Valpo and recently opened up a second one in New Lansing. Now, he could gamble as much as he wanted. Morland had sent scouts out with some of the other historians but no one seemed to have the knack Ovard did for determining which worlds were worth raiding.

Someone asked what Morland planned to do. "I will take the *Zama* to Vishnu and talk with Vin. We'll figure something out."

That caused another uproar, the gist of which was that it wasn't safe for him to be seen on Vishnu and that he should have a fighting ship with him.

"I want to leave the *City of Emesh* here, if the other ships are gone," he said, the prospect of a visit from the Empire ever present on his mind. "We built her to defend this world, not to make ordinary trips between worlds."

"Then take the *Skull Splitter*," DeBorder said.

He shook his head emphatically. "No, even with the *Emesh* here there is no need to advertise our presence to the Empire. I am sure there are paid observers in every civilized world's port looking for the *Skull Splitter*. That's what I would do in Vandarvant's place."

There was silence for a moment and Rivera spoke up. "Take the *Zama* and the *City of Emesh*. Leave the *Emesh* next to one of Vishnu's outer worlds, where it can be summoned quickly if you need it. We will rotate the ships traveling to Nissaba so that at least two ships are always here to protect Sarpanitum. Plus, we have over two dozen interplanetary ships in-system."

Everyone nodded, showing they all liked that idea. He started to object but they all looked firmly at him.

Apparently even newly minted Admirals had to follow orders, occasionally.

VISHNU III

As soon as the *Zama* had landed on Vishnu, Morland brought Arvin Morrison, his head of Security, to Vin Qual's office to confirm one of his suspicions. Arvin took out his detection equipment and ran it over Qual's desk and across the walls.

Arvin nodded twice, signaling him that the office and the communication screens were bugged. He had to get Qual outside of his office where they could talk freely.

"Let's go for a short walk, Vin."

"What do you mean, go for a walk?" Qual asked loudly.

Morland tried signaling him to leave the room.

"This is serious, Admiral. We need to figure out what to do. None of my crews will leave Vishnu now...." Qual looked around helplessly, then threw his hands out shaking them in frustration.

"Come with me. I've got a man, a ship captain, that is, who I want you to meet. I think he can help us," Morland said, signaling again with his hands for Qual to follow. Shrugging his shoulders, Qual gave up and followed him as they left his office.

Qual had spent a good portion of his profits from the last few years buying most of the derelict and run-down property on his block and fixing it up. The street didn't look threatening anymore; in fact, there was a pleasant-looking bar nearby that he steered Qual into.

"Isn't it a little early in the day for drinking?" Qual asked as they entered the bar. They joined a middle-aged man with a gray beard seated at a booth in the back corner. Before Qual could say anything Morland raised one finger to his lips, silencing him.

"The bar's clean," Arvin Morrison said. He held out a detection device and ran it around the edge of Qual's body. "He's clean, too."

A light started to dawn in Qual's eyes. "My office is bugged!"

"Yes," Morland said. "That's how they were able to know your freighter's schedule and what was on its manifest."

He introduced Qual to Morrison and the other man, Hugh Westfield. Westfield was a Space Viking who had been recruited by Javen DeBorder on Jagannath. He had served a couple of voyages on the *Gift Horse* as a senior officer, but had not liked working for Tylor Ragnarsans. He had left the *Gift Horse* and had been training crews on the interplanetary vessels until the *City of Emesh* was launched and Morland made him an officer of planetary security.

Morland had been impressed by Westfield and had brought Westfield and Arvin Morrison along as part of a scheme to teach the pirates—whom he believed weren't pirates at all, but employees of one of larger shipping companies on Vishnu—to leave Morland's and Qual's ships alone. He explained his plan to Qual. "So we'll be waiting on Ammut in the *City of Emesh* to turn the tables on them," Morland concluded.

"But how will I get a crew?" Qual asked. "After the last attack, everyone's afraid to serve on one of my ships."

"You don't have to worry about a crew. That's why I brought Captain Westfield and another crew with me on the *Zama*. If we use the *Zama*, the pirates might be suspicious, so you're going to use one of your own freighters, only it will be crewed by my men."

Vin Qual still looked worried. *Nothing in his life so far has prepared him for this*, Morland thought. Off-World Imports had been small potatoes until Morland had brought him all his off-planet business, because none of the large import/export outfits would deal with a Space Viking. Qual had told Morland, more than once, that his dream had been to continue his father's business and make a good living for his family.

Now he was head of the fastest growing import/export firm on Vishnu and his nerves were stretched to the breaking point. "I thought we had problems when I had to deal with politicians and diplomats, but those were nothing compared with these pirate raids. And the threats we've been getting."

"What kind of threats?" Morland asked, his voice rising.

Vin turned white as a bed sheet. "Late at night we've been getting dark-screen calls telling me to give up my business. Or terrible things will happen to me, my wife and children."

Morland turned to Arvin Morrison. "Before we lift-off, engage the services of the best security firm on Vishnu. I want the Quals given twenty-four hour protection."

"That's going to cost, boss," Arvin said.

"Hang the expense," Morland said, his face twisted in a snarl. "I want the best protection money can buy. And their best agents on the job, and plenty of them. Tell them that if anything happens to Vin or his family, I'll rain hellfire down on them."

Morrison pulled back. "Yes, sir!"

"What if your plan doesn't work?" Qual asked.

"It will work, Vin," Morland said. "I'm betting my ship on it."

Finally Qual nodded, "I'll do it."

"Good," Morland said. He splashed a little of his drink on himself so he could go back to Vin's office and play the happy-go-lucky, slightly drunk fellow who didn't worry about things like threats to freighters. "Now, let's go over everything we will say in your office again so we've all got our parts down."

AMMUT

"Nothing new, sir," Reese Duggan, Astrogator of the *City of Emesh*, said as he entered the wardroom at 0600 hours in the morning. The majority of ships in Terran-occupied space followed the Galactic Standard twenty-four hour day and night phases. This system of marking time had the advantage of keeping everyone aboard the ship on the same schedule; otherwise, everyone went by their own internal clock and scheduling was shot to hell and back.

Morland nodded and selected some breakfast from a robot server. They had been on Ammut over three weeks. They were sitting on the bottom of a deep ocean canyon in hopes that any ships from Vishnu would not be able to detect them. He had read about such a feat in Harkaman's biography on King Lucas I of Tanith. It was the only way he knew of to cloak a large ship's presence on the surface of a planet. Some of his officers were concerned about the plan.

"The Mardukans have had an underwater detection system on their ships for over a century," Arvin Morrison had said. "What if the Vishnuians have one as well?"

"It's a chance we'll have to take," he'd told them. "Otherwise, the moment they spot the *City of Emesh*, they'll be micro-jumping out of range." Since Vishnu hadn't been involved in any kind of a war in over four hundred years, Morland thought the chances were slim indeed that they had adopted any new detection systems. Vishnuian society as a whole was resistant to change and he suspected their military was just as conservative.

In this case, Morland was betting a freighter, a good officer and a crew on it.

They had sent up a small sensor to the surface of the ocean to stay in communication with the outside world. They had also built a couple of crude towers that could relay a narrow-beam line-of-sight transmission to the receiver without, hopefully, being tapped. He didn't want to depend on them, but it was good to have a backup.

They had baited their trap with gold. In his office, Vin had mentioned that the freighter would be carrying a large shipment of gold so he could pay off his debts to Prince David. That, plus the usual shipment of Ammut rum, would hopefully attract the vandals who had hijacked the last freighter. Any experienced naval captain would find the suggestion that a veteran captain could somehow dodge a fast warship with a slow freighter humorous—if not outright laughable, to say the least.

Qual's freighter, the *Varani*, had arrived three days ago and was scheduled to leave today. Morland had finished his breakfast and found the rest of the bridge crew was ready. They waited as patiently as possible until they heard Captain Westfield announce his departure to the base on Tisel Island.

Ten minutes later they heard the freighter announce, "Three ships detected in the outer atmosphere!"

The bridge crew tensed up. Other than the senior officers, most of them had not been in combat before.

Morland wondered why so many ships; he'd only expected one or two pirate craft, more than likely converted freighters drafted into use by Qual's competitors. Maybe their statements about an experienced captain had caused a change in plans after all. Well, they would just have to deal with the extra ship. *In any case, this is what the* Emesh *was built for.*

The pirate ships were ordering the freighter to surrender or be shot down. Westfield had taken evasive action, and was arguing with them via radio.

"Who do you think you are to threaten us? You will face retaliation from Prince David of Sarpanitum!"

There was scornful laughter coming from the radio. "What do we care about a threat from some Neobarb so-called prince? We're Vishnu Naval ships. No Neobarbarian would ever dare attack us."

Well that's illuminating, Morland thought. He hadn't expected that. If the Vishnu Navy was involved, they'd be facing a much higher caliber warship than from pirates.

"You're in violation of your own Naval orders by attacking us," Westfield said scornfully. "I don't believe you're a Navy ship. You're just pirates trying to sound important. No Vishnuian Naval ship would be involved in a private dispute."

"You're wrong, Captain. We're here on direct orders from the Vishnuian government," the voice thundered from the radio. "We're going to put an end to this disruption of our society. No more off-world recruiting. No more commoners getting out of their place. This is your last warning. Surrender immediately or we will blow you out of the sky!"

"You'll never catch us in the Hubertz Mountains," Westfield said.

That was the signal; Westfield had successfully lured them to the other side of the mountain range about three hundred miles from Tisel Island. They would have a few moments before they were likely to be detected.

"Go," Morland ordered. The *City of Emesh* rose out of the water, like a surfacing Morglay sea-kraken, and headed toward the pre-arranged rendezvous point, moving as fast as possible in hopes of avoiding detection. They had been underway barely a minute before someone spotted them.

"This is the Vishnu Naval ship *VNS Sky Wheel*, Captain Casimir Thackeray commanding. Identify yourself!"

"Hello, *Sky Wheel*. Who are your friends?" Morland replied.

"I am accompanied by Vishnu Naval ship *God's Mace* and the freighter *Malvina*. I repeat, identify yourself!"

"We have them in range, Admiral," Reese Duggan said.

"This is Admiral David Morland of Sarpanitum, commander of the *City of Emesh*," he announced. "You have tried to hijack a ship under my protection. If you do not surrender to me immediately, your ships will be destroyed."

All he heard was cursing, then the radio broadcast terminated. "Admiral, they're separating and trying to box us between them," one of the bridge crew said.

"Let them," he replied. "What size are they?"

"They're both fifteen-hundred-footers," Rovard Harvan reported.

"Full speed ahead, begin firing at extreme range."

The three ships rushed at each other. At two hundred miles, the Vishnuian sprayed the air with missiles. He saw them growing in size on some of the bridge repeater screens, and then their counter-missiles began firing.

"Fire the starboard battery!" Weapons ordered.

Several hundred missiles streaked out of the *City of Emesh's* battery. The sky was filled with explosions, as missiles and anti-missiles detonated, reminding Morland of fireworks. It was different fighting in an atmosphere; he could hear the exploding missiles and warning klaxons through his earplugs.

It was soon obvious that the sheer number of the *Emesh's* missiles were overwhelming the Vishnuian ship's missile defenses.

"We got one!" cried someone to general cheering.

Morland saw a slowly blossoming fireball of red and orange on one of the screens from where the *God's Mace* had been. The *Emesh* shook gently from the shockwave because of the atmospheric disturbance. There were only a couple of lights blinking on the battle stations' board and as he watched, all but one light steadied as the breaches were sealed and functions restored.

"Where are the other ship and the freighter?" Morland asked.

"The *Malvina's* fleeing," a junior signals-and-detection officer reported.

"The other ship, the *Sky Wheel*, is heading back toward Tisel Island," Rovard Harvan reported. "She's hurt, but not too badly." Harvan looked up suddenly, a frightened look on his face. "She's going after our freighter!"

"Get us over there!" Morland cried. "NOW!"

"I'm heading toward her as fast as I can, sir," his normal space astrogator reported. Milsap was busy pressing buttons. He looked back toward Morland and shook his head. "It'll be close, sir."

Morland looked at the board. They were already going as fast as their Abbott drives would take them. When they reached extreme range, missiles began going out, but there were already missiles headed toward the freighter from the *Sky Wheel*. With a lump in his throat, he saw the freighter vanish in a series of fiery explosions. Then he had to turn his attention to the *Sky Wheel* as she approached, missiles spewing from her.

"Send them two Hellburners!" he ordered.

He watched as the Hellburners arched out accompanied by a flock of missiles. Suddenly the *Sky Wheel* came apart in flaming chunks of metal and the *Emesh was* rocked by the mother of all shock waves.

"Where the Nifflheim did that come from?" Duggan asked.

"They shot-off a Hellburner and one of our antimissiles hit the launcher just as it got into the tube," Reginald Mathes explained. "We got 'em good."

"Good job, everyone," Morland announced quietly. He was thinking of Captain Westfield and the freighter's crew, all gone because they hadn't arrived fast enough. The bridge group was somber, undoubtedly thinking the same thing.

"How are you doing, *Emesh*?" a voice called out.

He looked at his signal's and detection officer, who looked incredulously at his instruments. "The freighter's okay," he cried joyously. The bridge crew whooped and hollered.

"Of course I am, *Emesh*," Westfield said somewhat sarcastically. "You don't think I would go into a fight without a few defensive missiles, do you?"

Morland laughed, slowly at first, and then with tears of relief running down his face. The *City of Emesh's* first battle had been a roaring success.

SARPANITUM V

I

"Everything hit the proverbial fan," Westfield said as he helped himself to a drink.

"What do you mean?" someone asked. They were enjoying the winter sun on a warmer than usual afternoon on the deck outside Morland's office. The deck, oriented so that it was shaded in the summer, was open to the sunshine in the winter. Westfield had just returned from Vishnu aboard the *Varani*.

Morland had returned home aboard the *City of Emesh* while the freighter hyperspaced back to Vishnu after the Battle of Ammut. He had transferred his Astrogator, Reese Duggan to the *Varani* to ensure that they reached Vishnu before the Vishnuian merchantman.

"Well, the *Malvina* got back to the Darveld System before us," Westfield said, "but we reached Vishnu first because Reese Duggan took fewer microjumps within the system and was able to calculate those jumps faster than the *Malvina's* navigator."

Duggan shrugged. "I've been to Vishnu enough times that I ought to be able to calculate the jumps in my sleep. I see those reference points in my dreams."

"By getting there first," Westfield continued, "we were able to release the photoplay of the battle to the telenews firms before the government could take any action to stop us. When it was later reported on the news that the *Sky Wheel's* Captain Thackeray said they were there by direct order of the Vishnuian government, it created a perfect storm of indignation and fury from the public. We refused to answer any transmissions by the telenews commentators, referring them to Qual. We just landed and emptied our cargo before returning to Sarpanitum."

"Did anyone mention the *City of Emesh*?"

Westfield laughed. "Their captain blamed a monstrous warship as the cause of their defeat. Apparently, the *Malvina's* detection system was overloaded during the attack so they didn't have any pictures or recordings to offer as proof.

"The telenews' reporters are having a field day and the opposition is hammering the government," Westfield said with some satisfaction. "The governing coalition appears to be splintering. There may actually be enough votes in the Senate to force an early election for the first time in over a century."

Odd how events on different worlds could parallel one another, Morland thought. There was also talk of an early election on Sarpanitum, in Nishun among states of the Union of Independent Nations. By threatening to resign from the ruling coalition, the Social Justice Party had managed to fulfill one of their campaign promises and pass a bill creating a national pension. To pay for those pensions they had raised taxes on businesses to such a degree they began laying off workers in order to pay the added taxes, which had managed to turn a flourishing economy into a recession within just a matter of months.

This in turn had offended those members of the government, especially the legislators from the Workers and Social Justice Party, who actually believed their rhetoric about the evils of big business. Apparently they assumed that businesses would always produce wealth, even beneath crushing taxes. Now they were talking about nationalizing the larger businesses for the nation's good.

The opposition and much of the country were in an uproar. Two votes of no confidence in the government had been held, with the most recent only failing passage by a handful of votes. This happened just as several hundred thousand troops, returning from the Lansing Peninsula, were demobilized and looking for work. It didn't help the Union that right next door the Kingdom of Lahar's economy continued to hum along just fine.

"We didn't have any problems once we landed the freighter, but Qual advised us, for the time being, to keep a very low profile," Westfield concluded. "The *Varani* is continuing onto Poictesme under her new captain. Then she'll go to Tanith."

Well at least one of his problems had been solved by Westfield's performance in the Battle of Ammut. With the completion of the *City of Emesh*, many of the skilled laborers had left Koshchei and come to Sarpanitum to work. They now had enough skilled workers at the port that they didn't have to stop work on a new ship whenever a Space Viking ship came in needing repairs. Consequently, the new ship would be completed in a month or two and Westfield was the logical choice as captain. Particularly since his other options were Reese Duggan, who liked being an astrogator, or Pavla DeLange, who wanted to focus on motherhood.

While there was plenty of sentiment in the local media for appointing a Sarpanitum native as captain, Morland felt none of the locals had enough shipboard experience. And almost no combat experience. The new ship's junior officers would all be Sarpanitans, and he was even thinking about appointing one or two of them as senior officers. The only question left was: What to name the ship?

II

As the self-created recession on Nishun worsened, the Union of Independent Nations' politicians cast about desperately for a solution, or, failing that, someone to blame. The Social Justice Party claimed that the Sword-Worlders were the source of the rising unemployment because the new technologies they'd introduced were throwing people out of work, particularly in the transportation industries, where more and more freight was being moved by contragravity lifters. They succeeded in convincing a majority of the legislature to enact a tax that applied solely to the various

Sword-World facilities that had been constructed or rehabilitated on the Nishun continent.

In retaliation, Morland closed all the Sword-World facilities in Siyawela and Kasrilapolis. Kas, as it was called, was the port located in the northwest of the continent and was the stronghold of the Workers Party. A delegation from the other two large cities in the Union, New Lansing and New Napier, came to see him begging him not to close the facilities in their cities. He was loath to do so anyway, especially in New Napier since it was their most profitable location. New Napier had been the original capital of Sarpanitum, during the Federation era, and had many buildings with collapsium exteriors. It was a lot cheaper and faster to rehab them than it was to construct new ones.

The delegations, particularly from New Napier, were more than willing to defy the national government. "We could withdraw from the Union," offered one of the New Napier leaders. "We have the Constitutional right. Triple Falls has already passed a resolution supporting secession." Triple Falls was a small city several hundred miles upriver from New Napier.

Morland asked them not to take any hasty action, noting that Consul Franc Huanca had asked him to come to Siyawela to discuss this and other issues. He was well aware that New Napier's threat to withdraw was based on the assumption that the Sword-Worlders would come to their defense if the government threatened war.

After the meeting he asked Manfred Trask, who had been working closely with the two governments, to talk with them and explain that he would not automatically come to their defense. His dilemma was whether to refuse to pay the tax and defy the government, or simply close down all their industry on the continent of Nishun.

The majority of his colleagues would have been more than happy enough to tell the Union of Independent Nations where they could stick their taxes. Laz Rivera thought they should encourage as many states as possible to withdraw from the Union. They would do business with only those states and leave the rest of the Union alone: "With a depression on the horizon, the Union will collapse in a few years and we can pick up the pieces at our leisure."

Others thought the Sword-Worlders should just withdraw from the Nishun continent altogether and leave them to drown in their own misery. Morland didn't want to give up on the continent or its government. What had made Sarpanitum so attractive to him as a base world was its advanced technology and large population base. As a Civ-Level 8 world, the Sarpanitum locals were advanced enough to easily learn and adopt Sword-World technologies. All of the Sarpanitans currently working in Emesh City and on their ships had proved that assumption correct. The last thing he wanted was to disrupt this progress over a dispute with the Union of Independent Nations.

Since Morland wouldn't make an immediate decision, the two factions, many of whom were involved in businesses on the continent, began squabbling with each other as to what should be done. That was when Vann Stenger reminded him, "And you were the one who wanted to find a more advanced world to call home."

"I know," he said, "but until this disruption, things were moving right along. I'm sure I can straighten things out when I meet with Consul Huanca. They need us more than they realize."

Arvin Morrison, head of Security, added, "I'm not sure you should attend that meeting without an escort."

"I've always gone to those meetings alone. I don't believe they're crazy enough to risk an all-out war with us. They saw what we did to the Communist Republic of Sarpanitum on Ashnan. I'll take Sergeant-Major Burris and a full squad of his hand-picked guards. I don't want our allies to think we're occupying Sarpanitum, even if we are. It's not like I'm going to Vishnu where we need a brace of troopers just to walk the streets."

Morrison shook his head. "I don't know. We've had the Union Assembly Hall and the Consul's office bugged for years, but lately nothing's been coming through but routine stuff. That worries me."

Morland laughed. "I know you, Arvin, you're not happy unless there's a conspiracy to report on."

Morrison reddened. "I think you should arrive in a pinnace with a full company of men. However, if you're going to be stubborn, let's just have the *Sky-Rover* stationed nearby—just in case."

"Sure. If it makes you all feel better. But keep the ship in low-earth orbit; I don't want the Union spotting it and using it as an excuse to blame us if the negotiations turn sour. They've been using a lot of anti-Space Viking rhetoric in their speeches and I don't want to provide them with fresh fuel."

All this ran through his mind as Xavier Burris circled the combat-car down toward Siyawela. The city was built at the junction of two rivers near the mountains that separated the west coast from the rest of the continent. It had been a tiny city at a natural crossing point of the river until settlers from the west had come across the mountains two centuries ago. The national government was totally contained on an island at the point where the two rivers joined.

He was not looking forward to this visit. Unlike Joao Molambo, Consul Franc Huanca had never met with him alone. In fact Huanca had always insisted on having at least half a dozen advisors along, each of whom seemed to represent one of the many factions in the governing coalition. A meeting with them was long and tedious, usually interrupted by speeches as each faction present tried to argue its own separate point. It was also the height of summer, which meant it was hot and humid in Siyawela, and the government buildings had no climate control.

Randa was the only advisor he had brought with him. She was familiar with many of the personnel in the upper echelon of the government and he had learned to value her insights on the sometimes baffling ways of her people. She had also listened patiently to his complaints about the heat and humidity before telling him he needed to attend the meeting. It was also the first time he had ever met with the leaders of the Union without King Altos present, but Consul Huanca had insisted on meeting with him alone. He knew he would miss the King, who was always a moderating influence with good suggestions on how to solve any problems that came up.

As usual, an honor guard of twenty-five men greeted him as they landed at the steps of the Consul's office. As he got out of the aircar with his bodyguards, the officer of the guard approached.

"I do not recognize you, Major," Morland said, looking at him quizzically. He had a bad feeling about that.

There was a long and awkward pause. Finally determining that the officer wasn't going to reply he continued. "Where is Major Balon? In the past, he's been the one who has always greeted me."

The officer replied coldly. "Major Balon has been reassigned." The new Major turned and directed Burris to take the combat-car to the edge of the plaza in front of the building. Morland nodded to Burris to comply with the request.

Sergeant-Major Burris approached him and said *sotto voce*, "Sir, I don't think you should leave without protection. I don't trust this guy."

After all they'd been through since the disaster at Agni, one thing Morland knew for certain was that he could trust Xavier Burris' judgment completely. He nodded, saying, "I don't either. Give me four of your men."

"I strongly suggest you take them all, sir."

Morland nodded.

The major frowned at the interruption. "Admiral Morland, we need to leave now. Also, I'm afraid I have to ask you to surrender your sidearm."

That was also something new. He started to protest and realized that the new major wouldn't pay any attention to him. *This is the price of diplomacy*, he thought, as he unbuckled his holster and handed over his sidearm. All this rigmarole just to attend a meeting that he didn't think was going to accomplish much anyway.

"Your bodyguards, too."

Morland shook his head. *Over my dead body!* he thought.

"I'm sorry, sir, but those are the new regulations. No one but the Consul's personal bodyguards can enter the building with a sidearm."

Morland looked the younger man in the eyes. "I disarmed as a courtesy, but if you demand that my bodyguards do likewise, I'll turn around right now and return to Emesh City without meeting with the Consul. You can tell him for me—this is non-negotiable."

The Major stepped out of hearing range, turned his back on them, then pulled out a hand communicator. He talked with his superior for a minute, then turned around. "You have the Consul's permission for your guards to bring their weapons."

For some reason that didn't make him feel a lot better.

"Maybe we should just go back," he said. "What do you think, Randa?"

"I don't like this, but we did come all this way. If we don't resolve some of these issues soon, they're only going to get worse."

He nodded. Several more states were already threatening to bolt from the Union and the last thing he wanted was a civil war.

The Major escorted them up the steps and into the building.

Morland ran his hand through his hair, shaking his head as they left the Consul's office. Randa looked at him with a puzzled expression. Seeing that the aide escorting them out was a little ahead of them, he spoke quietly. "That was the oddest meeting I have ever had with this crew."

"Why, dear?" Randa asked.

"It was short," he said, looking at his watch. "Only about an hour, hardly any speeches and—"

"And nothing resolved," she said. "Most of what I heard was the Consul blaming you for his government's own incompetence. It reminded me of the meetings I attended at the Presidium."

He didn't reply as they had reached the honor guard. The officer in charge had changed again. It was a young lieutenant, not more than twenty, and he didn't know where Morland's gun was.

"I'm very sorry, sir," he said, and seemed to mean it. "I got a call from Major Atombe about an hour ago. He had an emergency to attend to. We just arrived fifteen minutes ago. I don't know anything about your sidearm."

That caused Morland to look around; he noticed that the honor guard had been replaced and reduced; there were only a dozen or so of them now. He was annoyed about the sidearm, but it wasn't anything special and he still had his hide-away pistol. He'd just demand it back before he attended any more meetings.

He gestured to the Lieutenant, who had introduced himself as Lieutenant Cronveldt, and he formed his squad up and led them to the door.

The corporal in charge of his bodyguards moved up beside him. "I don't like the looks of this, sir."

"Me, neither," he answered.

"I'll have my men form up around you and your wife. Let the honor guard exit the building first and act as our shield."

When he reached the door, Morland noticed that there was a huge crowd on the plaza, numbering in the high thousands. *Where did they come from?* he wondered. The plaza had been empty when they'd arrived.

He looked closer and saw they were carrying hundreds of colorful signs, all of which seemed to refer in one derogatory fashion or another to the "Butcher of Bennetown."

The low murmur of the crowd rose as they exited the building, turning into a roar.

"What is going on here?" he asked the Lieutenant.

"I don't know, sir. We came in the back way."

He called Burris on his personal communicator but there was no reply. Suddenly the crowd began chanting, "Death to the Butcher! Death to the Butcher! Death to all off-worlders!"

The crowd started to toss rocks and moved en masse towards them. The escort troops began looking around uneasily.

Morland turned around. "Open the door," he said, to the soldier closest to the door. The man tried to re-enter the door but it wouldn't budge.

"It's locked" he said.

"It's a trap," Morland yelled. "Form your men in close order, Lieutenant! And we'll make a stand behind that row of statues."

Lieutenant Cronveldt looked like he wanted to argue, but he formed his men into a line. The crowd seemed to surge forward in irregular waves.

He turned to his bodyguards. "Protect my wife at all costs."

She started to protest. "It's you the crowd is after—"

He shushed her with a hand motion. "Without you, all this means nothing!"

The crowd was growing louder and Lieutenant Cronveldt looked back and forth between the mob and Morland.

"Fire over their heads," Morland ordered as he continued to press the button that should summon Burris. He had just reached the conclusion that Burris was probably incapable of responding when Cronveldt said, "I can't fire on civilians, sir."

"My men can and will," Morland replied.

The issue became moot as shots rang out from the crowd and two of the honor guards dropped. He quickly pushed Randa down behind one of the statues in front of the building, at the end of the wide stairway. "Take cover," he yelled to the remaining escort, when something hit him.

He became aware that he was lying on his back and one of his escorts was standing over him pulling at his shirt with an odd look on his face.

"There's no blood!" the soldier cried. "He's not hurt. It's a miracle!" Just then he threw up his arms and fell out of sight as a bullet struck him in the face, splashing Morland with blood.

As Morland rolled behind the statue he became aware that the other members of the honor guard were not firing at the crowd and Randa was looking down at him anxiously. "Are you all right, David?" she asked. "What happened?"

He reached down and pulled a hide-away gun out of his boot. He realized that his left shoulder wasn't doing what he wanted. "A bullet must have hit me in the shoulder."

She grabbed at him. "But there's no mark, no blood there, either!"

"I'm wearing armor." When she gave him a questioning look he continued, "I wore light armor for climate control because of the damned humidity. And it made Burris happy."

As an expression of comprehension dawned on her face, he rose and fired several shots around the statue. The nearest person, a rough-looking man, fell, dropping what appeared to be a club. Several others started shrieking. His squad was formed up around him and they were firing their rifles on full auto. The resulting carnage had brought the entire mob to a complete halt; they hadn't expected stiff resistance.

He fired his hide-away pistol and saw a big man grab his stomach and topple over. The crowd was packed so tightly that even small caliber shots took casualties. His corporal moved up. "We're short on ammunition, sir. We need to get into the combat-car."

"Why haven't the honor guard been using their weapons?"

"The bloody bastards gave them rifles with no bullets!"

Morland rang off a string of curses. "Give any of them that look like they want to fight the weapons from our casualties. Use single shots to hold off the crowd for now." He pointed to the two or three hundred dying and wounded men who littered the ground. "It'll take them a while to bolster their courage again and we want to be able to hit them with a large volume of fire when they regroup."

The corporal nodded and went off to talk to each of his soldiers.

One of the soldiers behind a nearby statue gasped and grabbed his arm, dropping his rifle. He noted that most of the honor guard, except the Lieutenant and one or two others, had fallen or melted away. He'd have been at the crowd's mercy without his bodyguard.

Morland pulled out his hand-phone and turned it up to the highest power. It probably wouldn't reach as far as New Napier but they were doomed without help.

The only reason they were still alive was that the crowd was more of a mob than anything else. They were willing to yell and wave their hands, but most of them were afraid to spend their lives against real weapons. The standoff would only last until they ran out of ammunition.

"May Day, May Day! This is Morland. I am under attack in the capital at Siyawela. May Day, May Day! Can anybody hear me?"

Suddenly the soldier next to him, the left half of his face a bloody pulp, lurched against him causing him to drop the communicator. He looked three hundred and sixty degrees around for the shooter as they were completely under cover. A soldier next to him threw up his rifle and fired toward a large tree on a small rise to the side of the plaza. He saw something drop out of the tree.

"Sniper," he said. "I got him, sir. They'll probably send someone else up there to replace him."

So much for Morrison's spies and tell-tales, he thought. However, he did warn me that something like this might happen.

He saw Randa rise to help one of the wounded.

"Stay down," he ordered. He wrapped his bad arm around her to make sure she complied.

The communicator crackled. "Admiral Morland, can you hear me?"

He picked it up. "Who is this?"

"This is Captain Clegg in the *Sky-Rover*, Admiral. We are almost directly above you sir. We are beginning our descent."

Morland swore. *Sky-Rover* was one of the interplanetary ships and it would take about a half an hour to descend from low orbit. Morrison had wanted it closer, but he'd overruled him because he hadn't wanted to make the Nishuns think he didn't trust them—*Ha!*

"Relay this distress call to all units," he ordered.

Clegg complied and he began to hear calls and questions coming in on the communicator from many sources. One of the men behind a nearby statue cursed. His rifle was out of ammunition.

Suddenly the communicator burst out: "This is Laz Rivera. Everyone off this frequency!"

After a few seconds that felt like an eternity to Morland, he spoke again. "David, can you hear me? What is your situation?"

He swore a choice swear word, then summed up the situation as succinctly as possible. Another member of his escort threw down his now useless rifle. He heard the corporal call for covering fire while several of the men went to collect the rifles off the fallen men. He stood up and added his fire to theirs. He felt something hit the statue just above him and jerked back, seeing another of his guards fall to the ground.

"David, according to his tell-tale Burris is alive but unconscious."

Some of the men in the mob were armed and shots were slapping against the bronze statues.

He wondered for a moment how Rivera could possibly read the tell-tale from this distance. The signal has to be relayed by the *Sky-Rover.* "He must have been gassed," he replied.

Another man fell. The guard next to him fired toward the tree again and looked over the statue. "They're going to rush us, sir," he said.

"Fire at the leaders," Morland ordered as he rose and began firing around the statue.

Those automatic weapons with enough ammo went on full auto, which took down the front ranks of the attackers. The charge broke less than fifteen feet away. The crowd retreated, again leaving several hundred dead and wounded behind.

The corporal pulled another clip out of his pocket and slapped it into his pistol. "That's the last one," he said.

Morland looked all around; besides the corporal and the man next to him, there were only five or six of his bodyguards still on their feet. The young Lieutenant was dead, but two of his men were still alive. Everyone else appeared to be dead, too. Randa was terrified but appeared uninjured. One of his bodyguards was shielding her with his body.

"Soldier," he yelled at one of the surviving honor guards, who was crouched next to a badly wounded man. "How much ammo do you have left?"

The man didn't respond and continued to stare at the ground.

"Soldier!" he yelled again.

"He's useless sir," the man next to him said, as he dropped his empty rifle to the ground. "He's been out of his head since he entered prison. Shell shock."

"Prison?"

"Yes, sir," the man replied while casting a look around the statue at the mob, which appeared to be reforming for another charge. The man wore a sergeant's stripes and appeared to be several years older than Morland. "They pulled all of us out of prison this morning to be your honor guard."

Before Morland could reply the corporal cried out and pointed toward the sky. Following his finger, Morland saw his combat-car, with the *Skull Splitter's* blazonry, rising up off the tarmac and into the air above the plaza. It weaved and swerved around as if an untrained drunk were at the controls.

"David," Rivera's voice called out of the communicator. "I've lifted the aircar up by auto-command. I'm opening the windows remotely. Maybe I can wake Burris up."

The aircar weaved around again, bouncing off the edge of the building. It tilted ominously. Morland swore. Rivera was just as likely to pitch Burris out a window as wake him up, but there didn't appear to be any other course of action.

While the mob's attention was focused on the lurching combat-car, the corporal made a dash for the adjacent statue and grabbed the unused rifle of a wounded bodyguard. He promptly fired a couple of bullets into the tree again at some movement that Morland hadn't seen.

The combat-car began to swerve back and forth over the crowd until it bumped into another building, knocking a corner off it. All of a sudden a gruff voice swore over the communicator. "What the Nifflheim?"

"Burris!" he and Rivera yelled simultaneously.

"What in the Gehenna is going on?" he heard Burris shout.

Morland quickly described the situation. Suddenly the combat-car swung around and hovered thirty feet over his head. It then dove down into the crowd, using its hull to smash through the tightly pressed protestors, tossing bodies left and right as the remaining soldiers fired at the leaders. The resulting carnage was indescribable.

It appeared that Burris was wide-awake now. The combat-car circled back down the center of the plaza, its auto-cannon and machine guns blasting through the mob, spraying death and dismemberment. By the time it reached the statue, a quarter of the protestors were lying in bloody heaps on the ground while the rest were hightailing out of the plaza as fast as they could run.

As the car pulled up in front of them and settled down on its air cushion, Morland pointed at the tree, yelling, "Snipers!"

The combat-car rose up fifteen feet and fired a missile, causing the tree and everything in it to explode into slivers. The car circled around the entire plaza before it set down again, hovering mere feet from Morland.

The door slid open and Burris yelled out. "All clear now, sir. I wouldn't stay here for long."

Morland grabbed Randa and dove into the vehicle while his surviving bodyguards picked up their dead and wounded. The corporal picked up another wounded man and one of the men pulled the frozen soldier to his feet and helped him to the car. As soon as all the survivors were in the combat-car, Burris shot straight up into the sky.

At a thousand feet elevation, Burris asked, "Where to, sir?"

He shook his head, then realized that Burris couldn't see him. "Stay right here. Do not leave until reinforcements arrive. Circle this island and do not let anyone off it. Put a missile up the tailpipe of any aircar or boat that tries to leave. The people that planned this massacre are still here and I intend to root every one of them out!"

In about twenty minutes, a dozen combat-cars and cavalry mounts vectored into the plaza from every direction. Under their cover, a contragravity medic lifter landed. They landed the combat-car next to the lifter and medics ran out to assist the wounded.

One of the soldiers began to shake, while Randa sobbed and threw her arms around Morland. He looked around and saw that the corporal was directing the medics to his wounded men. *It could have been a lot worse*, he thought. Then his shoulder really began to hurt.

III

Everyone appeared to be in on the scheme to keep him attached to the robomedic.

"Sorry, sir," Xavier Burris said firmly after a nurse had summoned him, pressing Morland back down into the bed. "Commander Morrison's orders. You're not to leave without his say-so."

"You wouldn't think I had been wearing armor from the way everybody's treating me."

It was the day after the assassination attempt. Condemnations of the attempt had poured in from government and non-government leaders alike. Consul Franc Huanca claimed that the communists had been behind the plot to assassinate Morland. He blamed dissident elements within the government.

Some—like those from Jura Salitros in Valpo and Hachmed Perkins in Emeshton—accused the Union itself of being behind the attack. The cities of New Lansing, New Napier and Triple Falls said almost the same thing and had called for the immediate resignation of the government. An official communication from King Altos condemned the attack and demanded an independent inquiry. His private note to Morland was more scathing.

"I see now why they didn't want me at the meeting, the damn fools!"

He also offered to send troops if Morland thought having some neutral soldiers would be helpful. He doubted it; if Arvin Morrison wouldn't brook any interference from Morland, he probably wouldn't want any help from the Northern Territories. Morrison had sealed off Government Island, and was letting people out only after careful interrogation with veridicators had established their innocence. Protests from the Union had been met with a short, pungent reply.

"You're just damned lucky I'm the senior officer present!" Morrison told them. "Captain Vann Stenger would have invaded Government Island, if only for the pleasure of personally shooting anyone remotely involved with the attempted assassination of Admiral Morland. And Captains DeBorder and Ragnarsans would have dropped a nuke on Siyawela without any concern for collateral casualties."

Randa had not only been shaken by the attack but also by seeing him hooked up to the robomedic, which looked frightening to someone not used to the latest medical technology. She was fine sleeping in the hospital lounge. They had promised him they would bring her into his room as soon as she woke up.

An hour after he had wakened, Laz Rivera came in to see him. "As near as we can tell, over half the people on the island have left. The government has refused to allow the full Assembly to meet, which has caused New Napier to threaten to secede."

Seeing Morland's exasperated expression, Rivera continued. "I thought you'd feel that way so I had Molambo located and flown to New Napier to reason with them."

Since retirement Joao Molambo had been traveling the world, saying that he always wanted to see the places he had only been able to read about. He was popular everywhere, even on Kabata, which surprised Morland, until Mayor Perkins told him why.

"In the years of our captivity under the Communists, Molambo's was the only voice we would hear over the radio telling us that we were not forgotten and that one day we would be free," he said.

Molambo had lost none of his authority in the west either. If anyone could persuade the New Napier to remain in the Union, he could.

A young officer came into the room.

"Sirs," he said, stopping and saluting, which identified him as a member of Morrison's security force. "Our hidden probes have discovered that only the Social Justice Party members and selected members of the Workers Party are in the legislative chamber. The rest of the assemblymen are being held under guard in another part of the building."

He rolled out a plan of the building, showing where they were. Morland and Rivera huddled over the plans.

"We can send a squad through the outer wall here," Morland said, pointing to a nearby corridor. "They can take out the guards and escort the legislators into the chamber. I think we can count on things to work in our favor once they break through. They have some guards, but no soldiers."

Rivera began speaking into his personal communicator to organize the attack. Morland began to lever himself up in bed, reaching out to begin disconnecting the robomedic.

Burris and Rivera reacted simultaneously just as Randa entered the room.

"No, you don't!" Rivera exclaimed, while Burris pushed him back down on the bed.

"What's going on?" Randa cried, running to the bedside. "Is David all right?"

"He's fine," Rivera said reassuringly. "David has a badly bruised and abraded shoulder injury. What would take months to heal on its own will be fine in only three or four days—if we can just get him to behave himself and stay in bed."

Randa glared fiercely at Morland. "He's not going anywhere! I've already had my sleep."

Morland relaxed, sighing in frustration. "All right. I know I have a good staff. I guess it's time to get out of the way and let them do their jobs." He turned to Burris. "Xavier, could you have someone bring a chair in here for my wife?"

Sergeant-Major Burris left the room. He nodded at Rivera, who turned on his heel and left with the beginning of a grin on his face.

Burris returned with several people carrying chairs and other equipment, which they began setting up. "I figured you would want to watch what's going on," Burris said, as several viewscreens were set up and tuned to local telenews channels.

Morland watched, sometimes patiently, sometimes impatiently, over the next three days as his troops stormed the capital building, overcame the guards and escorted the legislators into the chamber. They turned on the cameras after they entered the chamber, televising the proceedings to the world. The debate that followed resulted in a no-confidence vote that ended the government.

The delegates appointed Joao Molambo, as the head of a caretaker government until elections could be held in eight weeks, as called for by their constitution. By that time, most of the conspirators had been captured. Although many refused to talk, enough confessed that all of the main parties were identified. Rivera made certain all confessions were given plenty of airtime on the telenews stations.

What came to be called the "Siyawela Summer Surprise" took place with the *de facto* leader of Sarpanitum griping in his hospital bed as everyone conspired to keep him out of action.

IV

"I am sorry for all of this, David," Joao Molambo said, as they sat on the terrace at Morland's home. "Using your truth machines we've identified the ringleaders who incited the mob in the Government Plaza. Most of the conspirators were reigning members of the Social Justice Party. Many of them were former communists, just as you suspected."

Morland nodded.

"All the conspirators have been hanged and their accomplices within the Workers Party dismissed or jailed."

"Why was my Sergeant-Major sleep gassed?" he asked.

"Plausible deniability. They wanted it to appear as if a spontaneous mob had caused your death. If your combat-car had been shot down or destroyed, it would have pointed to a conspiracy within the government. Even the die-hards were worried about reprisals from your Space Viking ships."

"It might have worked, too," Morland said, "if Morrison hadn't been so concerned."

Joao Molambo agreed. "In part, it was my fault. I told myself I should stay out of endorsing anyone in the last election. Then the Party, thinking they were doing me a favor, went ahead and endorsed old Hachipuka. I would have never supported him; he's too old and set in his ways."

Molambo shook his head. "I should have supported Vondelay immediately," gesturing to Vondelay van Schalk, new Consul of the Union of Independent Nations. "Then none of this would have happened."

"Everything worked out," Morland said. Van Schalk, personally endorsed by Molambo in the recent election, had led the Peoples Party to a resounding victory. He had not only rallied the troops, bringing people back to the party, he had also brought in many members of the Conservative and Workers' parties, who had been shaken by the assassination attempt and the subsequent revelations about the people involved, into the Peoples Party.

Even though the Peoples Party had achieved a majority of the vote, Van Schalk had immediately asked members of several parties to join his cabinet in a unity government. The Social Justice Party, which had received only four percent of the vote, was pointedly excluded. The special taxes on business and Sword-World property had immediately been rescinded, and the economy was already on the rebound.

Morland had then made a donation, just coincidently the size of the unpaid Sword-World taxes, to the new government.

"Yes," King Altos said. "Now we must take steps to insure that nothing similar happens again."

They all looked at Altos, intrigued.

"What do you suggest?" Morland asked.

"First, I suggest that you take the title of King of Sarpanitum," Altos stated. "I, of course, will promptly step back to being a prince."

That shocked them all.

"What!" Morland exclaimed, as the others gasped. More and more people had been using the title of prince when addressing him. While he was chained to his hospital bed for four days, Laz Rivera had consistently referred to him in that fashion. Most of the other governments had promptly adopted the title as well.

"We should not allow the people, or any political parties, to be confused about who is in charge," Altos said. "You have established your rule informally," he gestured to Morland, who was trying to interrupt him, "Let's make it formal."

Altos continued, suggesting an agreement be drawn up, leaving internal matters to each nation, with the king to arbitrate any disagreements between nations, and the king to be responsible for all off-world policy, including trade. "Implicit in this, of course," he concluded, "is that you are responsible for the defense of Sarpanitum from any off-world aggressor, a goal to which you are currently working toward anyway."

Morland was surprised to find that Joao Molambo didn't disagree; he merely suggested some minor changes on how such an agreement could be drafted and approved. Altos waved off Morland's objections, continuing, "This is the perfect time to do this, now that your succession will soon be provided for."

Randa had told him that she was pregnant while he was in the hospital room. The news had leaked out a few weeks later, principally because she was so happy she couldn't stop talking about it. Shocked at first, he had become as excited as she was about it.

Finally he stood, lifting his hands. "You're right. It's time I took more responsibility, I'm going to declare myself Prince of Sarpanitum. It only makes sense since just about everyone's granted me that title in absentia."

"It's about time, Your Highness," Vann Stenger stated. "Now you can grant titles and present land grants like they do back on the Sword-Worlds. There's a lot of territory abandoned by the communists that you can declare for the crown."

Morland nodded, thinking, *that's a damn good idea!* "I appreciate all your support and as your prince I ask all of you to work with me in concert to make our world safe and prosperous."

"Hear, hear! Hear, hear! To Prince David!"

They all stood, raising their glasses to that goal. *At least I hope so*, he thought, downing his drink.

V

"I hereby name thee *DaSilva*!" Princess Randa cried, pressing the button that launched a bottle of cheap wine against the side of the ship.

The crowd of over thirty thousand people cheered heartily on a sunny spring afternoon. Everyone who was anyone had come to the ceremony. Local citizens, politicians and business people from every continent, all were there to celebrate the first ship built on Sarpanitum. Every rehabbed building in the entire city of Emesh was full to bursting. As for Emeshton, Hachmed Perkins said it best, "We got 'em stacked like cordwood everywhere we can squeeze 'em in."

Morland had spoken to Hachmed only briefly before his sister Zandra had hustled Perkins off to help with something. Those two were slated to be the next wedding of a Sword-Worlder and a Sarpanitum. There had been a lot of those lately as everyone settled into their new homes and lives. The growing population meant there were fewer buildings in Emesh City to be rehabilitated or torn down every year. As far as new ones, they couldn't build them fast enough Now that the ceremony was over, the crowd started to stream off the landing field to attend one of the many parties held as part of the festivities.

"Congratulations, kid," Captain DeBorder said to Hugh Westfield, *DaSilva's* first captain. Morland laughed with the others. *Kid*, he thought, *Westfield's got gray hair. How old is DeBorder anyway? I was a kid when I took command of the* Nebula. *Now, how many years ago was that? No, I don't want to know.*

Morland did allow himself some brief nostalgic thoughts about his old ship, now captained by Rovard Harvan. He missed the planning and executing of a daring raid.

Funny, but Rivera said he didn't miss it at all. Will Haversham said the same thing and was very happy in his new life as a country squire.

Haversham had done a tremendous job of organizing and pacifying most of the uncontrolled areas of the Ashnan continent. Not only had he stopped the flow of refugees across the great bridge, but he was attracting people from other parts of the continent who wanted a more stable political situation. Those Sword-Worlders who indicated an interest in owning land, he sent to Will Haversham. Those who Will judged as good candidates were granted ownership of one of the vacated estates in the area. They were manufacturing agricultural equipment in Emesh as fast as they could and still couldn't keep up with the demand.

Tylor Ragnarsans came up to join them, offering his congratulations to Westfield, as did many of the other Space Vikings. *I'm going to miss Tylor*, Morland thought. While he had been getting shot at in Siyawela, Ragnarsans and DeBorder had been exploring planets looking to establish another base. The world they had chosen was called Ashur. Ashur had actually been identified as a possible base years ago by Ship's Historian Ulrik Selner, but it had been in the opposite direction of where Morland had wanted to go at the time.

Ashur was over eight hundred hours away from Sarpanitum and, based on the information they had brought back, more industrialized than Poictesme had been—about Civ-Level 7 or 8—at first contact. Now Ragnarsans would fulfill his long-held dream of having his own base and running his own show. Morland hoped the dream lived up to his expectations. He promised to make Ashur part of the Sarpanitum Trade Alliance.

DeBorder and Tylor Ragnarsans congratulated him as well on the construction of the *DaSilva*. Javen heartily, Tylor less so. Ragnarsans seemed to think that Morland should be investing more goods for his new base. In particular, he wanted more fissionables than they were willing to supply. Consequently, Ragnarsans had talked DeBorder into accompanying him on another raid on Tashmetum, that being the nearest place to loot plutonium. They were preparing to leave in a few weeks.

Vann Stenger was going to escort Westfield and the *DaSilva* to Ammut, and then go on to Poictesme. For the first time in several years a ship returning from Poictesme would not be carrying back any interplanetary ships. They had over thirty ships in orbit acting as missile platforms. Even Morland thought that was enough. He didn't have a big demand for trained crewmembers anymore, since they were not intending to construct any new ships for a while.

It was time to start bringing money in again, he decided, after watching the larger portion of his reserves go out to construct the *City of Emesh*.

He would be switching many of those working on ship construction into other areas as there were plenty of items that he wanted to manufacture on Sarpanitum rather than import from Poictesme, Tanith or anywhere else.

Randa came up and put her arms around him and leaned into him. It was time to head over to Randa's restaurant and start the going away celebration.

VI

The Odin captain was unhappy that he had to wait to see Morland, since even before reaching orbit he had radioed in that he had an important matter to discuss. He was unhappier still when he landed in the evening and Morland refused to see him until the following morning.

Morland intended to enjoy the evening with his wife rather than spend the rest of the night dickering over cargo prices. He wondered why the captain was in such a hurry, probably just a tight schedule.

The captain was forced to wait even longer since Morland was moving slowly that morning. Randa was very restless in the final months of her pregnancy. It was disrupting his sleep and he wasn't in a hurry to get to his office.

The captain was already waiting in his office when he arrived. Sipping slowly on his coffee, Morland asked the captain to repeat himself.

"Prince David, I said that I have information that you will want to hear very badly," Captain Holenbeck said. "I think this information is of such value to you that I would like a hundred-million stellars worth of free cargo in return."

Morland jerked back. He couldn't imagine what news was that valuable, nor did he like the captain's tone of voice. He studied Captain Holenbeck, whose face was as solemn as a stone carving. The inhabitants of Odin tended to view everyone else as less civilized and most of them carried their sense of superiority wherever they went. If this was some sort of scam he would soon find out, and there would be hell to pay.

"All right," he said. "If your information is valuable enough, you may have your hundred-million stellars worth of free cargo."

"My choice."

"Yes, but trade goods only." He offered his hand to seal the bargain.

Holenbeck shook his hand. "I was trading on Mara," he began. "I was surface-side, in their government center, where they were asking me to sell them the hyperdrive secret."

They both chuckled over that. Morland refilled his coffee cup and settled in for a long morning, as most merchants loved to gossip almost as much as they loved to bargain. Despite the fact that students from Mara had been on Sarpanitum for several years studying hyperdrive mechanics and related subjects, many in the Marian ruling class continued to believe there was some sort of secret to hyperdrive that Morland was withholding from them.

Possibly that was because the Marians had initially responded to his offer to teach them hyperdrive mechanics by sending only the sons of their titled nobility to the classes. Most of them had lacked the necessary mathematical background to even begin to understand the subject. The Marians eventually learned their lesson and started sending commoners with advanced mathematical backgrounds. These subjects were doing a better job of slowly learning what Morland conceded was a very difficult subject. This delay had cost Mara at least two years, and they continued to agitate for hyperdrive ships.

"I think, because I was already there, they allowed me to stay when the Mardukan flotilla arrived and contacted them," Captain Holenbeck continued.

Morland sat forward in his chair. He suddenly didn't need to finish his coffee to wake up.

"They discussed a good many things while the Imperial ship was descending from orbit. The Marians called out their military forces, even though I told them there was indeed such a thing as the Mardukan Empire and that they were not in the habit of raiding planets. They did not believe me."

Morland winced. The Marians had never forgotten the *Skull Splitter's* raid and the destruction it had wrought. One reason they were so anxious to obtain hyperdrive ships was so they could protect themselves from future Space Viking attacks.

"Before the ship landed," Holenbeck continued, "the Imperial commander asked if they had any knowledge of a ship called *Skull Splitter*. Of course the Marians did, describing the raid of years ago in great detail. The Mardukan Commodore said that the *Skull Splitter* was his enemy, and—"

Morland interrupted him. "Who was this Commodore?"

"After he entered the government center, he introduced himself as Commodore Vandarvant. His ship was the *Challenger*."

Morland groaned. From what he had been able to determine, Vandarvant was the commander of the Imperial base at Belphegor, so it was no surprise that he was now a commodore. If he could trace the *Skull Splitter* to Sarpanitum, he undoubtedly had a large force of ships at his immediate disposal. He also appeared to be a first-rate grudge holder.

"It's worse than you think," the Captain said, almost seeming to relish Morland's predicament. "During his discussions with the Marians, this Vandarvant found out that the *Faerie Queene* traded on Mara. Apparently, he had already determined that the *Pay Dirt* and *Faerie Queene* were allies of yours. The Marians told Commodore Vandarvant that the *Faerie Queene* came from Sarpanitum. They were most angry when they discovered that Space Vikings were the true masters of Sarpanitum. When Vandarvant said that the Mardukan Empire would protect them from any future raids, the Marians immediately repudiated all trade agreements with Sarpanitum."

At long last, here it was: What he had long feared. How had Vandarvant tied the *Skull Splitter* to the *Faerie Queene* and *Pay Dirt*? A comment by some crewman overheard on a Space Viking base world? A report from an observant trader or diplomat on Vishnu? It could have been any one of those things.

"How long ago did this happen?" Morland asked.

"I left Mara as soon as I could," Captain Holenbeck said. "But, first, I had to wait for the Mardukan flotilla to leave. I had overheard enough that I figured it was more profitable to trade this information with you than to continue arguing with the Marians. I left Mara a little over seven hundred hours ago."

The Captain paused. "Did I figure correctly?"

Morland didn't answer. He was calculating where all his ships were and how fast they could get back to Sarpanitum. If he sent one of the pinnaces off immediately he could probably catch Vann and the *Faerie Queene* at Poictesme. The *DaSilva* must have already left Ammut for Vishnu and she wouldn't get back for at least two months. The *Gift Horse* and *Pay Dirt* were out on a trade-and-raid run which included several planets in addition to Tashmetum. He had no idea where they were.

Captain Shawley had taken the *Grim Reaper II* on a long trading voyage and visiting tour of his old friends on Xochitl and other Space Viking base planets. That was Shawley's right as he had long since paid all of the upfront costs and now owned the *Grim Reaper II* outright. He wasn't expected back for at least a year. *Hopefully he'll have something to return to,* Morland thought.

Whether the rest would make it back in time would depend on how fast Vandarvant could get here, and with how many ships. With only the *Challenger*, he would certainly return to his base for more warships. There could be anywhere from five to eight Mardukan warships based on Belphegor and nearby planets like Rhiannon. All Morland had in-system were the *Skull Splitter* and the *City of Emesh*, but the *Emesh* was no ordinary ship. The two of them could probably take on four or five ships, but he didn't know about eight. If Vandarvant went directly from Mara to Belphegor, and stopped at Rhiannon on his way to Sarpanitum, he could be on-system within eight hundred hours.

He suddenly realized that the Captain was waiting for an answer.

"Yes, you did right. You'll get your cargo."

Holenbeck clenched his hands in ecstasy. A hundred-million stellars of free cargo was something he would eat off of for the rest of his life, just in the telling of the tale.

VII

Vann Stenger burst into the command room at a dead run. "Anything yet?" he asked.

"No," Morland replied. One of the pinnaces had detected a ship emerging at about six light-minutes away from Sarpanitum. All of the senior officers had immediately been summoned, since everyone was on a heightened state of alert. Rivera, living closer, had arrived at the command center before either of them.

"They've jumped again, Your Highness," one of the technicians on duty announced. "It's only one ship, sir."

"One ship. But the *DaSilva* couldn't possibly get back for at least another month," Vann Stenger said.

"If it was the *DaSilva*, she would have stopped and sent a message," Rivera said. That was the protocol they had established for their own ships. Jump in five light-minutes from Sarpanitum, then send a message before proceeding closer. Morland knew it couldn't be DeBorder and Ragnarsans since they had left with two ships.

The past two Galactic Standard months had been a whirlwind of activity as they prepared for an attack by the Mardukan space-navy. They had passed his earliest estimate for an attack three weeks ago. Vann Stenger had returned four days ago. Morland was glad that Randa was more than two weeks overdue with the baby. He didn't want to think about anything else, no matter how important.

In truth, he reflected, Sarpanitum was as well prepared as it could be. Every ship was fully outfitted, everyone on full alert. The *Skull Splitter* and *Faerie Queene* were both in orbit. Vann and Harvan could get to their ships within a few hours, long before any attacking ship could reach them. The *City of Emesh* had been moved to Emesh Spaceport and was also ready to leave at a moment's notice.

There was a sudden reaction from one of the technicians. "The ship has jumped to one light-second away," he announced. One light-second was cutting it pretty close, Morland thought. They either had an excellent astrogator or they had been here before.

"Message coming in," Rivera announced. The screen flickered a few times then Tylor Ragnarsans face appeared on it. His face looked strained and his uniform disheveled.

"Tylor, where's Javen and the *Pay Dirt*?" Morland asked.

There was a delay longer than the necessary time for the message to reach the *Gift Horse* and return. He'd never seen such a stricken look on Ragnarsans face before, not even when he was badly injured on Mara. "Since our last visit, the bloody bastards on Tashmetum went and got their hands on some nuclear missiles," he said, with deep anguish. "The *Pay Dirt* was destroyed—Javen's dead."

Morland almost doubled over, as if he'd been slammed in the stomach. Javen had become one of his best friends, and, true, he'd always teased him that he'd die someday with his boots on. But not so damn soon.…

"Where did they get the nukes from?"

"We ran across reports of Mardukan ships all over the quadrant."

More of Vandarvant's revenge? he wondered. Mardukans didn't normally trade nuclear weapons with Neobarb worlds, but a man bent on revenge might. *It should have been me, not DeBorder who died there.*

He would have to mourn later, when the battle was over. And, if they won; if they didn't—it wouldn't matter. Then there would be time for a proper going-away ceremony, even if there wasn't anything of DeBorder left to cremate.

"Are you all right, David," Rivera asked.

He didn't trust himself to speak, so he simply nodded his head. When he had his emotions under control, he said, "We're going to win this battle with Vandarvant and we're going to dedicate it to our old comrade."

"Of course, David. Of course...."

VIII

"What is this?" Morland asked, astonished by the number of people in the antechamber. His sister rose to her feet.

"David, we've just been waiting to hear the news." He stared at her for a moment. His mother also rose to her feet with an expectant look on her face. Somehow he couldn't quite connect them with what he had been through in the past day. He ran his hand through his hair and wondered for a moment why it felt so greasy.

"Well?" Zandra said impatiently. "Boy or girl?"

Finally things started to register with him. "A boy," he announced, grinning.

They cheered and his sister Zandra hugged him. His mother following behind. He looked at her strangely, because she looked more tired than he had seen for a long time.

"Your father is on his way," she said, thinking he was looking for his father. Hachmed Perkins was behind her, also offering congratulations. Perkins' oldest daughter followed, hand-in-hand with his nephew Richard.

There was another Sarpanitum and Sword-Worlder romance that looked as if it was destined to end in marriage, based on how they appeared to feel about one another. As they released him, Richard kept one hand on his shoulder, steadying him. "What's his name, David?"

"Henry," he replied. "Henry DaSilva Morland."

There was a brief silence, then more cheering.

Perkins shook his head, grinning. "That had to be Randa's idea," he said.

He nodded his head, puzzled by Perkin's statement, but before he could say anything else everyone was on him with a flurry of questions.

Randa's health, the baby's health, weight, height and eye color. He let them know she was fine and all of the particulars before he turned to look quizzically at Perkins.

"You'll find out in a few days," Perkins said. "That girl really knows her, ah, stuff."

After rousing himself from a long sleep the following day, he realized exactly what Perkins meant. All of the telenews stations and papers were cheering his son's name and saying the same thing. The name of his son meant that Prince Morland had become a true son of Sarpanitum. He would have passed this on to Randa but she was sound asleep.

The good news continued when the *DaSilva* returned two weeks later. Westfield reported that things were a little chaotic on Vishnu but that Vin Qual and his family were fine. Apparently no party had achieved enough of a majority in the elections to form a government. More information had come out about the former government's attempts to block people from leaving Vishnu, which touched off a series of protests.

The military threatened to intervene, until information came out about certain senior officers' involvement in the attack on Ammut, which created more protests and caused a split between some of the junior and senior officers. Another election had been scheduled.

Morland received the invitation to the gala in the cafeteria through interoffice mail. Zandra led the way via the contragravity lift. Gasps of amazement came from everyone as they entered the room, soon followed by slowly building applause which continued until everyone was clapping and cheering. Laz Rivera stood there, looking embarrassed and gratified, while trying not to look too proud.

Laz's magnum opus, which he had been working on for several years, had just been unveiled. A dozen or more canvases over thirty feet high covered the cafeteria walls. The paintings told the story of the Sword-Worlders who had left Joyeuse, the worlds they raided, the adventures they had and their life on Sarpanitum.

Morland even noticed in the corner, where the story started, a painting that showed him taking over the *Nebula* on Agni after the death of the senior officers. Laz must have obtained the information from others, because Morland had never discussed that raid with anyone but Vann Stenger. The final image was of him holding his son up for everyone's review.

He was sorry Randa couldn't be here to attend the party, but—right after his son was born—he had sent her and Henry to stay with King Altos at his palace in Port Chatham. If the Empire did attack and were successful, he decided she would be safer there. Then he noticed there were several blank canvases hanging on the wall and asked Laz why?

"The story's not finished," Rivera said. "I have to leave room for future events."

He felt a touch on his elbow. He turned and found it was Alex Feraday, the historian who returned from Tashmetum with Tylor Ragnarsans after the last raid. Ragnarsans had contacted Feraday after the *Pay Dirt* was destroyed, telling him that no one would be returning to Tashmetum, and asking him if he wanted to be removed. Feraday was accompanied by his two-year-old son and his wife, a Tashmetum native who still looked a little bewildered and out of sorts.

Feraday gestured toward Ragnarsans and a group of *Gift Horse* officers, who were exclaiming and pointing at the scene showing the destruction of the *Pay Dirt*.

He was glad to see Tylor was out and about. He had been very depressed over Javen DeBorder's death and hadn't left his home for days. He blamed himself for convincing Javen to make another raid on Tashmetum. At the funeral service they'd held for *Pay Dirt* personnel, Tylor had broken down, utterly despondent.

He was pleased that Tylor wanted to stay around and help defend Sarpanitum instead of leaving to start his new base at Ashur. But he was no longer certain how Tylor was going to react to anything given his black mood.

People were calling out for Rivera to speak when an announcement came over the loudspeaker, "Attention, attention please. There are numerous emergences over ten light-minutes away."

Everyone turned and looked at him, then exploded into action, racing for the exits. Burris was already setting down the aircar as he came out of the cafeteria entrance. As sirens blared he climbed in and they headed for the *City of Emesh*. The Empire had finally come to Sarpanitum.

IX

"The pinnaces report ten ships, Admiral, sir," said the junior signals-and-detection officer as he entered the bridge of the *Emesh*. "They have just jumped to about one and a half light-seconds."

That would put them a little over sixteen hours from orbit, plenty of time for everyone to get to their ships and be ready. Pavla DeLange and Astrogator Reese Duggan entered the bridge a moment later. He nodded to them and said "Take off as soon as everyone's aboard."

As the *City of Emesh* was rising up into the air a message came over the communication system. "This is the Mardukan Empire ship *Challenger*, Commodore Vandarvant commanding. Your world is now under the authority of the Mardukan Empire. If you surrender and turn over the Space Viking David Morland and his ship, the *Skull Splitter*, to us, I promise you no one will be harmed. If you do not do this, I promise you that everyone who resists will be killed."

"Send them our screen code," Morland ordered. In a few seconds Commodore Vandarvant's face appeared on the screen. At first, he thought he was looking at an apparition: a closely cropped skull with hollowed eye-sockets holding two burning orbs. Then he looked again, and it was Vandarvant wearing the same short reddish-blond beard.

"Welcome to Sarpanitum, Commodore," he said. "I see that I was being much too civilized," he stressed the word civilized, "when I let you live at Rhiannon."

Vandarvant sneered. "Big talk from Sword-World trash on a Neobarb world. I hope you won't surrender. I've dreamt of nothing but this moment for seven years."

Has it been that long, Morland wondered? *Maybe it has at that.* There had been a lot of water under the proverbial bridge during that time. He saw that Vandarvant was waiting for a reply and spoke. "Really. I've built a trade alliance and brought peace and prosperity to half a dozen worlds during that time. You really should have gotten out more."

The Commodore's face turned red, and he looked as if he'd just swallowed an egg whole. "You insolent barbarian. Surrender or die!"

"No, we will not surrender. If you attack us, we will use whatever force is necessary to repel and destroy you."

He saw a triumphant grin form on Vandarvant's face, and then the connection was terminated.

"Maintain formation and commence jamming," he said, as they continued to rise to orbit with the *Skull Splitter, Faerie Queene* and *Gift Horse* to meet the *DaSilva*. They had found during their many training exercises that if their ships were grouped closely together, and they jammed the radar and micro-ray detectors, it was impossible to tell how big the *City of Emesh* was until someone was very close. He wanted to conceal the *Emesh's* size until the last possible moment.

The missile ships had moved together until they were in two closely aligned clumps. During training exercises, they had found that the missile ships had a greater impact this way than if they acted independently. One of the keys to the upcoming battle would be to keep the missile ships close to his capital ships in order to take advantage of their collective firepower.

As they made orbit and joined up with the rest of the fleet, the Mardukan ships continued their approach. Vandarvant was not going to repeat his mistake at Rhiannon. The ships were approaching slowly enough that they could easily get into orbit and engage the Sarpanitum fleet. He ordered food sent around, and ate a little himself even though he didn't feel hungry. It would still be several hours before they engaged and he wanted everyone ready.

"We have the ships identified," DeLange said, handing him the list. Besides the *Challenger*, there were three more of the newer two-thousand foot diameter Mardukan ships: the *Centurion, Champion* and *Queen Myrna*. Since, unlike Space Viking ships, the Mardukan ships did not have to use precious deck space for cargo and ground fighters, these ships were formidable opponents and out-gunned Space Viking vessels of the same tonnage. Morland knew he'd been very fortunate in his first encounter with the Vandarvant.

The other Mardukan warships were the older fifteen-hundred-footer ships. These were the *Vindex, King Mikhyl,* and *Adiutrix*. There were two other fifteen-hundred-footers from Baldur that were identified as the *Valhalla* and the *Hringhorn*. The tenth ship was two thousand-feet in diameter but they could not identify it until they picked up a transmission. It was the *Grendelsbane* from Beowulf.

The Mardukans approached in a loose wall formation. Just before they reached maximum firing range, Morland gave orders to move into the formation they had practiced. The ships were formed into a ring. The idea was that the enemy ships would approach from above, allowing volley fire from around the circumference of their formation without hitting their own ships.

They accelerated quickly so the Mardukans wouldn't have time to adjust their own formation.

"Weapons, fire missiles," he ordered.

Missiles began firing. He was happy to see the *Challenger* was the first ship they encountered. The *Challenger* was returning fire with missiles and counter-missiles. He hoped that once they realized the *Emesh*'s size it would distract them, but he couldn't count on it. Red flares were going off between the two ships as the missiles met counter-missiles. The *Challenger* was taking missile fire from the entire fleet. As they approached the *Challenger*, their short-range batteries began to fire. The *Challenger* was taking heavy damage, since the *City of Emesh* had eight-times the number of batteries as that of the typical two-thousand foot warship.

With the combined firepower of the fleet concentrated on one ship, the *Challenger* was beginning to break-up. The communication screen lit up. On it he saw Vandarvant expressing a remarkable number of unfavorable opinions about his parentage, ethics, looks—and lack of honor.

He gave up listening as more missiles began streaking out.

"Hellburner incoming," someone cried.

"Send him two of ours in reply." Due to its great size, the *City of Emesh* carried two dozen Hellburner missiles. He checked the screens just in time to see the *Challenger*'s Hellburner intercepted and blown-up. The screens went white and when they were back up he could see the *Challenger* rapidly approaching on both of their Hellburners' screens, all of its counter-missiles failing to stop them. One of the missile screens went blank as it was destroyed, and then the other missile reached the ship.

Cries of delight arose from everyone on the bridge as the *Challenger* suddenly blew apart.

"Have a nice time at Em-See-Square, Vandarvant!" Morland yelled.

Next it was the *Valhalla* coming up along with the *Centurion*, *Champion* and *Queen Myrna*.

"Concentrate fire on the *Valhalla*," he ordered.

Morland glanced at the board. He hadn't felt any impacts but it showed a few blinking lights where missiles had hit. He glanced at the screens showing his other ships all busy engaging the incoming Mardukan ships. They continued firing and being fired upon until all of the enemy ships had passed through the ring.

"The *Valhalla* is gone!" a signals-and-detection officer cried.

"Fleet status?" he asked DeLange. He noticed numerous blinking lights on the board but all of them were still red, which indicated that the missiles had only penetrated a handful of decks. If anything had broken through the second layer of collapsium shielding the lights would be green. There were also blinking red lights where some of the missile tubes had been damaged or severed. As he watched, several of them were restored by repair crews and robots and the lights grew steady again.

"The Mardukans have entered orbit. No severe damage to any of our ships," DeLange reported. "*Faerie Queene* and *Gift Horse* report moderate damage."

"We've hurt them bad," Duggan said. "One ship," he looked at his instruments again, "the *Queen Myrna*, is moving off slowly. She's badly damaged."

He looked and saw that all of his ships were still in formation around the *Emesh*.

"Another ship's moving off," someone reported. "It's the *Grendelsbane*; she's moving at full speed away from Sarpanitum!"

"Keep an eye on her," Morland said, "it could be some sort of diversion."

"I don't think so, sir," one of the communication officers said. "Listen."

At first Morland couldn't understand the words he was hearing due to the accent and the staccato way in which the person was speaking. Then he realized that most of the words were swear words directed at the Mardukans, the gist of which was that Vandarvant had promised that they would be facing three ships, not five ships with a giant dreadnaught among them.

They all had a quick nervous laugh as the *Grendelsbane* jumped into hyperspace and disappeared off the screens.

DeLange brought them back to business. "The Mardukans are about half a minute away from Point X." The survivors had passed through the ring and were now approaching the missile ships.

Morland looked at the communication board and the technicians nodded that the other ships had received the information. When the Mardukans reached the point almost equidistant between the two formations of missile ships, he gave the order.

"Fire!"

As the missile ships opened up on the Mardukans, the Sarpanitum fleet immediately accelerated to top speed so that they could strike the enemy while they were engaged. "We got one!" someone cried, as the shields went up and the viewscreens blanked. *Good!* he thought, *another one down, many more to go.*

"The *Hringhorn* has left the Mardukan wall and is heading for the missile ships," someone announced.

He cursed; the missile ships couldn't survive a battle with a real ship and most weren't fast enough to escape.

"*Adiutrix* coming," Duggan said. Missiles went out again as the two ships closed in on each other and then as the short-range guns let loose the *Adiutrix* veered off, leaving orbit and heading away.

"What's everyone's status?" Morland asked.

"The *DaSilva* is right with us, sir," DeLange said. "The other three are still okay but far behind."

He looked at the screens and saw the *Skull Splitter* and *Gift Horse* were close together and that the *Faerie Queene* was moving toward them. He punched a button.

"Vann, what's going on?"

"We ran the *Vindex* off after a brief fight," Stenger replied with a grin. "The *King Mikhyl* and *Centurion* are headed for the *Gift Horse* and the *Skull Splitter*. I'm moving in to support."

He thought about helping them, but *Emesh* was much closer to the missile ships. "Send to the *DaSilva*, we will relieve the missile ships," he ordered.

As the enemy approached the missile ships, he saw that they were overwhelming the Mardukans' counter-missile defenses. Two missile ships exploded, but the rest were firing waves of missiles. One of the small Imperial ships blew up as they approached, then another. The *Hringhorn* finally noticed them and tried to run but they were too close. The *City of Emesh* and *DaSilva* came in on either side of her, as the *Hringhorn* spewed missiles as fast as possible, desperately trying to get away. They closed up and let loose with a barrage of missile fire.

Suddenly the *Hringhorn* vaporized spectacularly in a kaleidoscope of colors.

Morland closed his eyes and when he opened them again he could see nothing but whirling colored globes.

As the cheers died down on the bridge he asked about the status of the other ships.

"We got another one," someone said.

"No, that was one of ours," someone else said.

Feeling a chill on his spine he quickly punched a button. "Was it Vann?"

"One ship moving off," Duggan said. "Two others still in orbit."

The screen cleared and he sighed in relief as he saw Vann's face. "Who?" he asked.

Vann Stenger shook his head. "They got the *Gift Horse*," he said. "We took out the *King Mikhyl*. Everyone else has fled the system."

Poor Tylor, he thought sadly. He would never realize his dream to run his own base. And the thousand other men and women on the *Gift Horse*, all their dreams were gone, too.

"No," Duggan said, "the *Queen Myrna* is still in-system. She's moving away slowly. I don't believe they have hyperjump capability any longer."

"I can take care of them Admiral," Rovard Harvan said from the *Skull Splitter*.

"No," Morland said. "No more butchery. There's been too much already. Send a message to the *Queen Myrna*. I want to talk to her captain"

He looked at the board. There were numerous blinking lights that indicated widespread but minor damage. As he watched, some of the lights steadied. He felt himself finally beginning to relax. They had won this round.

Then the main screen lit up, displaying the captain of the *Queen Myrna*. He had a slender, clean shaven face, with thinning blond hair that was starting to go gray. Currently that face was set in a determined expression.

"We have nothing to talk about," he said. "Mardukan ships do not surrender."

"I'm not asking you to surrender," Morland said.

"What are you asking, then?" he asked.

"I suggest that you direct your ship back to Sarpanitum and land at the Emesh spaceyards. We will repair your ship to a state where you can leave."

Now the captain looked even more puzzled. "Why would you do that? We're at war."

Morland shook his head. "I do not regard us as being at war. You attacked us, we did not attack you."

"That's not what I heard."

"You have been the victim of false information, Captain," Morland said. "I give you my word, both as Admiral and as Prince David, ruler of Sarpanitum. If you agree not to continue hostilities, you may land your ship and we will repair her so you can leave."

He could see the captain struggling with the idea, and then his face relaxed. "Very well. My name is Captain Ericson. I accept your terms."

Morland didn't let his pleasure show. "Welcome to Sarpanitum, Captain Ericson."

X

I'm getting tired of memorial ceremonies, Morland decided. The mess was the only room in the *City of Emesh* big enough to hold everyone who wanted to attend, no matter how incongruous the area was for a memorial. He found himself staring at the blank canvas on the wall unsure of how the story was going to end. They had won the battle; now he had to use that victory to win the war.

"*Pixie, Fawzi,*" A person was listing the missile ships that had been destroyed in the attack yesterday. He wasn't going to win the war by winning any more space battles that was for sure. If another Mardukan force showed up, it would undoubtedly be so large that they wouldn't stand a chance against it. "*Pegasus, Sky-Rover, Centaur.*" They had already mentioned the *Gift Horse*. He thought again of his mixed feelings toward Tylor Ragnarsans; one thing was certain, this was not how he'd wanted their relationship to end.

He suddenly realized the list of ships had stopped, and that they were waiting for him to say the final words. He rose to his feet. "We honor our brave comrades, who gave their lives to defend our world and their homes. May they never be forgotten."

The normal end to the ceremony would have been for him to lead the procession out of the room. Instead he spoke again, "I invite Captain Ericson of the *Queen Myrna* to say a few words for his comrades on the *Challenger, King Mikhyl, Champion, Hringhorn,* and *Valhalla*." Ericson looked surprised, but then he had looked that way almost throughout his brief time on Sarpanitum—especially during the service. He could guess how the captain felt. Not only had his fellow ships been beaten by a Neobarbarian fleet, but his conquerors were actually proving themselves to be civilized.

After Captain Ericson had finished his short eulogy, Morland asked Ericson to join him while they led the procession out of the room. Once they were outside, he gestured to the Mardukan to follow him away from the crowd. Ericson's escort, a young officer and a man who seemed to be a combination of bodyguard and valet, followed along. They both wore sidearms, while Ericson was unarmed. The young officer had gradually relaxed since arriving on Sarpanitum, but his bodyguard was as alert as ever.

"I'd like to thank you for giving me the opportunity to honor my comrades, Admiral Morland," Captain Ericson said. "Or should I call you Prince David?"

"I think Admiral is fine."

"Very well, what's next, sir? Do you want us to confine ourselves to the ship while the repairs are being made, or what?"

During the battle a missile had reached deep enough into the *Queen Myrna* to wreck her hyperdrive engines. It was a tribute to her crew that they had managed to keep the engines, and the ship, from blowing up. However, they needed brand-new Dillingham engines, which would take a couple of months to build and install.

"No, your crew can have the freedom to roam this world like any ship's crew on leave. I have already issued orders to that effect. I would recommend however, that none of them leave Emesh Spaceport without an escort. The rest of this world has little experience beyond Sarpanitum. I am afraid they would have a difficult time keeping their anger toward your crew in check."

That was putting it mildly. The papers and telenews stations seemed to alternate between slavish praise of the defenders of Sarpanitum and severe condemnation of the attackers. It wouldn't be safe for the crewmen anywhere else on the planet.

"You said none of them, referring to my crew. Does that mean you have other plans for me?"

Despite Morland's assurances, Ericson seemed to believe that he would receive some sort of punishment or sanction for the attack. He had already volunteered that he was senior captain of the fleet after Commodore Vandarvant.

"Yes," Morland said. "I would like you and, of course, your escorts," he gestured to the men accompanying him. The young officer reddened slightly. The bodyguard didn't change expression a bit. *I would hate to play cards with that one*, Morland thought. "To take a trip with me," he finished.

"Where?"

"To Vishnu."

VISHNU IV

"The ambassador will see you now, gentlemen," said the secretary outside the Mardukan Ambassador's office. They had made the trip to Vishnu in the *City of Emesh*. Morland saw little reason to conceal the *Emesh's* existence anymore, as the story of the Battle of Sarpanitum would be all over Federation space within the year. However, since Vishnu was only weeks away from a hotly contested election no one seemed to pay them any attention at all.

Captain Ericson had told him that he thought the remnants of the Mardukan fleet would jump straight to Marduk without stopping anywhere. This would mean that they were still in hyperspace. He thought the *Grendelsbane* was most likely on its way to Beowulf. Either way, there would not be enough ships to threaten Sarpanitum anywhere but on Marduk.

"That's if they decide to attack you again," Captain Ericson said ruefully. "We have always understood that we acted without the sanction of the Emperor. In the past he has looked the other way when we were successful. I have no idea how he is going to react to this defeat."

If the reaction of Ambassador Edvard Jonson was any indicator, probably not well. Jonson was aghast when he heard about the attack. "Captain, you attacked a planet we have a trade agreement with! Prince David leads a trade alliance of half a dozen worlds. How are we ever going to persuade them to join the Empire now?"

Captain Ericson's eyes were downcast, and he gave no answer. The ambassador kept fuming. "Some of you officers believe everything can be determined by military might."

Morland assumed he was talking about the aggressive faction of the Emperor's court.

"I should have thought you learned your lesson at Manannán." He flung his hands up in disgust. "Knowing Commodore Vandarvant, he probably paid no attention to the list of worlds we recognize as trading partners."

Captain Ericson shook his head.

"On the other hand," the Ambassador said, "I must admit, I had no idea that the Prince David of Sarpanitum that I negotiated a trade agreement with was also the Space Viking David Morland, who without provocation, attacked one of our ships on a Neobarbarian world."

His eyes bored into Morland. "Or did you attack our ship, Prince David?"

"No, I didn't, Your Excellency." He repeated a short version of his first encounter with the *Challenger*.

Ericson, who had already heard the story, kept his eyes down.

Morland felt sorry for him. He was probably envisioning his career going down in flames.

Ambassador Jonson looked thoughtful when he finished. "Would you be willing to repeat that story under a veridicator, Prince David?"

Morland reached inside his jacket, removed a data tab, and handed it to him. "Ambassador, I have already done so. This was witnessed by Captain Ericson and his aides." He gestured toward the bodyguard and a junior officer. "Captain Ericson took part in the questioning."

The Ambassador looked at Ericson, who nodded in agreement. Johnson sighed and took the tab. "Prince David, I can only offer you my unofficial apology for this unprovoked attack. You understand, don't you, that any official response must come from Marduk?"

"Yes, I understand, Your Excellency."

The Ambassador continued. "I will send all of this information to Marduk immediately. It shouldn't get there too much later than the remnants of our battle fleet. I do not believe they will have finished their inquiry before my briefing arrives."

He turned to Ericson. "Captain, it would be in your best interest to return to Sarpanitum with Prince David. Remain there with your ship until you are relieved."

Ericson immediately protested, as did the young officer.

The bodyguard didn't so much as blink an eye. Morland had heard he'd done very well in the card games aboard the *Emesh* on the journey to Vishnu.

The Ambassador held up a hand. "I am aware that the diplomatic corps cannot order the military to do anything. You should consider this a strong suggestion. And Captain Ericson," he added as the captain still seemed unsure, "should you do so, I will be happy to forward a statement of your cooperation in this matter."

The Ambassador looked straight at the young officer. "I would also recommend that you return to Sarpanitum with Prince David and remain there with your ship."

The young man began to protest. "But—"

The Ambassador cut off his words with a wave of his hand. He turned toward the bodyguard. "You may go with whomever you wish."

The bodyguard said nothing.

The young officer continued to protest until Ericson turned to him. "Consider yourself so ordered."

"It's probably my last order," he muttered under his breath. He rose and saluted the Ambassador, and shook hands with Morland, who had already risen. "I will await your instructions, Your Excellency."

He strode out of the room. The bodyguard followed him. The young officer wavered for a minute, and then followed them as well.

The Ambassador stood and extended his hand to Morland, saying "Prince David, again, I want to apologize for this matter."

Morland shook the hand, saying "Thank you, Your Excellency." Then he went for broke. "I understand former Commodore Vandarvant's hostility toward me, after we defeated him in battle. However, I am surprised, that no one ever asked me if we would have been willing to join the Empire."

"What?!"

EPIL⊕GUE

"Don't!" Randa said, wrapping her arms and legs around him tightly. "Don't move."

He relaxed, holding her and enjoying their closeness. He could feel her whole body smile as she hugged him even tighter. "I've been kissed by an Emperor and now I'm married to a King," she said happily.

Yes, he thought, it had been a big day.

They had all signed the Treaty of Vishnu earlier today. Even Odin had signed it as an Affiliated Union to the Empire, a nice vague phrase which presently meant nothing. It had taken over three years of negotiations, offers and counteroffers. He hadn't had to give up much. Just turning over trading rights to Tashmetum and Mara that he didn't actually have and agreeing to support the Empire's expansion.

As Morland had hoped, wiser heads had prevailed. An Empire that was facing challenges from Aton and Isis couldn't afford to turn down an offer from a Neobarbarian prince that would greatly expand its boundaries and bring over half a dozen additional worlds into the Empire, even if that prince had destroyed several Empire ships. Especially when one of those planets was the civilized world of Vishnu.

The new Vishnu government had been grateful to David Morland for the fact that he had, unintentionally, caused the downfall of the old government. They were also responding to public opinion, which was much more interested in being part of something beyond Vishnu than the old nobility had ever suspected.

David guessed that he owed more to King Rodrik of Tanith than he would ever know. His son Manfred had faithfully reported every rumor his father heard about the Empire in general, and the negotiations on the treaty in particular. From Prince Manfred he had learned that the aggressive faction at the court had been totally discredited, with a number of naval officers and ministers being forced into retirement.

When he met the Emperor he also heard that King Rodrik had personally vouched for him.

Meeting the Emperor had been much more nerve-racking than he had ever anticipated. It put him in mind of when he had first met King Alwyn after Count Benedik's rebellion, when he'd been afraid Alwyn was going to punish him because he had gotten the *Nebula*, as she was called then, shot up so badly. That meeting had ended with him being appointed Captain of the *Skull Splitter*.

He finally relaxed when it became apparent that the Emperor was mainly interested in reaffirming previously made assurances that David would give him all the plans for the *City of Emesh* and assist him in the construction of similar ships for the Empire.

His offer to construct those ships on Koshchei was met with polite thanks. That told him that Emperor Lucas did not intend for his main shipyard to be anywhere but in the Daveld System. As an aside, the Emperor did mention that he thought his negotiations with Aton and Isis would improve if a couple of Emesh-class ships appeared in their skies.

Ambassador Jonson had mentioned the same thing to him at the celebration afterward. He was leaving soon after the party to take up his new position as ambassador to Odin. He hoped to convert Odin's vague statement of affiliation with the Empire into a more solid agreement.

He had also mentioned that he hoped the Treaty of Vishnu would prove to be the new standard for how civilized worlds joined the Empire.

The Ambassador had noted, "It's all well and good to take over and dominate primitive Neobarb worlds when we bring them into the Empire. But there's no reason why we can't come to more judicious agreements with the civilized worlds. After all, the important thing is *that* they join the Empire, not *how* they join."

David had happily agreed with him. He had enjoyed the celebration, visiting with King Rodrik and meeting his wife Melissa, who was already pregnant with the King's eighteenth child, and dancing the few dances he knew with Randa. When Rodrik had learned that Sarpanitum was joining the Empire, the King had decided the time had come to reconcile with

Marduk and become a subject world. "There's no room for freebooters anymore," had been Rodrik's words on the subject to David. "The Space Viking Era is over, kaput!"

Randa had even managed to talk the Emperor, who was not known to be fond of dancing, out onto the dance floor. Vann Stenger and one of the local beauties had also joined them. He felt some comfort that Vann had looked even more out of his element than he did.

Laz Rivera had skipped the celebration. He had more fun hanging out in Malverton's art galleries and discussing painting techniques with other artists.

He was just about to suggest to Randa that they all leave when Ambassador Jonson came up to him and said the Emperor had a special announcement to make.

The Emperor made a short speech, thanking everyone again for their hard work on the treaty, and then he introduced the new ambassador to Vishnu.

Thinking that the Emperor was finished, David moved over to Randa, when the Emperor spoke again. "To show our appreciation for all his efforts on behalf of the Empire, we hereby appoint Prince David Morland as Planetary King of Sarpanitum, and charge him to protect and defend the people of Sarpanitum and the Empire."

As David stood there gaping, Randa flung her arms around him and the Emperor strode over and congratulated him, shaking his hand. Randa then seized the Emperor and kissed him as the crowd laughed and applauded. He had been in a daze as he accepted the congratulations of Vann, Duke Ladbrok, Gytha and others.

King Rodrik also offered his congratulations. "I had a good feeling about you, David," he said. "The galaxy needs more people like you to reunify all the human worlds."

Reunify all the worlds, he thought happily later, as he snuggled with his wife on their way back home. *I'll leave that to the Emperor. One world's enough for King David.*

The End

CPSIA information can be obtained at www.ICGtesting.com
Printed in the USA
BVOW05*1701190315

391737BV00001B/5/P